"Paul, I don't know what the truth is," Grace said.

"I don't know whether I'm Elizabeth or not. And... and I'm frightened to find out. But I must, if I ever hope to find peace."

Her words rang with conviction, Paul thought. It would be so easy to fall under her spell. "You can save your breath," he said. "I'm not fooled by your innocent look. You're still just another fortune hunter."

She looked at him for a long, silent moment. The only sounds in the room were the ticking of the clock on the wall, and the creaking of the house as a gust of wind blew up under the rafters.

"Think whatever you want," she finally said. "But know this. I'm not leaving until I find out the truth. Whatever the truth may be."

Dear Reader,

Welcome to Silhouette **Special Edition**...welcome to romance.

Bestselling author Debbie Macomber gets February off to an exciting start with her title for THAT SPECIAL WOMAN! An unforgettable New Year's Eve encounter isn't enough for one couple...and a year later they decide to marry in *Same Time, Next Year*. Don't miss this extraspecial love story!

At the center of Celeste Hamilton's *A Family Home* beats the heart of true love waiting to be discovered. Adam Cutler's son knows that he's found the perfect mom in Lainey Bates— now it's up to his dad to realize it. Then it's back to Glenwood for another of Susan Mallery's HOMETOWN HEARTBREAKERS. Bad boy Austin Lucas tempts his way into the heart of bashful Rebecca Chambers. Find out if he makes an honest woman of her in *Marriage on Demand*. Trisha Alexander has you wondering who *The Real Elizabeth Hollister* is as a woman searches for her true identity—and finds love like she's never known.

Two authors join the **Special Edition** family this month. Veteran Silhouette Romance author Brittany Young brings us the adorable efforts of two young, intrepid matchmakers in *Jenni Finds a Father*. Finally, when old lovers once again cross paths, not even a secret will keep them apart in Kaitlyn Gorton's *Hearth, Home and Hope*.

Look for more excitement, emotion and romance in the coming months from Silhouette **Special Edition**. We hope you enjoy these stories!

Sincerely,

Tara Gavin
Senior Editor

Please address questions and book requests to:
Silhouette Reader Service
U.S.: 3010 Walden Ave., P.O. Box 1325, Buffalo, NY 14269
Canadian: P.O. Box 609, Fort Erie, Ont. L2A 5X3

TRISHA ALEXANDER

THE REAL ELIZABETH HOLLISTER...

Silhouette®

SPECIAL EDITION®

Published by Silhouette Books

America's Publisher of Contemporary Romance

This book is dedicated to the men in my life:
Dick, Sandy, Mike and Ryan.

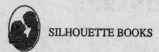 SILHOUETTE BOOKS

ISBN 0-373-09940-1

THE REAL ELIZABETH HOLLISTER...

Copyright © 1995 by Patricia A. Kay

Printed in U.S.A.

Books by Trisha Alexander

Silhouette Special Edition

Cinderella Girl #640
When Somebody Loves You #748
When Somebody Needs You #784
Mother of the Groom #801
When Somebody Wants You #822
Here Comes the Groom #845
Say You Love Me #875
What Will the Children Think? #906
Let's Make It Legal #924
The Real Elizabeth Hollister... #940

TRISHA ALEXANDER

has had a lifelong love affair with books and has always wanted to be a writer. She also loves cats, movies, the ocean, music, Broadway shows, cooking, traveling, being with her family and friends, Cajun food, "Calvin and Hobbes" and getting mail. Trisha and her husband have three grown children, two adorable grandchildren and live in Houston, Texas. Trisha loves to hear from readers. You can write to her at P.O. Box 441603, Houston, TX 77244-1603.

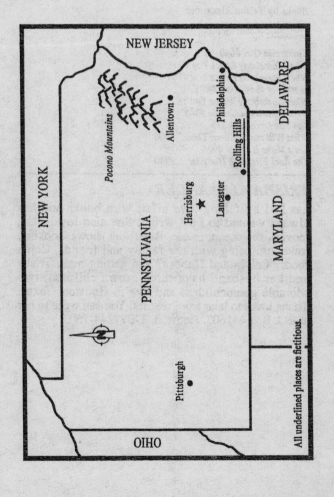

NEW JERSEY

Pocono Mountains

Allentown •

Philadelphia •

DELAWARE

Harrisburg ★

Lancaster •

Rolling Hills •

NEW YORK

PENNSYLVANIA

MARYLAND

Pittsburgh •

OIHO

All underlined places are fictitious.

Prologue

The Rolling Hills Record November 27, 1963
Foul Play Feared in Disappearance of Local Heiress
by Teresa Block, Staff Reporter

Elizabeth Hollister, thirteen-month-old granddaughter of local resident Virginia Fleming Hollister, disappeared along with her nanny, Josie McClure, early Friday.

Chief Newton Gilliland, of the Rolling Hills Police Department, disclosed that Miss McClure took the Hollister child for her daily walk in Lancaster Park at ten a.m. When the two failed to return at the usual time, Mrs. Hollister and Wilbur Davis, an employee, went out to look for them. When their search yielded nothing, they returned to the Hollister home and called local police.

Chief Gilliland said because foul play is suspected, with kidnapping and transport across state lines a possibility, the FBI have been notified.

The Hollister family, owners of the Hollister's Department Store chain nationwide as well as a vast network of office buildings and real estate, have offered a $100,000 reward for information leading to the recovery of Elizabeth. When last seen, she was wearing a dark blue corduroy one-piece garment, a heavy knit sweater and matching cap, white wool mittens, and white high-top shoes. Elizabeth weighs 21 pounds, is 26 inches tall and has blue eyes and blonde hair.

The nanny, Josie McClure, is 25 years old and has been in the Hollister family's employ for seven weeks. She is also blonde and blue-eyed, weighing approximately 120 pounds, and is about 5'4" tall. When last seen, she was wearing low-heeled black shoes, a dark blue skirt and white sweater, and a tan trench coat.

Anyone with information should call the Rolling Hills Police Department.

Chapter One

"I don't know if I can go through this again, Paul." Virginia Hollister rolled her wheelchair to the big bay window of the first-floor library and stared out at the wintry Pennsylvania landscape surrounding the estate.

Paul Hollister walked over and placed his hand on the thin shoulder of his great-aunt. He gave it a comforting squeeze. "Then don't, Aunt Virginia. Let me call Ned and tell him you've decided not to see this woman."

Virginia sighed. Her bony hands with their arthritic fingers clutched at the armrests of her chair, the great emerald she wore on her left hand glowing in the waning rays of November sunshine slanting through the window. She was silent for a long moment. "Is that what you think I should do?" she finally said.

"It seems the wisest course, don't you think?" he hedged.

"I just keep thinking, what if this time...?" Virginia's voice trailed off.

Paul heard the wistfulness in the uncompleted question and felt like strangling his aunt's attorney for getting her hopes up again. Paul had thought they were finally through with the endless series of fortune hunters who had claimed to be Virginia Hollister's missing granddaughter over the years. Now it seemed they would have to endure yet another blonde con artist whose only goal was to get her hands on the Hollister millions.

"Aunt Virginia," he said, choosing his words carefully, "you *do* realize that the likelihood of this woman's turning out to be Elizabeth is practically nonexistent, don't you? We've got to face it. It's been more than thirty years since Elizabeth disappeared. If she was alive, she'd have surfaced long ago."

Virginia nodded. "Yes, I know, Paul, I know. Don't think I haven't told myself the same things—many times. But Ned thinks I should see this woman. He said there are elements to her story that are hard to explain. Otherwise, he said he never would have told me about her."

Paul wanted to answer that he no longer trusted Ned Shapiro's judgment, that the man should have retired years ago. He wanted to say the only outcome possible from this newest claim to the Hollister name was heartbreak and disappointment for his aunt. He wanted to tell her to spare herself the ordeal and order her attorney to tell this woman to get lost.

But how could he? Now that his great-aunt knew about this Grace Gregory person, she would have to see her. Otherwise, she would always wonder about the woman.

He grimaced. And if she didn't see her, Virginia would eventually wonder about his reasons for dissuading her from a meeting.

After all, Paul thought, he was adopted, not a true flesh-and-blood Hollister the way Elizabeth had been. Wouldn't it be natural for Virginia to wonder about his motives? In her place, he would, especially since as things now stood, when Virginia died, Paul would inherit the bulk of her estate.

He frowned. No matter how much he wished he could shield his aunt from additional disappointment, no matter how much he wished he could call Ned and say they'd decided against seeing the woman, no matter how much he wanted to pretend this dilemma had never come up—Paul's hands were tied.

His aunt would have to find out for herself that Grace Gregory was just another fake in a long line of fakes. The best Paul could hope for was that the truth would be evident quickly, and that his aunt would not be hurt too badly in the process.

His decision made, he released Virginia's shoulder and sat on the window seat facing her. Her blue eyes, still bright, still full of intelligence, met his gaze. He couldn't help voicing one final warning. "Don't count on too much."

She nodded. "I'm not. I know what the odds are. But Paul, I'm eighty-six years old. I don't know how much time I've got left. And if there's any chance at all that this woman is Elizabeth..." The yearning note in her voice was unmistakable.

"I know. You have to check her out."

"Yes. You understand, don't you?"

"Of course I understand."

"And you don't mind, do you?"

He shook his head. "No. I don't mind."

She sighed, giving him a relieved smile. "Good. I didn't want you to think—"

"The only thing I care about," he said, interrupting her, "is you. My *only* concern in all this is the effect it'll have on you if..." He wanted to say *when* but restrained himself. "If this woman turns out to be an imposter."

"You don't have to worry about me. I'm prepared for the worst. I'll be all right."

He nodded. "Okay, then. That's settled. How soon did you want her to come?"

Virginia's blue eyes twinkled as an impish smile appeared. "Tomorrow?"

Paul's aunt had been a renowned beauty in her day, and when she smiled, that beauty was still apparent. He chuckled. He was glad she could joke about the situation. He loved his aunt very much. She'd been the one person he could count on, the mainstay of his life, since he was thirteen years old.

"Tomorrow might be pushing it," he said. "From what Ned told me, the woman has a job in New York and will have to arrange for time off." That was a point in the unknown Grace Gregory's favor, he guessed. Several of the other pretenders to the name of Elizabeth Hollister hadn't seemed to have any visible means of support.

"It's just that since we've decided to have her come, I'm anxious to meet her," his aunt said.

"I agree. If we're going to do this, it's best to do it quickly. I'll call Ned and tell him to make the arrangements for her to come as soon as possible." He stood, then bent down to kiss his aunt's cheek.

As he straightened, Virginia's bright blue gaze, filled with love, rested on his face. "Paul," she said softly, "there's something I want you to know. No matter what happens in the future, my feelings for you will never change."

A few minutes later, Paul left the library and headed for his office on the second floor. He knew his aunt really believed what she'd said when she'd assured him that nothing was going to change, if by some miracle this woman should turn out to be Elizabeth.

There were a lot of unknowns in this situation, but one thing Paul knew beyond a shadow of a doubt.

If Grace Gregory turned out to be Elizabeth, everything would change.

* * *

After Paul left the library, Virginia sat thinking for a long time. When Ned Shapiro, who had been her lawyer for the last thirty-five years, had called this morning, she hadn't been prepared. It was nearly eight years since the last girl claiming to be Elizabeth had shown up on the doorstep, and Virginia had almost come to accept that there wouldn't be another.

She had told herself Elizabeth was dead.

She had told herself to stop thinking about her granddaughter. To stop wondering what had happened to her.

And she'd thought she'd been successful.

But the moment Ned had said, "There's a young woman in New York who could be Elizabeth," Virginia knew she had still been clinging to a small sliver of hope.

For the past thirty years, Virginia had never stopped hoping. Although she loved Paul unconditionally and that love would never waver, the link between Virginia and Elizabeth had been special. The first time she'd held her newborn granddaughter in her arms, Virginia had known how pure and unselfish love could be. Even now, remembering that magical moment, tears filled Virginia's eyes.

When Elizabeth had disappeared, along with her nanny, Virginia felt as if a piece of her heart had been cut out. She had never experienced such pain. Not even when her son and his wife—Elizabeth's parents—had died so young and so tragically. Of course, then she couldn't afford to wallow in grief. When Evan and Anabel died, they had left their three-month-old daughter behind. All of Virginia's energy and love had been poured into the care of the orphaned Elizabeth.

Virginia wiped away her tears.

She would never stop missing Elizabeth. That's why she was seeing Grace Gregory. Because if there was any chance, no matter how faint, Virginia had to take it.

She owns a locket like the one you gave Elizabeth.

As Virginia remembered Ned's words, her heart quickened and she twisted her hands together in her lap. *Please, God,* she prayed. *Please, God.* She knew Paul was right. She knew she shouldn't count on anything. She knew if she gave way to the emotions struggling to burst forth, she would be setting herself up for another bitter disappointment.

After all, there could be dozens of explanations for the similarity of the lockets, the most logical one being that someone had designed it to look like Elizabeth's.

On purpose.

But even as Virginia told herself all of this, she couldn't stop the ache of yearning that filled her heart. "Maybe this time will be different," she whispered. "Maybe Elizabeth is finally finding her way home."

Grace Gregory undid the top two buttons of her black wool coat. It was warm in the taxicab, and the driver had told her it would be about twenty minutes before they would reach Hollister House.

Hollister House.

Grace could hardly believe she was on her way to meet Virginia Hollister. Ever since the day Grace had unearthed and read the newspaper stories detailing the disappearance, more than thirty years ago, of Elizabeth Hollister, heiress to the massive Hollister department store and real estate fortune, she had been in a precarious emotional state, hoping for, yet dreading a possible meeting with the woman who might be her grandmother.

What if she didn't like Virginia Hollister? What if the woman turned out to be awful, someone Grace had no desire to know or be connected to?

She reached inside her coat to touch the small gold locket she wore around her neck. The locket was the reason she was here. The locket had started everything. From the moment she'd received it more than six months ago, Grace's life had been turned upside down.

One day she was an ordinary woman who led a quiet, almost dull life in New York City as an editor of children's books, the next she was having disturbing dreams that suggested she might be the missing heiress to a vast fortune.

The fortune didn't tempt Grace—money had never been important to her. The possibility of finding out her origins did. From the time she was old enough to understand that she was a foundling, left on the doorstep of a convent when she was a baby, and that her parents were unknown, Grace had longed to know who she was, longed to know her roots.

And now, unbelievably, she might be on the verge of that discovery. And all because of the locket. All because of the dreams.

"This is it," the taxi driver said, catching Grace's eye in the rearview mirror.

Grace's heart skipped a beat. She craned her neck to see out the window as the cab pulled up to a small, stone gatehouse. The driver rolled down his window and pushed a button. A speaker crackled into life. After identifying himself, the driver entered through the remotely controlled iron gates and drove up a long, winding driveway to a circular turnaround in front of an enormous three-story redbrick house.

Grace paid her fare and, taking a deep breath to still her jittery stomach, she climbed out of the taxi. Just as she closed the car door behind her, the front door of the house opened, and a tall, dark-haired man stood framed in the doorway.

For a long moment he gazed down at her, then, unsmiling, said, "Miss Gregory?"

Grace suppressed the desire to shiver. His eyes were the coldest gray she'd ever seen. "Yes."

"I'm Paul Hollister, Mrs. Hollister's nephew." He inclined his head. "Come in, please." There was no warmth in his voice.

His barely concealed hostility took Grace aback. She wasn't sure just what kind of reception she'd expected, but it certainly wasn't out-and-out animosity. She wondered why Virginia Hollister had consented to see her if she and her nephew felt this way.

Chilled, Grace climbed the steps and walked past him into the foyer. Her low-heeled pumps made a hollow sound on the highly polished, hardwood floor. Once inside, she was assaulted by a jumble of impressions: rich jewel-toned colors and gleaming wood heavily scented with lemon oil, fresh-cut flowers in a beautiful Chinese vase sitting atop a heavily carved oak refectory table, an ornate crystal chandelier and a graceful, curving staircase, and from somewhere upstairs the muted sounds of a Brahms violin sonata.

A young, dark-eyed maid stood off to Grace's right. "May I take your coat, miss?" she said.

Grace shed her coat and told herself not to be intimidated by any of the obvious trappings of great wealth and power that surrounded her. After all, she was not claiming to be Elizabeth Hollister. She was simply here to find out if there was any possibility she could be the missing Hollister granddaughter. As long as she was truthful about her own doubts in this respect, she had no reason to be afraid of the Hollisters.

Feeling a lot calmer, she raised her eyes to meet Paul Hollister's cool gaze.

"My aunt is in the library," he said.

Now that Grace was closer to him, she realized he was very attractive. *Could* be very attractive, she amended, if he would only smile. That hostile stare couldn't be considered appealing by anyone. She guessed he was in his mid-to-late thirties and about six feet tall. Grace was fairly tall herself at five feet seven inches, and he was at least a head taller than her.

He had a strong-looking face with high cheekbones, a prominent nose and a firm chin. It wasn't a classically handsome face, yet Grace knew it was one that would appeal to women with its combination of ruggedness and character.

And even if Grace hadn't known who he was, she would have known he came from a privileged background. The soft leather of his loafers, the impeccable cut of his gray slacks, the fine detailing and texture of his open-necked blue shirt, the gleam of real gold from his watch—all screamed money.

He led the way through the entrance hall and into a hallway that intersected the house horizontally, turning right. Grace followed him to the far end of the hall and into a large, square room lined with bookcases. A small, frail-looking old woman wearing a dark blue dress trimmed in lace sat facing them in a wheelchair. Her white hair was twisted into a topknot, and a white crocheted lap robe lay across her knees.

"Aunt Virginia," Paul Hollister said. "This is Grace Gregory. Miss Gregory, my aunt, Virginia Hollister."

Virginia's bright blue gaze met Grace's.

The sensation that skidded through Grace had only happened once before in her life. She looked into Virginia Hollister's eyes, and there was instant recognition. It was the strangest feeling—as if she knew Virginia Hollister, *had* known her before today.

Grace had felt this same jolt of recognition with Melanie Beranchek, her roommate. They were introduced, their gazes met and Grace knew that Melanie was going to be a very dear, very close friend for the rest of her life. There was no getting-acquainted period, no feeling her way with Melanie, and later Melanie told Grace that she'd felt the same way. They simply *knew* each other.

Thus it was with Virginia Hollister.

And Virginia felt it, too. Grace could see the knowledge in her eyes as the seconds ticked away and their gazes clung.

Paul Hollister cleared his throat. The sound visibly startled Virginia, but she recovered her aplomb quickly. She held out her hands. "Hello, my dear. I'm so glad to meet you."

Grace walked forward, leaning down to clasp the older woman's hands. They felt brittle, the skin papery and fragile. "Hello, Mrs. Hollister." Yet as Virginia returned Grace's handclasp, her grip was surprisingly strong.

"Please. Sit here by me." Virginia patted the arm of a small, chintz-covered love seat to her left.

Grace sat, tugging her narrow black wool skirt down in a futile effort to cover her knees. As she looked up, her gaze briefly met Paul Hollister's and she suddenly wished she'd worn something with a fuller skirt. She felt vulnerable with her legs exposed.

Telling herself not to be an idiot, she turned back to Virginia. The older woman smiled at her. "Would you like some coffee or tea? Or a glass of sherry?"

"I don't—"

"I feel the need for some fortification, myself," Virginia said. "Paul, would you pour us some sherry?"

Grace took a deep breath. Yes, maybe a glass of sherry was a good idea. Having a glass in her hands would give her something to do if she got frazzled or needed time to think. "Thank you," she said, her eyes drawn to Paul Hollister, who had moved to a small rosewood chest where an ornate silver serving tray held crystal sherry glasses and a half-filled decanter.

A few minutes later, he handed them each a glass filled with a light-colored sherry. Grace avoided his assessing eyes and took a sip. She felt him move out of her range of vision and knew he was standing somewhere in the distant recesses of the room—closely watching her every move.

She swallowed and looked at Virginia again, giving the older woman a tentative smile.

"I'm glad you were able to come so quickly," Virginia said. "I've been so anxious to meet you."

Grace nodded. She'd been anxious, too.

"You're very lovely," Virginia said softly. "Exactly the way I've imagined Elizabeth would l-look." Her voice broke and there was a sheen of tears in her eyes.

Virginia's words, the warmth in her voice, and the touching evidence of her fragile emotional state combined to push Grace ridiculously close to tears, herself. She fought against them, gulping down another swallow of sherry.

Get a grip! She *had* to remain calm. She could just imagine the censuring look on Paul Hollister's face if she succumbed to tears or made a fool of herself here. She knew he would be sure to think she was just making a dramatic play for sympathy.

"Thank you," she said as evenly as she could.

Virginia's gaze dropped to the locket. She pushed her wheelchair closer and reached out a trembling hand. "May I see it?" she whispered.

Wordlessly, Grace unfastened the chain. She gently placed the locket into Virginia's outstretched hand. At the contact, Grace trembled, too, and once more she felt absurdly like crying. What was wrong with her?

Virginia's hands continued to tremble as she fingered the locket, then brought it closer. "It's Elizabeth's locket," she finally said, her voice firmer and filled with conviction.

"Aunt Virginia, you can't know that," Paul said sharply. His voice held a warning note.

Grace turned. He gave her a hard stare, then stood and walked over to his aunt's side. "Just because my aunt

thinks this locket belonged to her granddaughter doesn't
mean a thing legally."

"Paul!" Virginia said.

Grace told herself not to get upset. She told herself not
to let his baiting rattle her. Instinctively, she knew he
wanted her to lose her temper. He wanted her to act in a
way that would make her look bad. "Don't worry," she
said. "I certainly expect you to investi—"

"I'm sorry," Virginia interrupted. "Paul is overpro-
tective at times. I'm sure he didn't mean to imply you
would try to take advantage of what I just said."

"You don't have to apologize for me, Aunt Virginia."
Once more, Paul Hollister's gray gaze met Grace's, and
if she'd thought his eyes were icy before, they were positively glacial now. "I think Miss Gregory and I understand each other perfectly."

*Yes, I'm certainly beginning to get the picture. You de-
spise me and think I'm out to milk your aunt of as much
of her money as I can get my hands on. Fair enough. I
guess I'll just have to prove you wrong.* Grace tried to
communicate her thoughts with her own I-won't-back-
down stare, and had the first inkling that perhaps Paul
Hollister wasn't quite as rigid and formidable as he would
have her believe when he was the first one to avert his
gaze.

Virginia handed the locket back to Grace with an apologetic smile. "I guess Paul is right. Later perhaps, we *will*
want to verify its authenticity," she said.

"Of course."

Virginia sighed deeply. "Now, I want you to tell me
everything. I understand that the first hint you had that
you might be connected to our family came from a
dream?"

"Yes."

"Will you tell me about it?"

"I..." Grace's gaze angled to Paul. Was he going to sit here and listen to every word?

"Paul," Virginia said, "I think Miss Gregory might be more comfortable if she and I talked alone."

"Aunt Virginia, I don't think—"

"Please, Paul..."

"It's okay, Mrs. Hollister," Grace said.

Virginia reached over and covered Grace's hand. "I'd feel more comfortable, as well."

Grace knew he must be furious. Sure enough, his eyes glinted dangerously.

Virginia released Grace's hand and turned to her nephew. "You can turn on the tape recorder before you leave," she said. "That way you can play the conversation later. All right?"

His jaw hardened, but he stood and said, "Yes, of course." Without looking at Grace he walked to the desk and removed a tape recorder from the top drawer. He fiddled with it a moment, then turned it on and placed it on the corner of the desk closest to his aunt. Bending down, he kissed her cheek.

She gave him an affectionate smile in return.

Just before he turned to leave the room, he looked at Grace. His hard gray eyes carried an unspoken message. *You might have won round one,* they said, *but there are still a lot of rounds to go.*

Chapter Two

Paul walked into his office and headed straight for the window that overlooked the front of the estate—the spot where he did his best thinking. He jammed his hands into his pockets and stared outside, the subtle beauty of the stark winter landscape making no impression on him.

His thoughts were entirely focused on the woman in the library with his great-aunt. He wasn't sure just how she had managed it, but it had been obvious to him that Grace Gregory had already won over his Aunt Virginia. He still couldn't believe how quickly his great-aunt had fallen under the woman's spell.

Paul had always considered Virginia to be a shrewd, intelligent, almost impossible-to-deceive businesswoman who always insisted upon a careful investigation before any commitment was made. Paul guessed her desire to find Elizabeth—made more urgent by her failing health and advancing age—had completely obscured the need for caution. Evidently his aunt so desperately wanted to find

Elizabeth, she was willing to completely suspend disbelief and accept Grace Gregory blindly.

In some ways, Paul could understand why his aunt had succumbed so quickly. Grace Gregory was a pretty slick customer. That reserved, almost-shy look in her wide blue eyes, that open would-I-lie-to-you expression, that all-American-girl freshness, her simple clothing—black skirt, white blouse and low-heeled black pumps—everything about her reinforced the impression that she was honest and trustworthy, simple and straightforward.

But Paul wasn't desperate like his great-aunt, nor was he foolhardy or gullible. Over the years, he'd tangled with some brilliant con artists masquerading as legitimate businessmen.

He'd also encountered plenty of women wanting to latch on to the Hollister fortune. Some of them had pretended to be Elizabeth, and some of them had pretended to be interested in him.

In the end, they'd all turned out to have one thing in common: they were clever liars. So it would take more than a locket similar to Elizabeth's, wide eyes and pretty packaging to convince him that Grace Gregory was Virginia's long-lost granddaughter. Just because Grace had an appealing exterior didn't mean she was principled or honest.

She might just be a damned good actress.

Paul's jaw hardened.

Someone had to be realistic. Someone had to keep a level head. Someone had to look out for his Aunt Virginia's interests if she wasn't going to do it herself.

And who else was there except him?

The tension in Grace's body slowly dissolved after Paul Hollister left the library.

Virginia spoke gently. "That's much better, isn't it?"

Grace smiled. "Yes."

"He didn't mean anything by his remark, my dear."

"Mrs. Hollister, please don't feel you have to explain. I think I understand how your nephew feels. Why wouldn't he be suspicious of me? In his place, I would be, too." Grace wondered how many other women had come calling over the years. She realized that the lure of the Hollister millions would be impossible for many people to resist.

"Yes, you're right, I know," Virginia said, "but I still wish Paul would keep an open mind." Now it was her turn to smile. "But enough of that. Let's talk about how you came to be here. Please ... start from the beginning, and don't leave anything out."

"All right." Grace settled back in her chair.

"Ned said you were a foundling."

"Yes. I was abandoned on the steps of a convent in the Hudson River valley region of New York."

"St. Mary's, I believe he said?"

Grace nodded. "The nuns told me that when they found me, I was just quietly sitting on the top step, holding a bedraggled teddy bear and sucking my thumb." As always, thinking about her abandonment produced an ache in Grace's chest.

Virginia's eyes softened with compassion. "And what year was this?"

"It was the day after Christmas, 1963." Grace shook off her momentary sadness. All of that was long ago. She had survived. She would continue to survive, no matter what.

Virginia twisted the emerald ring she wore, and it glittered in the lamplight. "Only one month after Elizabeth disappeared," she murmured.

"Yes." When Grace had made the connection between her dreams and Elizabeth Hollister's disappearance, the time element involved was one of the most important factors in her decision to go forward, to investigate whether she might be the missing Hollister heiress.

"How old were you then?"

Grace shrugged. "The nuns guessed I was anywhere from twelve to fifteen months old." She smiled fondly. "Later, when they realized they would probably never know for sure, they decided to make the day I was found my first birthday."

"Elizabeth would have been fourteen months old on December 21." Virginia's voice seemed strained, as if each disclosure took a little more out of her. Yet her gaze was steady and she kept her hands clasped together tightly. "So the ages fit."

"Yes."

Virginia sighed deeply. "And there was no note or anything when the nuns discovered you?"

"No. Nothing. They said I was dressed in very ordinary clothing. Corduroy overalls, an inexpensive T-shirt, a down jacket with a hood. I also wore a locket around my neck."

Grace instinctively reached up to touch the locket. As always, its warmth surprised her. She quickly released it. Each time she touched it, images surfaced, sometimes immediately. These images were always hard on her. She could only imagine the effect it would have on Virginia if Grace were to experience anything like them now.

"I gave Elizabeth that locket when she was ch-christened." Virginia's voice wobbled on the last word, and her lower lip trembled. "I—I remember how, the morning she disappeared, when I was fastening the clasp, I noticed she was outgrowing the chain, and I knew I needed to get her a longer one." Virginia's throat worked as she swallowed. "I never did."

Grace's chest constricted, and she leaned forward, reaching for Virginia's hands in an instinctive gesture of comfort.

Virginia made a visible effort to get her emotions under control, then in a firmer voice, said, "It looks as if the original chain was replaced. Did you wear the locket all the time?"

Grace shook her head. "I don't think so. In fact, I didn't remember anything about it until only recently. Mother Gregory, the nun in charge of the convent, had put it away. I think her intention must have been to keep it for me and give it to me when I got older. But Mother Gregory died when I was twelve, and somehow, when the nuns disposed of her effects, the locket got overlooked. Six months ago, one of the nuns contacted me and said they had found something that belonged to me. That's how I got the locket."

Grace knew she'd never forget that day. The moment she'd taken the locket into her hands, she'd felt an eerie awareness...a premonition, almost, and the locket, which should have felt cool, felt warm to her touch. Because her feelings disturbed her, she had quickly slipped the locket into her purse. Then she had hugged and thanked Sister Mary Clare, who had always been her favorite of the nuns.

For the remainder of the day, Grace had tried to forget about the locket. Although she normally enjoyed visiting the nuns and especially enjoyed seeing Sister Mary Clare, she had been unable to relax. Throughout the afternoon, as she and the nuns talked and drank tea and ate the festive lunch they'd prepared in honor of her visit, she'd been disquieted and all too aware of the locket in her purse.

It was almost as if the locket were calling to her, and Grace couldn't wait for the afternoon to end so she could make the return trip to New York City where she could finally take it out and really examine it.

As Grace told Virginia all of this, she was amazed that she was able to discuss her feelings so openly. She knew this was a testament to the instant rapport she'd felt with the older woman, but it was still surprising, because Grace had always been a very private person.

"You mentioned Mother Gregory. Is she the reason your surname is Gregory?" Virginia asked.

Grace smiled. "Yes. The nuns asked me my name, but evidently because I was so young, I couldn't tell them. I said things like 'no' and 'teddy' and 'mama,' but no names."

Virginia stared at her. "E-Elizabeth used to call me mama because she couldn't say grandmama."

Grace's heart skipped a beat at the look in Virginia's eyes. She didn't know what to say. Virginia's statement revealed just how desperately she was grasping at anything—no matter how minute or coincidental—that might link Grace to Elizabeth.

In an effort to dilute the intensity of the emotion vibrating between them, she said, "Mother Gregory decided to name me Grace. She said I had come to them by the grace of God." Grace smiled in warm memory of the kindly old nun.

Virginia's brow knit. "Didn't she wonder about the 'H' engraved on the locket?"

"I'm not sure she realized it was an 'H.'"

Virginia nodded. "Were you unhappy at the convent?"

Grace swallowed. "No. Not unhappy." But there had always been an empty place in her heart. When her classmates had proudly introduced their mommies and daddies at school open houses or plays, her own parentless status had hurt unbearably. She was the only one in her elementary school class who didn't have at least one parent. The only one who lived such a strange existence.

From the time she was old enough to understand her situation, she'd yearned for a family of her own, an ordinary life like the other kids had. She'd wondered who her parents were, and why they had abandoned her. Even now, as an adult, she still felt as if a part of her were missing, and that until she found that missing piece, she could never be whole.

"So what happened when you returned to New York City after picking up the locket?" Virginia probed gently.

Grace sighed, shaking off the painful memories of her childhood. "After I got home, I almost immediately started having dreams."

"About Elizabeth."

"Yes, but at first I didn't know they were about Elizabeth. All I knew was that I was dreaming about a little girl, and I could feel her fear and loneliness and sense of abandonment. I wasn't sure if the girl was me or not. You know how it is with dreams."

Virginia's face had twisted when Grace mentioned the words *fear* and *loneliness*.

"This is too hard on you," Grace said. "Maybe I shouldn't contin—"

"No, no! I must hear this. If..." Virginia closed her eyes briefly. When she opened them again, she said, "If you...if my granddaughter had the strength to endure whatever it was she endured, I can certainly be strong enough to hear about it."

Grace wished she had the right to hug the older woman and tell her how much she was beginning to admire her. Suddenly, Grace, who had tried to remain philosophical about the outcome of this visit—telling herself that if it turned out she wasn't Elizabeth, she wouldn't have lost anything except a week or so of her time—knew that her rationale was no longer true.

She would be losing a lot, and the loss would hurt, because she wanted very much to claim Virginia as her grandmother. Wanted very much to actually *be* Elizabeth Hollister. Wanted more than anything in the world to finally belong to someone.

"Please, my dear," Virginia said, "continue."

Grace took a deep breath. "Gradually, over a period of about three weeks, the dreams intensified, and I began to see and feel the presence of another person."

"Josie McClure."

"Yes. Of course, I didn't know her full name until I read the newspaper story."

A bleakness dulled Virginia's eyes. "I was so impressed with that young lady when I hired her. I just couldn't believe that Josie was a part of Elizabeth's disappearance. For weeks, I really thought she had been abducted along with Elizabeth. I kept expecting the police to call and say they'd found Josie's body." She shook her head. "She had such excellent references. She had worked for the son of an old friend, and even though there was a long gap between jobs, I accepted her explanation that she'd taken time off to care for her sick mother. When she told me her mother was dead and she was alone in the world, my heart went out to her. I thought how her situation and Elizabeth's were similar, so she was bound to empathize with Elizabeth." Virginia sighed shakily. "I trusted Josie implicitly."

"If my dreams are accurate at all, Mrs. Hollister, Josie was almost as frightened as Elizabeth."

"Was she?"

"Yes."

"Did your... did your dreams actually show you how Elizabeth was abducted?"

Grace shook her head. "No. I..." She hesitated, unsure if she should say what she was thinking. She looked at Virginia, saw the desperation to know everything that shone from her eyes. "I was hoping that coming here, where it all happened, might trigger those...memories...if that's what they are."

"Did...did Josie...did she mistreat—" Virginia broke off.

Grace knew Virginia had been about to say *you*, but had stopped herself. "Mrs. Hollister, we don't know if I'm Elizabeth, and it would make me feel more comfortable if we just acted as if I'm not." She left unsaid that acting as if she wasn't would make it easier for both of them to bear later on if it turned out she wasn't.

Virginia nodded. "I'm trying, but I've waited so long, and you *are* wearing Elizabeth's locket, I'm convinced of that."

Yes, Grace was convinced of that, too. There was no other logical explanation for the dreams. The locket had to be the catalyst, and if it wasn't Elizabeth's, then none of this made any sense at all. "To answer your question," she said, "Elizabeth, as far as I know, anyway, wasn't mistreated."

Virginia nodded slowly, bowing her head so her gaze was hidden from Grace's. She knew the older woman was trying valiantly to keep her emotions controlled. She could also imagine how difficult it was for Virginia to hear what Grace had to tell her. "Do you want me to go on?" she asked after a moment.

"Yes, please," Virginia whispered.

Grace guessed it was better to tell Virginia everything now, quickly, and get it over with. "The dreams got so disturbing, I finally decided to see a psychologist who specializes in dream interpretation. Over the next couple of months, I met with Dr. Coleman several times a week, and, as more information was revealed to me, she helped me understand that I had to investigate."

"What kind of information led you to Elizabeth's disappearance?"

Grace was glad to see Virginia was composed once more. "In one of the dreams, Josie was crying, talking to herself about a man named Frank. She said things like 'Why did I let you talk me into this?' and 'What will I do if the Philadelphia police find me?' That's what triggered my decision to go to Philadelphia and try to find out exactly what Josie was talking about."

"But how did you know where to begin?"

Grace grimaced. "In one of my later dreams, Josie said something that really pinpointed the time frame for me. She mentioned how it was just a wild stroke of luck that they had pulled off their job the same day President Kennedy was assassinated. I didn't understand the meaning of that, but at least I knew what time period I needed to investigate."

"I understand what she meant," Virginia said.

"Yes, I do, too. Now. It's obvious that because of the assassination and all the coverage, Elizabeth's disappearance didn't get much media attention, and what it did get was relegated to back pages, several days after the fact."

"Which explains why the nuns at St. Mary's wouldn't have connected you with Elizabeth's disappearance."

"Yes. They're a bit isolated, anyway, not very concerned with the secular world, but even if they hadn't been, they probably wouldn't have heard much about the disappearance of a child in a small town in Pennsylvania."

"Ned said you found the local newspaper stories through the library," Virginia prompted.

"Yes."

"And then?"

"Then I went back to New York and tried to figure out what to do. Once I decided I had to follow up on my discovery, it was fairly easy to find Mr. Shapiro."

"Because of the reward we'd offered through his firm."

"Yes."

"And then he called me," Virginia said.

For a long moment, neither woman spoke. Grace sat quietly. She felt much calmer. She had told Virginia everything, and now, whatever happened next was out of her control.

The loud buzz of the intercom startled Paul. Pressing the button that activated the speaker, he said, "Yes?"

"Paul, would you mind coming back to the library, please?" his aunt said.

"Of course not. I'll be there in a few minutes."

Paul told Susan, his secretary, where he was going, and exactly three minutes later, he knocked on the library door to announce his arrival, then opened it and walked into the library. His aunt now sat behind the cherrywood desk, and Grace Gregory was nowhere to be seen.

"Did you send our visitor packing?" he asked.

"No, she's still here. I wanted to talk to you privately, so I asked Anna to take Grace into the sun room and serve her some tea. I told Grace we'd join her there in a little while."

Every afternoon at four o'clock, Paul and his aunt observed the English tradition of afternoon tea, complete with freshly baked scones and anything else the cook took it in her head to concoct. Tea with his aunt was usually a pleasant interlude that Paul looked forward to. Grace's presence today would spoil that.

"Paul, I believe we've found Elizabeth."

Alarm arrowed through Paul, but he picked his words carefully as he lowered himself into one of the two leather Queen Anne chairs flanking the desk. "Based on what?"

His aunt raised her chin almost defiantly. "Based on the fact that there are too many things that fit that theory to be coincidence. The locket Grace is wearing belonged to Elizabeth. They are the same age, have the same blonde hair and blue eyes, and Grace was found abandoned on the steps of that convent only one month after Elizabeth disappeared." Her own blue eyes glittered with passion. "She even looks like Elizabeth."

"Oh, come on, Aunt Virginia," Paul said, unable to stop himself. "You have no idea what Elizabeth would look like today."

"Of course I do. I know what her mother and father looked like, now, don't I?"

Paul had no answer for her logic. And even though he didn't want to admit it, Grace *did* bear some resemblance to photos he had seen of Anabel Hollister, Elizabeth's mother.

"And Paul, when you listen to the tape of our conversation—" his aunt pointed to the tape recorder "—you'll hear for yourself all the things Grace couldn't know unless she'd experienced them herself."

"Like what?"

"Like Josie's name."

"Aunt Virginia, think for a minute. Of course she could know Josie's name. Josie's name was plastered all over the newspaper stories."

"But Grace knew Josie's name before she knew about Elizabeth's disappearance."

"That's what she says. Did you ever stop and think that she might have read the stories first, then *pretended* to have these dreams?"

"No."

"No, you never thought of that? Or no, you don't believe that's what she's done?"

"No, I don't believe that's what she's done. How do you explain the locket? I believe her story. I believe *her!*"

Paul studied his aunt carefully. He knew, from experience, just how stubborn she could be once she'd decided on a course of action. He also knew how much this meant to her.

"Fine," he said. "But I'm afraid I can't let you just take this woman on faith alone. Every single one of her claims must be investigated thoroughly, and we must have the locket examined and authenticated, if possible." The fact that his aunt had had the locket specially fashioned by a famous jewelry designer would help, Paul thought. There should be experts out there who would be able to verify whether or not Grace Gregory's locket had been designed by the same person.

"Of course we'll investigate everything." His aunt smiled happily. "But, Paul—it won't matter. You'll see. Grace is Elizabeth. I know it." She touched her heart. "I know it here, where it counts."

Paul sighed. He started to rise, but his aunt waved him down again.

"There's one more thing," Virginia said. "After tea, I want you to take Grace back to the Rolling Hills Inn, wait until she's packed her belongings, then bring her back to the house. I want her to stay here, with us, for the duration of her visit."

"Aunt Virginia, that's not a good idea."

"Why not?"

Because the more you're around her, the more she can get her hooks into you. "Because it's dangerous to get too attached to her until we know if she's legitimate."

His aunt appeared to consider his argument. After a few moments, she slowly said, "I know you're probably right, Paul. I also know your suggestion is prompted by concern for me. But I feel so strongly about this. About *her.* I want to spend as much time with her as possible. There are still so many things I want to ask her. So many things I have to tell her." She took a deep breath. "Please, Paul, try to understand."

"I do understand. I just—" He broke off. What was the use? He'd voiced his objections already, and obviously his aunt was not going to listen.

"Paul, I'm not worried, really, but *if* . . . if your concerns turn out to be accurate, well, you warned me, didn't you? I'll just have to deal with it. But until then—" she paused, her eyes beseeching him "—please don't fight against everything I suggest. Let me enjoy this time with Grace.''

He nodded. ''I just don't want to see you get hurt.''

''I know. And I love you for that.''

Actually, in one way, it *did* make sense to have Grace stay here. If she was here, he would be better able to watch her and study her. There was more of a chance she might slip up and commit a fatal mistake.

A mistake that would prove, once and for all, that she was not Elizabeth.

Chapter Three

The same dark-eyed maid who had taken her coat when she'd arrived served Grace tea in the sun room.

"Milk and sugar, miss?" she said.

"Yes, please," Grace said as the maid poured the steaming tea from an ornate silver service, added milk and one teaspoon of sugar.

"Is there anything else you'd like?" the maid asked, gesturing toward the scones and cakes and tiny sandwiches displayed on the tea cart. "I'll be happy to fix you a plate."

"Thank you, but I can serve myself."

The maid smiled. "Very good, miss."

Before leaving the room, the maid turned on a couple of lamps to dispel the afternoon gloom. Grace glanced outside. She had an unobstructed view of a terraced backyard with a flower garden that was probably magnificent in the spring and summer. Beyond the garden was a small pond containing several ducks. The pond was the perfect size for ice-skating, Grace thought, wondering if it was ever utilized in that way.

Behind the pond and gardens stretched rolling hills dotted with pine and spruce trees. It was the perfect setting for a large family. Grace could just picture laughing, boisterous children at play, surrounded by barking puppies and gamboling kittens, all of them watched over by doting parents.

She smiled at the romantic image she'd conjured. That's what came of being an editor of children's books, she thought. She spent her life in an idealized world.

Sighing, Grace buttered a scone, then as she sipped her tea and ate the scone, studied her indoor surroundings. The sun room was about twenty feet square, with windows and French doors on two sides. One of the inner walls contained a massive fireplace with a thick mahogany mantel.

The room was probably much nicer during warm-weather months, she thought, although today there was a cheery fire going in the fireplace, and the chintz-covered sofas and chairs lent an air of homey comfort to the room. Adding to the cozy impression were dozens of indoor plants that looked well-tended and healthy.

So far, what Grace had seen of Hollister House had impressed her. Although the house was very large and old, it wasn't forbidding or gloomy. No, she thought wryly, the only gloomy thing she'd seen so far was Paul Hollister.

Grace had been sincere when she'd told Virginia that she understood why her nephew was acting the way he was. Why he was suspicious. But that didn't make his behavior or his suspicions easier to bear.

Grace knew people liked her, even though she was quiet and reserved and mostly preferred to remain in the background. She thought the reason they liked her was that she was the kind of person who treated people the way she wanted to be treated—with respect, honesty and kind-

ness. As a result, today was one of only a few times in her
adult life that another person had reacted toward her in an
antagonistic way.

So, despite her understanding of Paul Hollister's motives, Grace wasn't happy being on the receiving end of his
hostility.

She shook off her thoughts as she heard approaching
footsteps. A moment later, Virginia Hollister, followed by
Paul, entered the room.

Virginia smiled.

Paul didn't.

Virginia rolled her wheelchair over so that she was facing Grace. "I see Anna has taken care of you."

"Yes," Grace said. "The tea and scones are wonderful."

"Would you like me to fix you a plate, Aunt Virginia?" Paul asked.

"Yes, thank you, Paul." Virginia turned her smile on
her nephew, and Grace could see the love shining in her
eyes. Grace couldn't help feeling a tiny stab of envy. Paul
belonged here. He would always belong here. Grace was
the interloper.

After Paul had fitted an obviously custom-made tray
across the arms of the wheelchair and had served his aunt,
he fixed himself a plate and a cup of tea, then sat a short
distance away in a high-backed chair placed at a right angle to Grace. She wondered what he was thinking as his
hooded gaze settled on her. Probably nothing good. She
crossed her legs at the ankles and told herself she didn't
care what he thought.

"Paul and I have been talking, my dear," Virginia said.
"And we've decided we'd like you to move out of the
Rolling Hills Inn and come stay here at the house."

"Oh, Mrs. Hollister, I don't think I should."

"Why not?"

"I just...well, don't you think...?" Grace tried to gather her thoughts. She hadn't expected this and wasn't sure what to say.

"I've already told you what I think. I think your coming here to the house would be the best thing all around. It'll give us a chance to get to know you better, and give you a chance to get to know us. Please say yes."

Virginia's voice was so eager, her eyes so bright, Grace knew she couldn't refuse. "Well...I...all right, I guess," she said.

Virginia beamed. "That's settled, then. When we're finished with our tea, Paul will drive you back to the inn. You can gather your things, then he'll bring you back here. That'll give you time to get settled in before dinner."

Grace glanced at Paul. His face told her nothing. He simply inclined his head, his eyes inscrutable. Even so, no one had to tell her that her moving here was not his idea. She wondered if he had given his aunt any argument over the suggestion or if, once it was made, he'd simply gone along with it.

Grace had made arrangements to be away from her job for a week. She hadn't been sure if she'd need that much time, but she'd wanted to be prepared, just in case. Now she wondered how she would be able to stand an entire week of the scrutiny she was sure to get from Paul Hollister. She guessed she would just have to stay as far away from him as possible.

Paul slanted a look at Grace. She had been silent ever since they'd left the house. He wondered if she thought her silence would bother him. If so, she'd thought wrong. Not having to talk to her suited him just fine.

He smiled to himself. He hadn't missed the looks she'd given him during tea. He hoped she was beginning to realize he would not be a pushover like his aunt. No, it didn't matter to him how good an actress Grace was, the only thing that would sway him was cold, hard facts and indisputable proof of her identity.

He continued to keep one eye on her as he navigated the familiar road. Her head was turned slightly away from him, so he felt safe studying her profile.

He was in agreement with his aunt on one count. Grace *was* lovely, in an understated, quiet way. Her beauty wasn't the kind to turn heads on the street. Instead, it was the kind that caused you to look at her again and again, and each time you did, her beauty seemed more obvious, and you wondered why you hadn't realized it was there in the first place.

Unexpectedly, Grace turned, and her eyes, as blue and clear as a summer sky, met his. "We're almost there, aren't we?"

"Yes." Paul was irritated with himself because she'd caught him staring at her.

"I thought so." She subsided into silence again.

Paul kept his eyes on the road for the remainder of the trip.

Grace packed her things at a leisurely pace. Why should she hurry? So far, Paul Hollister had been barely civil and had shown her no consideration at all. Why should she care how long he waited downstairs in the lobby? She would take her own, sweet time, and if he didn't like it, let him leave. She was perfectly capable of calling a cab for the return trip to Hollister House.

Yet even as she told herself all of this, she knew she was just whistling at the wind, pretending she didn't feel uncomfortable, pretending Paul Hollister's opinion of her didn't matter, pretending this was an ordinary situation.

Sighing, she forced herself to move quickly and efficiently, and within fifteen minutes, she had repacked her clothing. After looking around the room to make sure she hadn't forgotten anything, she picked up the phone and asked for a bellman.

Ten minutes later, she followed the bellman out of the elevator and into the lobby. She headed straight for the front desk. A perky, red-haired clerk smiled at her as Grace approached.

"I'm Grace Gregory. Room 22. I'm checking out and want to settle my bill." Grace placed her key on top of the counter.

The clerk smiled brightly. "Thank you, Miss Gregory. Your bill has already been taken care of."

Grace frowned. "Excuse me?"

The clerk's smile faltered slightly. "Uh, the bill's already been paid."

"By whom?" Grace already knew who had paid her bill. She just wanted it confirmed.

The clerk wet her lips. "Uh, Mr. Hollister paid your bill."

"Thank you," Grace said tightly. She didn't need Paul Hollister to pay her bill. She had always paid her own way.

Grace turned, spying Paul immediately. He stood talking to an attractive dark-haired man who looked to be in his mid-forties. Paul's back was to her, so he didn't see her.

"You want me to take these outside?" the bellman said.

"Oh...yes, please," Grace said. She had forgotten the bellman was there. She wondered if she should walk over to Paul or just wait for him to finish his conversation and turn around. While she was trying to decide on a course of action, his companion's gaze met hers, and, smiling, he said something to Paul.

Paul slowly turned, his cool gaze connecting with hers.

Grace walked slowly forward and wondered how he managed to show no emotion whatsoever. The man must have ice water in his veins instead of blood.

"Ready to go?" he said as she drew abreast of him and his companion.

"Yes. The bellman just took my bags outside."

Paul nodded. "Okay." He glanced at the other man. "Geoff, it was good to see you. Give me a call about that idea of yours."

"Aren't you going to introduce me to your friend?" the man called Geoff said. He gave Grace a dazzling smile. His dark eyes were both curious and admiring.

Grace glanced at Paul. If he was irritated by his friend's question, he didn't show it. He smiled easily and said, "Sorry. Forgot my manners. Geoff, this is Grace Gregory, a houseguest of ours. Miss Gregory, Geoff Hastings, an old friend."

"It's nice to meet you," Grace said. She extended her right hand.

"It's a *great* pleasure to meet you, Miss Gregory," Geoff said, taking her hand and holding it too long. "Are you planning to be in Rolling Hills long?"

Grace smiled as she extricated her hand. "I'm not sure."

"Well, a beautiful woman is always a welcome addition to our town."

"Thank you." Even though she knew Geoff Hastings was probably the type of man who routinely flirted with every woman he met, Grace couldn't help feeling gratified by his attention, especially since Paul had been so singularly unimpressed by anything about her.

"Well, Geoff, we'd better be going. Aunt Virginia is expecting us for dinner," Paul said smoothly. He took Grace's arm.

"Will I see you at the country club tomorrow night?" Geoff said.

"Probably not."

"Why not? I'm sure Miss Gregory would enjoy our weekly dinner-dance."

"Listen, Geoff, we really have to go," Paul said.

"I see," Geoff said. His eyes twinkled and he winked at Grace. "You want to keep her all for yourself. Can't say as I blame you. But still, don't you plan to provide any entertainment at all for your houseguest? That's damned selfish, don't you think?" He grinned at Grace. "You tell him, Miss Gregory. Get him to bring you tomorrow night. It'll be a lot of fun."

Grace almost felt sorry for Paul, although the only indication she had that he was annoyed was the slight clenching of his jaw. "Goodbye, Geoff," he said evenly.

Once her bags were loaded in the big Lincoln and they were on their way to Hollister House, Grace said, "I'm sorry if I put you in an awkward position back there."

"No problem," he said. He didn't look at her.

"I just wanted you to know that I certainly don't expect you to entertain me while I'm here."

He looked at her, his expression enigmatic. "I'm glad we understand each other, because I have no intention of entertaining you."

Grace gritted her teeth. It was getting harder and harder to remain polite to this man in the face of his stubborn determination to give her no quarter. "By the way," she said, forcing her voice into an even tone. She'd be darned if she'd let him see how angry he made her. "How much was my room bill? I want to pay for it myself."

"Really?" he said, his disbelief transparent as his mouth curved into a cynical smile.

"Yes, really!" Grace was immediately chagrined that he had managed to provoke her into answering sharply. "I always pay my own way."

He didn't answer for a long moment. When he did, his voice was hard. "Forget it, Miss Gregory. That act of yours hasn't fooled me for a minute."

Grace opened her mouth to retort, then thought better of it. Fine, she thought. If this was the way he wanted

things, that was fine with her. Silently, she opened her
purse and withdrew her wallet. She extracted four twenty-
dollar bills. She placed the bills on the seat between them.
"That should take care of it." Then she turned and looked
out the side window. From now on, she would only talk
to him when she absolutely had to.

When they arrived at Hollister House, she opened her
door before he could come around to open it for her, got
out and walked to the back of the car.

Without a word, he opened the trunk and removed her
bags.

"I'll take those," she said, reaching for the garment bag
and suitcase.

"Don't be ridiculous." He easily lifted both bags out,
holding them in one hand while he closed the trunk.

Grace had never felt so frustrated in her life as she followed him into the house. He was infuriating. All the
sympathy and understanding she'd felt for him earlier in
the day had completely disappeared.

Paul placed her bags in the foyer. "I'm not sure where
my aunt intends to put you, so let's just leave these here
until we find out."

The maid named Anna materialized from one of the
rooms off the foyer. She reached for Grace's coat.

"Do you know where my aunt wants Miss Gregory?"
Paul asked.

"Yes, sir. She's to go into Miss Elizabeth's room."

"Miss Elizabeth's room?"

In his voice, Grace heard incredulity, which, in this instance, matched hers. She darted a glance his way and saw
anger sparking his eyes. Well, the man wasn't a completely cold fish. He could feel *some* emotion.

"Excuse me," he said tightly, meeting her gaze. "I have
work to do. Anna will take care of you." He turned to the
maid. "Anna, get Wilbur to carry Miss Gregory's bags
upstairs."

"Yes, sir."

After Paul disappeared down the hall, Grace, with mounting trepidation, followed the maid up the winding staircase and down the second-floor hallway into the right wing of the house. They passed six or seven closed doors before coming to one on the left, which by now Grace knew faced the back of the grounds.

Anna opened the door and stood aside. Grace, feeling a nervous flutter in her stomach, slowly entered. The room was lovely. Grace wasn't sure what she'd expected—a little girl's room filled with dolls and toys, perhaps—but this room wasn't like that at all. This was a room intended for a woman.

A large canopied bed occupied the center of the room. The bed hangings and spread were a soft rose satin. The furniture was dark, highly polished walnut, by an English maker. In addition to the bed, there was a tall armoire, a dressing table containing several crystal bottles and containers as well as a silver-backed brush and mirror, a desk and matching chair and a smaller chest. There were also two bedside tables, and a chaise longue covered in rose velvet sat in one corner of the room. The drapes were rose-and-cream-striped silk, and a thick sea green carpet covered the floor.

The room looked charming with fresh flowers atop the chest and golden lamplight softly illuminating the interior. The drapes were closed against the early-winter nightfall.

All in all, a very inviting room, Grace thought with relief.

"Your bags will be up in just a few minutes, miss," Anna said. "You have a private bathroom in there..." She pointed to a partially opened doorway on the right side of the room. "Dinner will be served in the dining room at eight, but Mrs. Hollister wants you to join her in the sitting room for cocktails first."

"I'm afraid I don't know where either room is."

Anna smiled. "I'll come up and take you to the sitting room at seven-thirty."

"All right." Grace hesitated. "Anna?"

"Yes, miss?"

"Do the Hollisters dress up for dinner?"

Anna smiled. "Mrs. Hollister always dresses up. Mr. Hollister, he's usually more casual."

Grace nodded. The dressiest garment she'd brought was a black silk crepe dress. Other than that, her suitcase contained the kinds of things she wore to work. Skirts and blouses and subdued dresses. Well, they would have to do.

When Anna left the room, Grace walked slowly over to the dressing table. She picked up the silver-backed brush. An odd sensation skidded through her as she looked at the elaborate scrolled *E* engraved in the metal.

Surely a child Elizabeth's age would not have owned anything like this expensive vanity set. That must mean that Virginia Hollister, through the years, had purchased items for Elizabeth in hopes that her granddaughter would someday use them.

How very sad, Grace thought. And yet, how heartening, too, and how rare to find that kind of faith.

For the next hour and a half, as Grace took a leisurely bubble bath, washed and dried her hair and polished her nails, she couldn't help thinking about everything that had happened since she'd arrived. She tried to empty her mind of everything and just relax. She knew that spending the evening in Paul Hollister's company was bound to be stressful, so recharging her batteries was essential, but she didn't have much luck. Still, she felt refreshed and ready to face the evening when the little clock on the bedside table chimed seven-thirty.

Only seconds later, there was a soft tap on the door.

Grace smoothed down the skirt of her violet wool dress and opened the door to Anna's smiling face. As they descended the staircase, Grace said, "How does Mrs. Hollister navigate these stairs?"

"Oh, she doesn't have to, miss. After her fall last winter, Mr. Hollister had an elevator installed."

"That's too bad. About her fall, I mean."

"Yes, miss, we all felt terrible. She tripped on the stairs and broke her hip. It just never mended properly. The doctors say it's because, at her age, her bones are too brittle. She can walk with the aid of a cane, but it's very painful, so she mostly uses her wheelchair."

By now they'd reached the first floor. Anna led the way past the formal dining room, which was accessed directly off the foyer, and Grace had a fleeting glimpse of rich Flemish tapestries and elegant dark wood.

Anna stood at the doorway of a smaller room that Grace could see was a pleasant mixture of traditional and antique furniture. "Here we are, miss," Anna said.

Virginia, wearing a long dress of burgundy silk and a double strand of creamy pearls, sat in front of the fireplace, where a fire burned brightly. She was talking animatedly, using her hands, and her emerald blazed with a fire of its own.

Paul leaned casually against the mantel. He looked incredibly attractive in dark slacks and a gray tweed jacket worn over a white turtleneck sweater, especially so because, as Grace walked in, he was laughing at something his aunt had just said.

The laughter transformed his face, softening the angles and hard edges.

Virginia turned, smiling up at Grace. "Hello! Don't you look lovely?" she said.

Paul turned.

And just before the smile slid off his face, just before his eyes turned aloof and unreadable, just before all of his thoughts and feelings were hidden behind that chilly mask he donned each time he was in Grace's company, something flared in the depths of his gray eyes.

Something that, if Grace hadn't known better, she would interpret as the awareness a man feels when he sees a woman who interests him.

Chapter Four

Grace sipped her glass of wine and wished Paul would stop studying her as if she were a specimen under a microscope.

She must have imagined his initial reaction to her when she'd first joined him and his aunt this evening, because he certainly hadn't evinced any thawing in his attitude toward her since. He had said very little, but she'd felt his constant scrutiny.

She knew he was looking at her right now. She shifted self-consciously and searched her mind for something, anything, to say.

"Is your room comfortable?" Virginia asked, finally breaking the silence that had stretched for interminable minutes.

"Yes, thank you," Grace said with relief. "It's quite comfortable... and beautiful." She hesitated, not sure if she should voice her thoughts.

"What? Is something wrong with the room? Did I overlook something?" Virginia asked.

Grace shook her head. "No, nothing's wrong. The room is perfect. It's just that I was kind of surprised. I guess I pictured you keeping Elizabeth's room exactly the way it was when she disappeared."

"For years I did." Virginia smiled sadly. "In fact, I wouldn't let anyone so much as move one toy." She glanced up at her nephew. "Paul is the one who convinced me to redecorate."

Reluctantly, Grace turned her gaze to Paul, who still stood in the same spot by the mantel.

"I suggested that if Elizabeth came home, she wouldn't want a room meant for a child." His eyes sent her a silent challenge. "Don't you agree that's how *she'd* feel?"

Grace hadn't missed his subtle emphasis of the word *she*. She wished he'd ease up, if only for this evening. He'd made his point. He didn't have to keep hammering at her. "Yes, I do agree... although..."

"Although what, my dear?" Virginia asked.

Grace shrugged and avoided Paul's gaze. "I—I guess I was hoping you'd kept Elizabeth toys and clothing."

Virginia smiled. "Don't worry. I did. In fact, I was planning to show you everything tomorrow when I give you a tour of the house. I'm hoping something will seem familiar to you."

"Yes, that's what I'm hoping, too," Grace admitted. She was dying to look at Paul and see his reaction to his aunt's statement and her own answer, but she forced herself not to. She was sure she knew what his eyes would reveal. She was also sure she wouldn't like it.

For the next ten minutes or so, she and Virginia talked about inconsequential things, with Paul occasionally adding a cryptic comment. Finally, to Grace's immense relief, Anna walked into the room and announced that dinner was ready.

Grace followed as Paul wheeled his aunt from the sitting room to the dining room. She didn't want to like anything about him, but she couldn't help respecting him for the way he attended to Virginia. It was obvious that he cared for his aunt a great deal, and that his concern was genuine.

You can always tell if a man will make a good husband by the way he treats his mother. Grace smiled as she remembered one of the things her best friend was fond of saying. She wondered if Melanie's observation extended to great-aunts. Not that it mattered. Grace certainly wasn't thinking of Paul Hollister as anything other than an adversary.

The dining room was immense. Long French casement windows, heavily draped in royal blue velvet tied back with gold braid, looked out over the front lawn. The furniture was dark oak and massive, with a sideboard at least ten feet long, and a dining table that would easily accommodate twenty people. Intricately designed wall sconces graced the flocked wallpaper and cast a soft, golden light over the room. The tapestries Grace had noticed earlier hung at the far end, their rich colors glowing in the lamplight.

Tonight, three places were set close together at one end of the table. As they drew nearer, Grace saw that the china and silver were ornate and elegant, the crystal heavy Baccarat, the tablecloth a fine Belgian linen trimmed in lace. Tall white tapers in frosted crystal candle holders flanked a centerpiece of fresh flowers arranged in a delicate Limoges vase.

A butler materialized from a door at the other end of the room. He helped Paul position Virginia's chair at the head of the table, then Paul walked over and stood behind the chair at Virginia's right as the butler came around and held out the chair to Virginia's left for Grace.

Grace sat, wishing Paul were not placed directly opposite her where she could not avoid his gaze. Once she was seated, he sat, too.

"Thank you, Wilbur," Virginia said, and the butler nodded and smiled, then moved to the sideboard and picked up a silver water carafe.

Grace spread her napkin over her lap. Looking at the intimidating array of silver, she was glad she'd spent so many weekends at Melanie's parents' home in Westchester County. The Berancheks were wealthy—not on the scale of the Hollisters, of course—but rich enough that Grace had attended some very elegant dinner parties. Otherwise, she might have been more nervous tonight than she already was.

After Wilbur had poured water into their goblets and Paul had tasted the wine that would accompany their soup, pronouncing it satisfactory, their wineglasses were filled with the white wine. Normally, Grace did not drink much in the way of alcoholic beverages, but tonight she welcomed the fortification the wine might afford. She would welcome anything that would help her get through the evening.

Over their asparagus soup, Virginia said, "Ned told me you've been working as an editor for the past ten years."

"Yes, that's right."

"I believe he said your specialty is children's books?"

"Yes." Grace smiled. "I started out as an editor of nonfiction, even though that's not what I had envisioned when I applied for jobs after graduating from college. I edited several books about antiques and furniture, then one on rare porcelains. I was very eager to do well, so I learned as much about each subject as I could. Then my publisher downsized, and I had to find a new job. It's funny how something that you initially think of as bad luck can turn out to be such a positive step. On my second try, I was able to find a job editing children's books, which is what I had wanted to do in the first place.''

"Kind of tough to make a go of it on an editor's salary, though, isn't it?'' Paul said.

He never gave up, Grace thought as she met his assessing gaze across the flickering candlelight. "My tastes are very simple, so I manage quite well.''

"Even so, living in such an expensive city as New York,'' he persisted.

"It's not that bad.'' Grace kept her voice light. "I live simply, and I share my apartment with a friend.''

Something flickered in the backs of his eyes. Then, as always, the emotion, whatever it was, quickly disappeared, and his enigmatic screen fell securely into place.

She wondered what he was thinking. Maybe when she'd said she had a roommate, he'd thought she meant a man. She barely suppressed a smile as she decided she'd just let him wonder.

She deliberately turned to Virginia, giving her a bright smile. "The soup is delicious.''

"I'm glad you're enjoying it.''

After their soup plates were cleared, and a warm spinach salad placed before them, Virginia turned to Grace. "Would you mind telling me about your life at the convent?''

"No, I don't mind at all.'' For fifteen minutes, Grace told Virginia about the friends she'd made, the schools she'd attended, how Sister Rachel had introduced her to Louisa May Alcott, Beatrix Potter, C. S. Lewis and other authors, and how she'd become enchanted with the world of books. "I loved books. They were my escape and my refuge. Living as I did, among all those quiet, gentle women, books were the only way I learned about how other people lived. I dreamed of becoming a writer, myself,'' she confessed.

"Why didn't you?'' Virginia asked.

Grace shrugged. "Unfortunately, I discovered I had no talent for writing."

"Paul once talked of becoming a writer, too." Virginia turned her smile on her nephew.

Grace slowly turned back to Paul.

"Surprised?" he said with something almost like amusement firing his eyes, which surprised Grace.

She met his gaze squarely. "Frankly, yes." Somehow she could not picture a man like him inhabiting a world created out of his imagination. He seemed too pragmatic, not to mention insensitive.

"And why is that?"

Grace took a sip of her water before answering. "You just don't seem the type."

That gleam was still there. "How can you make a judgment like that? You don't know me at all."

"That's very true. Just as you don't know me." *But you're judging me, anyway, aren't you?*

Now his amusement—if that's what it had been—was replaced with something very like admiration. "That's a point well taken, Miss Gregory."

"Oh, for heaven's sake," Virginia said. "Her name is Grace. Would you stop calling her Miss Gregory?"

"Sorry, Aunt Virginia."

Grace almost laughed at his meek reply. It was good to know that someone could cow Paul Hollister, even if only briefly. "Why did you change your mind about becoming a writer?"

"Like you, I found my talents lay in other directions."

"So what do *you* do to earn a living?" Two could play this game, Grace thought.

He gave her a knowing smile. "To start with, I'm chairman of the board of Hollister's Department Stores. I'm also Aunt Virginia's business manager."

"Which means?"

"Which means I oversee all of the family investments and real estate holdings." His smile faded. "Would you like me to enumerate them for you?"

"Paul!" Virginia said.

His eyes remained fixed on Grace. "Well, she asked. And I'm sure she's wondering. Unless, of course, she's already checked us out thoroughly." His tone left no doubt that's exactly what he believed.

"Paul, I'm ashamed of you. Grace is our guest. I can't imagine what's come over you."

"It's okay, Mrs. Hollister," Grace interjected. "I don't mind answering his questions."

Virginia was still looking at Paul. "She doesn't care about our holdings."

He continued to stare at Grace. "I'm sure you're right, Aunt Virginia. I'm sure the Hollister fortune is a matter of no importance to her at all."

Grace met his gaze evenly. "Actually, it isn't, even though I know you don't believe that."

"Paul, you promised me," Virginia said.

He shrugged and lapsed into silence, but Grace felt his gaze—ever watchful for the slightest slipup on her part.

Although Grace felt she'd given as good as she'd gotten, the barbed exchange had taken its toll. She felt drained and edgy. Throughout the main course of broiled lamb chops and fresh green beans, then their dessert of a mouth-watering berry cobbler, Grace couldn't wait for the meal to be over so she could escape to her room.

She found it more and more difficult to respond to Virginia's questions and the older woman's equally watchful gaze. She knew Virginia's reasons for questioning her and studying her so closely were probably vastly different than Paul's, but the constant scrutiny from both of them was still hard to endure.

Grace felt as if every word, every physical action or re-action, was not only being watched, but examined and dissected and evaluated. It was even hard for her to enjoy the superb food.

Finally dinner was over.

"It's been a long day," Virginia said, sighing and pushing back from the table. She gave Grace a warm look. "You're probably tired."

"Yes," Grace said gratefully, "I am."

"Paul and I always have breakfast together in the sun room at eight-thirty. I'd be pleased if you'd join us. Unless, of course, you're a late sleeper, in which case, I'll leave instructions for the cook, and you can have breakfast in your room."

Grace noticed that Paul did not echo his aunt's invitation. For just a second, she thought about taking the coward's way out and opting for a peaceful breakfast alone. Instead, she smiled and said, "I'm usually up before seven. I'll be happy to join you at breakfast."

Virginia smiled. "Good. Afterward, we'll take that tour I promised you."

Grace rose, and so did Paul. She stood awkwardly for a moment, then impulsively walked around the table, leaned down and kissed Virginia's soft cheek. A faint scent of roses clung to Virginia's skin.

Virginia's eyes shone with pleasure as she met Grace's gaze. "Good night, my dear. I hope you sleep well."

"Good night, Mrs. Hollister." Grace finally looked at Paul. "Good night...Paul." It was the first time she'd addressed him by his first name, and it felt strange on her lips.

"Good night...Grace."

Keeping her head high and her back straight, Grace walked out of the dining room and up the stairs. She knew without looking that Paul was watching her.

Later, as she lay in bed and tried to fall asleep, she wondered if she'd made a mistake in coming here. She'd been so sure it was the right thing to do, but now she wasn't sure about anything.

She reached for the locket, which she'd placed on the bedside table. Its scrolled surface felt familiar, even comforting. She held it for a while, knowing she would dream tonight, then slipped it under her pillow and closed her eyes.

"Mama!" Laughter bubbled out of the child's mouth, and she rocked back and forth.

"Careful, Elizabeth," warned the attractive woman standing by her side. She put out a cautionary hand. "You'll fall off the horsie."

The toddler shrieked and rocked faster, teetering dangerously.

The woman grabbed the little girl, keeping her from falling off the big rocking horse. She hugged her close, nuzzling her face against the child's neck. The child giggled.

"No!" she shouted in her piping baby voice, pushing at the woman. "No, Mama."

The woman laughed. "Elizabeth, you're getting big enough to spank, you know." But the words held no real threat, and she hugged and kissed the toddler before putting her back atop the rocking horse again. This time she stood right next to her, holding her as the child began to rock.

The child rocked back and forth, back and forth. As the motion of the horse became faster, something around the child's neck bounced up and down, gleaming golden in the sunlight.

The object grew bigger and bigger as if a zoom lens were trained upon it, moving closer all the time. Finally, the golden oval was the only thing visible in the camera's eye. The closer the locket came, the more dazzling was its light.

The brilliance of the light blinded Grace. She put her hand over her eyes to shield them.

Grace sat up in bed. Her heart was beating too hard, the way it did when she was afraid. She took a long, shaky breath and removed her hands from her eyes. Light from the half-open bathroom door illuminated the bedroom. For a minute, Grace was confused. Where was she? Then, like water bursting through a hole in a dam, memories of the day and evening flooded her mind.

She was at Hollister House.

Sleeping in Elizabeth's bed. In Elizabeth's room.

It took her a few more minutes to remember the dream. Closing her eyes, she reached under her pillow and touched the locket. As she stroked the rough metal, the images from her dream came rushing back, vivid in their detail.

A large room with casement windows on two sides. Window seats and sunlight streaming in. Bookcases filled with books, toys and puzzles. A large, gaily-painted rocking horse in one corner. Next to the rocking horse, a chair.

Grace clutched the locket tighter and closed her eyes. The little girl from all of Grace's dreams, the girl she now knew was Elizabeth, sitting on top of the horse. Laughing. Laughing. Her heart filled with joy. And next to her, her grandmother, Virginia. A younger Virginia. Smiling indulgently. Holding the toddler firmly so she wouldn't fall.

The images were so real, Grace felt as if she could reach out and touch them. She wanted to. These images were happy ones, good ones.

Grace rubbed the locket, and the images merged, separated, then merged again.

Elizabeth held out her pudgy arms. "Mama, Mama!" Virginia lifted her from the horse and held her close.

Grace felt Virginia's warm, comforting arms going around her, holding her close, and an overwhelming sense of peace and security enfolded her.

The room shimmered around them, filled with love and safety.

Grace slowly opened her eyes. Clutching the locket in her hand, she blindly reached for her satin robe. She put it on, tied it tightly around her waist, then, like someone being guided by an unseen hand, she walked slowly toward the door.

Paul couldn't sleep. He kept seeing Grace's face, Grace's eyes. He kept hearing her soft voice, remembering the way she'd looked when she first walked into the sitting room earlier that evening.

He'd been startled by his completely unexpected response to her. He took one look, and it was as if he'd had no control over either his body or his emotions.

She had looked irresistibly beautiful in a violet dress, made out of a soft wool that swirled around her shapely legs. She'd piled her golden hair on top of her head in a more sophisticated fashion than she'd worn it earlier, and her face looked fresh and natural under light makeup.

The locket had gleamed around her neck.

Paul's breath had caught, and he knew his eyes had revealed his awareness of her. His attraction to her. It disgusted him that his body had so betrayed him.

For the rest of the night, no matter how he tried to keep his thoughts about her objective and impersonal, he kept losing himself in the depths of her deep blue eyes. Worse, he kept imagining what she'd look like with her hair tumbling loose around her shoulders.

He kept remembering what a beautiful smile she had and wondering what her laughter would sound like.

He kept trying to force those thoughts away. Kept trying to maintain his emotional distance. Sitting across from her at the dinner table, he'd told himself, just as he was telling himself now, that the worst thing that could happen would be for him to be swayed by Grace's delicate beauty, her undeniable charm and feminine appeal.

He told himself she was a con artist, that the way she looked was deliberate. She was clever, sophisticated and practiced at deception—everything he despised in a woman. She was no better than any of the others who had paraded in and out of this house or in and out of his life. She just had classier packaging.

Yet no matter how many times he reiterated these cold, hard truths, he was having trouble believing them. Grace's entire persona belied his arguments.

Around and around, his thoughts whirled. Finally, after hours of lying awake, he got up, turned on his bedside light and reached for his thick terry-cloth robe. He drew it on, belted it and headed for the place that had been his haven since childhood.

Five minutes later, he stood looking out the third-floor windows of the playroom. He hadn't turned on any lights, but the room wasn't dark. It was filled with moonlight. As always, a certain peace enveloped him as he gazed down at the backyard.

As a child, this room had been the first place he headed when his father and mother came to visit.

After his father's death in Vietnam when Paul was ten, and after his mother had left him more and more in Virginia's care, this room became even more important to him—the one constant in a no-longer-secure world. The playroom, even filled with Elizabeth's toys, was his special place.

It was here, in this room, where his aunt had told him that his mother had decided to leave him at Hollister House permanently.

"Why?" he'd asked stoically. At thirteen, he was already a master at concealing his emotions.

"Well, you know, Paul," Virginia had said gently, compassion shining in her eyes, "your mother has a new husband, and she's trying to get adjusted to her new life." She'd put her arms around him, holding him close even as he held himself rigid. "And she knows I'm lonely and how much I love you. It'll be wonderful to have you here with me."

"It's 'cause I'm adopted, isn't it?" he'd said, trying to ignore the awful lump in his throat.

He still remembered the look of horror that had twisted his aunt's face. "Oh, no!" she'd exclaimed. "Oh, Paul, how could you even *think* that? Of course, it isn't because you're adopted. Sweetie, your mother loves you! She's just being pulled in so many directions right now, that's all."

He'd swallowed hard. *Don't cry,* he told himself. *Who cares, anyway? If she doesn't want me, I don't want her!*

Paul grew up that day. And in so doing, he cut his mother out of his heart. In subsequent years, during the few times he was in her company, he called her Jennifer and did his best not to even think of her as his mother. His stepfather, an obnoxious braggart, and his step-siblings— three greedy, whiny brats who had grown up to be even more greedy and whiny—he totally ignored.

The stepsisters and stepbrother weren't really related to him, anyway. After all, he was adopted, and they were Jennifer's natural children.

Paul never acknowledged how much it hurt that his mother obviously didn't feel *they* were a burden to her but he was. Instead, anytime he felt scared or lonely or less brave than he wanted the world to think, he escaped to the playroom.

Even now, as a thirty-seven-year-old man, whenever he felt troubled or lonely or beset by his private demons, he came up here.

He stood there at the window for a long time, thinking and remembering. And just as he decided it was time for him to go back to his room and try to get some sleep, he heard a noise.

He whirled, eyes widening in surprise.

Grace stood in a patch of moonlight in the open doorway.

"What are you doing here?" he asked.

"I—I couldn't sleep." She shivered and hugged herself. "I—I had a dream. It... it upset me."

It was only then, as his shock subsided, that he noticed she was barefoot and trembling, that her clothing appeared to be insubstantial—some kind of satin robe that revealed generous curves and couldn't provide much warmth. Other details stood out, too. Her tousled hair, loose around her shoulders the way he'd imagined it, and her toes peeping out from the bottom of a gossamer-thin nightgown—toes that looked oddly vulnerable in the moonlight.

Once more his body betrayed him as a deep yearning filled him. "Bad dream or not, you shouldn't be wandering around," he said, his voice deliberately harsh to disguise the unwanted feelings her appearance had provoked.

She looked around slowly, as if she hadn't heard him. Her voice trembled. "Th-this is the room from my dream. There's the rocking horse. And there are the bookshelves."

Her words caused a tremor to snake down his spine. What an actress she was!

She walked closer, and as she did, the soft folds of her robe undulated against her body, clearly outlining her rounded breasts with their hard little nipples. The sexual attraction and desire he was trying so strenuously to deny surged hotly through him, and it took all his self-control to tear his gaze away.

"You don't believe me, do you?" she murmured, so close now he could reach out and touch her.

He licked his lips. "No, I don't believe you." He willed her to leave this room. To leave him alone.

She looked up. He could see the soft rise and fall of her breasts. He could even see the little pulse that beat at the base of her throat. He could smell her, too—a tantalizing mixture of flowers and musk.

He instinctively backed away from her. He felt threatened in a way he hadn't felt threatened in a long, long time.

"I—I guess I don't blame you. In your place, I'd probably feel the same way." Her voice was soft and urgent, her eyes dark, shining pools. "Paul, I don't know what the truth is. Whether I'm Elizabeth or not. And...and I'm frightened to find out. But I know I must if I ever hope to find peace."

Her words rang with conviction. It would be so easy to believe her, so easy to fall under her spell as his aunt had. He set his jaw, knowing he couldn't weaken.

"Oh, I'm sure that's what you'd like me to believe," he said. "That you've got some high-principled reason for being here. But you can save your breath, because I'm not fooled by your innocent look, or by what you've said. You may be more clever than the others, but underneath, you're still a fortune hunter."

"No! That's not true. I don't care about the money." Her voice broke. "I—I just want to find my family."

"Even if you break my aunt's heart in the process?" he challenged.

She looked at him. Her throat worked. "I would never hurt your aunt," she whispered.

He stared at her. "Prove it."

"How?"

"Leave. Go away. Make up some story tomorrow morning, and get out."

Her shoulders slumped, and she didn't answer for a long moment. When she spoke, her voice was filled with resignation. "I can't do that."

He smiled cynically. "Why is it I knew that would be your answer?"

She looked at him for a long, silent moment. The only sounds in the room were the ticking of the clock on the wall, and the creaking of the house as a gust of wind blew up under the rafters.

"Think whatever you want," she finally said. "And do whatever you have to do. But know this. I'm not leaving until I find out the truth. Whatever the truth may be." Then she turned and walked out of the room.

Chapter Five

The next morning, Grace felt sluggish and tense. She always felt this way after she had a dream about Elizabeth—as if all the energy had been drained out of her. Even a hot shower didn't do much to revive her. Her bravado of the night before had completely deserted her, and she had almost decided Paul was right.

Maybe she *should* leave.

Maybe she should tell Virginia that's what she'd decided, when she saw her at breakfast this morning.

Mulling the situation over, Grace dressed carefully in cranberry wool slacks with a matching turtleneck sweater and soft brown boots with flat heels. Instead of twisting her hair into its usual chignon, she brushed it back from her face and tied it with a cranberry ribbon.

Then she slowly fastened the locket around her neck. She looked at herself in the mirror and wondered if this would be the last time she'd ever wear the locket. In fairness, she should leave it with Virginia if she decided to go back to New York.

Her heart ached at the thought. Both the locket and Virginia had come to mean something to her.

Virginia.

Grace could hardly stand to see the disappointment in the older woman's eyes if she decided to leave. But wasn't that really the smartest thing she could do? No matter what Virginia had said, Grace would never be accepted here. Paul was determined to make her life miserable. She couldn't fight against his anger and suspicions indefinitely. She wasn't sure she even wanted to.

Virginia was an old woman. It was obvious, just by looking at her, that she was frail. How much longer did she have to live? Grace, picturing Paul's cold dislike, could just imagine what life would be like once Virginia was gone.

Intolerable.

Who needed this? She'd been happy with her life before the dreams started. She could be happy again.

And in the end, Virginia would probably be better off, too, if Grace left now. There would be much less heartbreak and disappointment in the long run.

Grace slowly walked downstairs. When she entered the sun room, both Paul and Virginia were already there, seated across from each other at a small round table placed in front of the windows.

Virginia looked up, her eyes lighting with happiness as she saw Grace. "Good morning!" she said eagerly. "Did you sleep well?"

Grace put her best effort into a smile, which felt stiff and fake. She didn't look at Paul. "Um, you know, a strange bed ..."

Virginia nodded. "I know, but you'll get used to it."

Grace sat down. Paul was at her left, Virginia at her right. Anna came in and poured coffee into Grace's cup, saying, "Good morning, miss."

"Good morning, Anna."

Paul still hadn't spoken, and Grace still hadn't looked in his direction, but she could feel his eyes watching. Her stomach gave a little nervous flutter. The scene in the playroom last night was vivid in her mind. She wondered if he was remembering it, too.

"Would you like a muffin?" he said.

Grace turned and accepted the basket of muffins. "Thank you." Her gaze finally connected with his, and with a jolt, she realized he was just as uncomfortable as she was. She hurriedly busied herself buttering her muffin and selecting melon and berries from the crystal bowl in the center of the table.

"There's scrambled eggs and bacon," Virginia said. "I don't eat them myself, but you're welcome to have some."

"No, thanks. This is fine."

Throughout their meal, Virginia seemed determined to ignore both Grace's and Paul's silence, and equally determined to pretend nothing was wrong. She kept up a casual conversation and forced each of them to respond.

Paul pushed away from the table before Grace had finished eating. "I need to get to work," he said.

Virginia smiled up at him. "Will we see you at lunch?"

Grace kept her gaze trained on her food. *Say no.*

"No. I have an appointment with William Singer to go over those new leases. But I'll join you at dinner."

After he'd gone, Grace could feel her body relaxing. She still hadn't come to a decision about staying or leaving Rolling Hills, but it would be easier to think with him out of the room.

Virginia, too, seemed to feel less inhibited, now that her nephew was absent. Her voice bubbled with enthusiasm as she said, "I can't wait to show you around."

Grace swallowed. Maybe she should tell Virginia now that she wasn't sure she would be staying on. She looked at the older woman.

Virginia's blue eyes shone with happiness. She smiled at Grace and reached over to grasp her hand. Her touch set off a deep yearning in Grace. "I'm so happy you're here," she said. "You can't know how happy you've made me. For the first time in a long time, I couldn't wait to start the day."

Grace fought against the tears that threatened to spill. She blinked and willed herself to stay in control.

Virginia squeezed Grace's hand, then released it. She wiped her mouth on her napkin. "Well," she said briskly, "are you finished?"

Grace bit her bottom lip. The time had come to make her decision. To go. Or to stay. She looked at Virginia. She saw the eagerness in the woman's eyes, the love she had to give. Grace took a deep breath. "Yes. I'm finished." She smiled. "And I'm looking forward to our tour."

Grace knew that Virginia was carefully watching her every reaction as they slowly toured the enormous house. Grace gradually lost count of the rooms. She had known there were people who lived like this; she just had never met any before. Even Melanie's parents, with all their money, seemed almost ordinary in comparison.

They started their tour on the first floor, which contained an elegant and formal living room, the dining room, sitting room, library and sun room—all of which Grace had seen yesterday—and across from the library, a smaller room Virginia called the morning room.

"This is my private place," she explained as she wheeled herself in ahead of Grace. "Anna is the only one besides me who comes in here, and that's just to clean." She smiled up at Grace. "Even Paul stays out."

The morning room was serene and beautiful, Grace thought, decorated in soft shades of peach and blue. There was an exquisite French writing desk positioned at the windows, which overlooked the front lawns, and Grace could see something that looked like a journal lying open on its surface.

"I don't expect this room to trigger any memories," Virginia said. "Elizabeth never came here."

Grace nodded. None of the rooms had triggered memories. She already knew that unless and until she rubbed the locket, no memories would surface.

On the other side of the morning room, opposite the sun room, lay Virginia's private quarters consisting of a large bedroom and adjoining bath. Nearby was the elevator.

"Paul had this installed after my fall."

"Yes, Anna told me," Grace said.

The remainder of the first floor contained several powder rooms and a cavernous kitchen and pantry.

Virginia introduced Grace to the smiling cook—a motherly-looking woman in her sixties. "This is Nora. Nora, Miss Gregory."

"Pleased to meet you, miss," Nora said. Her rosy cheeks glowed. "If there's anything special you'd like to eat while you're visiting . . . just let me know."

"Thank you."

After they exited the kitchen, Virginia said, "I've saved the best for last. She led the way down the central corridor and into the left wing, throwing wide the double doors at the end of the long hallway.

Grace gasped.

An immense ballroom lay beyond. As she slowly followed Virginia into the room, she realized it ran the entire width of the house and was two stories high. Long casement windows ringed the room on three sides, and the fourth wall contained long gilt-framed mirrors. Four crystal chandeliers hung from the ceiling, one in each quadrant of the room.

The floor was a highly-polished dark wood. At one end, it was raised about six inches, and Grace could picture a small orchestra positioned there.

Sunlight poured through the windows. As Grace moved deeper into the room, she saw that some of the windows were actually French doors. Beyond the ballroom was a huge flagstone patio, and beyond that the grounds of the estate.

"It's incredible, isn't it?" Virginia said.

"Yes, incredible," Grace echoed, imagining what the room would look like at night with the chandeliers blazing and hundreds of beautifully dressed guests whirling on the floor to the strains of a Strauss waltz.

"My husband told me that some of his earliest memories were of wonderful dances held in this room." Virginia sighed. "When I came here as a bride, my in-laws held a huge dinner-dance for Evan and me, and four hundred people came." Her eyes grew cloudy with memory. "And every Christmas, there was the most fabulous Christmas Ball." She looked down at her hands. Her emerald looked brilliant in the sunlight. Her voice softened. "The Christmas after Evan, Jr., was born, my husband gave me this ring. I'll never forget it. I wore an emerald green velvet dress to the ball that year. I was so happy. So very happy. I thought I was the luckiest girl in the world."

Grace swallowed against the lump in her throat.

Virginia smiled sadly. "I stopped having the balls after Elizabeth disappeared. I just didn't have the heart for it anymore." Her gaze met Grace's. "This ballroom hasn't been used in thirty-some years." She took a deep breath. "Enough of that. Let's go upstairs."

When they reached the second floor, they turned to the left wing first—the ballroom wing. Virginia indicated a set of double doors at the end of the hall. "Paul's private quarters are in there." She gestured across the hall. "And his office is there."

Grace noted that he was at the opposite end of the house from both her and Virginia.

The right wing contained a bewildering array of bedrooms and bathrooms as well as a cozy room that Virginia said was the upstairs sitting room. "You're welcome to use this anytime you like," she told Grace.

The third floor, which was only about half as big as the other two floors, held the servants' rooms, storage rooms and the playroom.

Grace wondered if she should tell Virginia that she'd already seen this room, both in her dreams and in actuality. She decided she wouldn't. Not yet. But when Virginia looked up at her hopefully and said, "Do you remember this room at all?" Grace couldn't lie.

"I dreamed about it last night," she admitted.

"You . . . Elizabeth spent a lot of time here."

Grace nodded. She couldn't meet Virginia's eyes. She knew if she did, she would be tempted to tell her more, and she didn't want Virginia to count on too much.

Instead, Grace walked to the windows where Paul had been standing last night. Once again, she remembered the tension in the room, the stiffness in his posture, the way he'd almost acted as if he was afraid of her.

She looked down over the grounds. The grass was still green, but it had lost its summer brilliance. All the trees except the evergreens were bare, and here and there a stray leaf, which had evaded the gardener's rake, provided a spot of color. As she watched, two frisky squirrels chased each other up one tree and down another. A few minutes later, she felt Virginia roll up beside her.

"Paul loves this room," Virginia said. "It has always been his refuge."

Why would *he* need a refuge? Grace wondered. He had everything. A home. A family. A place he belonged. Not to mention all the money anyone could possibly need.

"He's adopted, you know," Virginia added.

Grace started. She hadn't known.

"He pretends he doesn't care, but the fact of his adoption has shaped his entire life."

Grace wasn't sure what to say. She looked down at Virginia. The older woman's gaze met hers. She grimaced. "The Hollisters don't seem to be very fruitful. My husband only had one brother, Andrew. Andrew was older than Evan, and he married late in life. He and his wife only had one child, too—a boy named Stephen. Stephen was Paul's father." Virginia sighed. "Stephen was a wonderful boy. I couldn't have loved him more if he'd been my own son. Although he was older than Evan, Jr., the two were great friends. Since we all lived here together, it was a good thing, wasn't it?"

Since she didn't seem to expect Grace to answer, Grace just smiled and waited for Virginia to continue. Grace found the family history fascinating.

"Anyway," Virginia said, "Much to Andrew's chagrin, Stephen showed no interest in the family business. All he ever wanted to do was fly. Andrew finally relented, and Stephen went to the Air Force Academy. Soon after he graduated, he married Jennifer, Paul's mother. After years of trying to have a child, they finally adopted Paul.

"Paul adored Stephen. Unfortunately, he didn't have his father very long. When Paul was ten, Stephen went to Vietnam. He was only there three weeks when his helicopter went down, killing him and the rest of the crew." She sighed heavily. "Paul took his father's death very hard. So did Jennifer, but their grief manifested itself in opposite ways. Paul turned inward. Jennifer looked for forgetfulness in the company of others. She married again within two years. I think Paul felt her remarriage was a personal betrayal. He hated his stepfather. He still hates him." Virginia gave Grace a sad little smile. "To be quite honest, I'm not very fond of Ron myself. He's—how do you young folks say it—a blowhard?"

Grace grinned.

"I'm sure Paul didn't mean to, but I think he made Jennifer and Ron feel so guilty and uncomfortable that they could no longer endure having him around."

Grace could understand that. If he'd looked at his mother and stepfather in the same accusing way he looked at Grace, she could understand it well.

"Anyway, when he was thirteen, she left him here with me permanently. That abandonment, on top of knowing that he was adopted, hurt him unbearably."

Grace didn't want to feel sympathy for Paul. She didn't even want to feel empathy. She, too, had grown up knowing she'd been abandoned, and she hadn't had *anyone* to call her own. It hadn't made *her* bitter and suspicious. Yet a tiny part of her ached for him. They had more in common than he might think.

"That's why he's acting the way he is," Virginia continued. "And that's why I can't get too angry with him for it."

"Thank you for telling me, Mrs. Hollister, but I'm not trying to take Paul's place."

"I know that, my dear. Even if you wanted to, you *couldn't* take his place. His place will always be there. And soon, I hope, he'll come to understand that."

I wouldn't count on it, Grace thought.

Paul returned to the house at two-thirty. He felt tired and out of sorts. No wonder. He'd barely slept last night. He waved at Tim, his aunt's chauffeur, who was waxing Paul's red Lamborghini in the driveway, and pulled the Ferrari into the six-car garage. Expensive, very fast cars were Paul's one big indulgence, the purchase of which he rationalized by telling himself they were a good investment.

As he walked toward the house, he wondered how his aunt's day had gone.

Oh, hell, he might as well admit it. He was wondering about *her*. He hadn't *stopped* wondering about her. Even William Singer, his luncheon companion, who wasn't exactly sensitive to the moods of others, had commented on Paul's preoccupation.

"Dammit, Paul, would you pay attention?" he'd said, his face red. "What the hell's wrong with you?"

"Sorry." Remembering their exchange, Paul gritted his teeth. That blasted woman was driving him crazy. He wondered what new way she'd managed to get her hooks into his aunt today. He could just imagine how she'd acted during the tour of the house. The soft looks and dramatic gestures. The sighs. The trembling lower lip.

She probably had Virginia completely smitten by now. So smitten that even if Paul were to uncover evidence that undermined or disproved Grace's story, his aunt would find some reason not to believe it.

Damn! He decided that as soon as he got into his office, he would call Ned Shapiro. Paul wanted a full-fledged, no-expenses-spared investigation started.

And he would tell that old man so. He'd also demand that Grace relinquish that locket so it could be sent off to be authenticated.

That decided, he entered the house through the back door, waved at Nora, the cook, and strode through the kitchen toward the back stairs. He took them two at a time.

Five minutes later he was in his office, seated behind his desk. Since it was Saturday, his secretary was off, but the message light on his answering machine was blinking. He ignored the messages and dialed Ned's number in Philadelphia.

"Ned," he said without preamble when the old man answered, "what progress have you made investigating Grace Gregory's background?"

"Well, I, uh," the lawyer sputtered, then finally seemed to regain his equilibrium. "The private investigator we hired is giving me weekly reports," he replied with dignity.

"And?" Paul demanded. He tapped his pen against his desk top.

"So far, nothing untoward has been discovered."

Untoward! Who the hell used a word like *untoward* in this day and age? Ned Shapiro was a fossil. They should have retired him years ago. "Where are my copies of the reports?"

"My secretary put them in the mail the day before yesterday. You should get them soon. And Paul?"

"What?"

"You should try to relax more. You're heading for a heart attack at a young age if you don't calm down."

Paul started to fire off an angry retort, then slumped back in his chair. Why was he taking his frustration out on Ned Shapiro? The older man hadn't done anything wrong. Paul grimaced. Ned was just the messenger. "You're right, Ned," he said. "I'm sorry I barked at you."

Paul could almost see the lawyer's smile. "Don't worry about it. I understand. I'm just as concerned that we get to the truth about this woman as you are. Do you want me to fax you those reports?"

"No. I can wait. They'll probably come in this afternoon's mail. There is one thing, though... I want you to try to have the locket authenticated."

"Of course. I've got an expert lined up already."

"Good. I'll plan to drive into the city Monday and bring it to you."

"I'll look forward to it."

They hung up, and Paul sat staring at the phone for a while. Then he sighed and punched his message button. Might as well see who had called while he was out. He'd return his phone calls, check and see if the mail had arrived, then he'd go looking for his aunt and Grace.

There were four messages pertaining to business, then he heard:

Paul, this is your mother. I'd appreciate it if you'd call me as soon as you return.

Paul frowned. Jennifer never called him unless she wanted money. And she'd already received her allowance for the year and had borrowed against next year's allowance.

The hell with her. He wasn't up to an argument.

He punched the intercom. When Wilbur answered, Paul said, "Has the afternoon mail arrived?"

"Not yet, Mr. Hollister."

"Bring it up as soon as it does."

"Yes, sir."

Paul decided he might as well wait until it was time for tea before going downstairs. He reached for the phone to return his business calls. Just as he did, it rang. He picked up the receiver.

"Paul Hollister."

"I told you to call me as soon as you returned," his mother said, a peevish note in her voice.

"I got your message."

She sighed dramatically. "Paul, I don't know why you're so hard to get along with."

"Most people find me quite easy to get along with," he said mildly.

"Name one."

Paul bit back a smile. No matter how angry Jennifer made him, her sharp answers had the ability to amuse him. "I'm busy, Jennifer. Did you want something in particular or are you just out to annoy me in general?"

"As much fun as it is to annoy you in general, I did need your help."

Just as he'd thought. His "help" always boiled down to giving her more money. He waited silently.

"I want to know about this woman who's claiming to be Elizabeth," Jennifer said.

Paul stared at the phone. "How did *you* hear about her?"

"I have my sources. So it's true then? There is another woman claiming to be Elizabeth?"

"Yes, it's true," Paul said reluctantly.

"Damn."

His sentiments exactly, although he wasn't about to admit it to Jennifer.

"Do you think she could possibly be for real?" Jennifer asked.

"I don't know."

There was silence for a long moment. "If she *is* real, that means you and I will both be cut out of Virginia's will."

"Is that all that concerns you? If it is, save your breath."

"No, it's *not* all that concerns me, despite what you might think," Jennifer said earnestly. "I really like the old lady."

Although he hated to admit his mother had any good qualities, Paul knew she was telling the truth. She *did* like his aunt. And for some damned reason, his great-aunt liked her. He had never understood why.

"And I'm worried about her," his mother added. "She's vulnerable."

"I know that. But I'm not going to let her get ripped off by anyone, so quit worrying."

"Will you at least call and keep me informed on what's going on?"

"Yes."

"Promise?"

"Yes, I promise," he said. "Now will you please let me go so I can get some work done?"

Grace stirred as a soft buzzing noise filled her head. She opened her eyes. The clock on her bedside table read three-thirty. She stretched, then slowly got up from the bed.

She had been so tired after lunch, she'd excused herself and come upstairs to take a nap.

"I'll see you in the sun room at four," Virginia had said, reminding Grace about afternoon tea.

A few minutes to four, face washed, hair combed, teeth brushed, fresh makeup applied, Grace descended the stairs and made her way to the sun room.

Virginia looked up and smiled as Grace entered the room. "Did you have a good nap?"

"Yes, thank you, Mrs. Hollister. I feel so much better."

"Good."

Grace sat down. She wondered if Paul would join them for tea. He'd said he'd see them at dinner. With luck, that meant she had a few hours' reprieve before having to endure the pleasure of his company.

Anna came in and poured their tea. She served Virginia, and when she'd finished, Grace served herself. When the maid left, Virginia said, "Ever since lunch, I've been thinking."

Grace waited.

"There has to be some way to prove whether or not you are Elizabeth," Virginia said.

"I don't know how—"

"My aunt is right," Paul's voice said. "And there *is* a way to prove if you're telling the truth."

Grace turned. Paul, dressed in a charcoal-colored suit that enhanced his dark good looks, strode into the room. He bent down and kissed his aunt. When he straightened, he looked directly down into Grace's eyes.

"I'm willing to do anything reasonable," Grace said. "Although I can't imagine what—"

"Can't you?" He smiled, triumph lighting his eyes. "It's simple. All you have to do is take a lie detector test."

Chapter Six

Grace looked at all the wires attached to her body. She had agreed to take the lie detector test, even though Virginia hadn't wanted her to. Grace could tell she wasn't going to enjoy this. She already felt vaguely guilty, as if she'd done something wrong, and the test hadn't even started yet.

She watched the technician, who seemed to be testing the machine by turning knobs. Paul had hired a private company to give the test, and the technician had come to Hollister House to administer it.

The equipment had been set up in Paul's office. It was the first time Grace had seen the suite of offices or met his secretary, a pleasant fortyish woman who introduced herself as Susan Webb. Paul's office was large and attractively furnished, with a modern light oak desk and matching credenza and file cabinets, a large leather executive chair, two leather side chairs, a beautiful paisley-print love seat, built-in bookshelves, and state-of-the-art computer equipment, laser printer, copying machine and fax machine. From somewhere in the attic, Susan had unearthed a schoolroom chair with a writing arm, which was where Grace sat now.

"Are you comfortable, Miss Gregory?" asked the technician, a soft-spoken man named Stewart.

"Yes, I'm fine." *I just want to get this over with.*

"Now remember, just answer yes or no to the questions. No qualifying. No elaboration or explanation. Understood?" His hazel eyes peered at her over his glasses.

"Yes."

"Are you ready to start?"

"Yes." She told herself to relax and took a couple of deep breaths.

"Is your name Grace Gregory?" he began.

"Yes."

"Do you make your home in New York City?"

"Yes."

"Do you work as an editor of children's books?"

"Yes."

Stewart asked her a dozen more routine questions about her background and her life. Grace answered them all calmly and could feel her body relaxing.

Then he said, "Have you been having dreams about Elizabeth Hollister?"

"Well, yes, I think—"

"Just answer yes or no, Miss Gregory."

"Sorry," Grace said, wetting her lips.

"It's okay." He smiled reassuringly. "Just relax. Let's try that question again. Have you been having dreams about Elizabeth Hollister?"

"Yes."

"Had you ever heard the name Elizabeth Hollister before you started having the dreams?"

"No."

"Had you ever heard the names Virginia Hollister or Josie McClure before you started having the dreams?"

"No."

"Had you ever heard of Paul Hollister before the dreams started?"

"No."

"Did you know the Hollisters were wealthy when you decided to come here?"

"Uh . . . yes."

"Did you know they were wealthy before the dreams started?"

"No, I told you—"

"Yes or no, Miss Gregory," Stewart said patiently, making a notation on his chart.

"Sorry," she said again. "No."

"Did you have the locket designed to look like the one Elizabeth Hollister owned?"

"No!" Grace frowned. Is *that* what Paul believed?

For the next half hour, Stewart questioned her on every aspect of her story concerning Elizabeth and continued to hammer on certain points. The experience was grueling and unpleasant. By the time the test was over, Grace felt drained, as if she'd had one of her dreams. Her mouth was dry, and she felt the beginnings of a headache.

Finally, Stewart removed all the wires and smiled at her. "That's it. You're done."

Gratefully Grace made her escape.

"Finished?" Susan asked as Grace walked out of Paul's office.

"Yes, thank goodness."

Susan gave her a sympathetic smile.

Grace went straight to her room. After entering, she shut the door behind her, leaned against it and closed her eyes.

Never again, she thought. Not for Paul Hollister. Not for anyone.

* * *

"Well, Paul? Are you satisfied?" Virginia rarely felt angry or even annoyed with her great-nephew, but ever since he'd suggested Grace take a lie detector test, she'd been upset with him.

The technician from the laboratory had called and given them his report only minutes earlier. Virginia couldn't prevent a small, triumphant smile as she faced Paul in the library. "I knew Grace would pass the lie detector test with flying colors."

He didn't even blink. "That's not what the report said."

"It most certainly is!"

"No," Paul insisted. "What the report said was that Grace believes that what she's told us is the truth. That doesn't mean it *is* the truth. Lie detector tests aren't conclusive. They can only tell when a person is consciously lying. Why do you think they are inadmissible as evidence in a court of law?"

"If you weren't going to pay any attention to the results of the test, why on earth did you want Grace to take it?" Virginia said, exasperated now.

"If you want to know the truth, I thought she'd refuse."

Virginia glared at him. "In which case, you would have declared her afraid to take the test."

"Yes."

"The whole test idea was a no-win situation for Grace, wasn't it?"

He shrugged.

"Even after she agreed to take the test, you thought she'd fail, didn't you?"

"Yes, I did."

"And if she had failed, you'd have considered *that* conclusive!"

"Because it would have been."

He didn't even have the decency to look contrite over his double standard. Virginia shook her head wearily. She'd thought he was coming around, but she knew now he hadn't accepted any part of Grace's story. "What's it going to take to convince you Grace is genuine?"

"More than this test, certainly."

"How about finding out that the locket is Elizabeth's? Will that be enough? Or will you still want more proof?"

"*If* we find out the locket is Elizabeth's, we—"

"No *ifs* about it," Virginia said, interrupting him. "That locket is the one I gave Elizabeth. I'm as sure of that as I am of my own name."

"Aunt Virginia," he said with a warning tone.

"Well, I *am.* You'll see." When he still looked skeptical, she added, "Just for the sake of argument, let's both assume the expert will confirm the locket's authenticity. Will that finally convince you?"

Paul shrugged. "Probably not."

Virginia chose her words carefully. She didn't want to hurt Paul's feelings or give him the idea that Grace was more important to her than he was, but his uncompromising attitude had become intolerable. "Paul, listen to me. I've gone along with everything you've suggested because I didn't want there to be any doubt in your mind concerning Grace. It's very important to me that Grace feel welcome here and that you accept her. I'm going to ask her to stay longer than a week, and she won't if you make her feel like an interloper."

"Aunt Virginia—"

"Please let me finish."

He sighed, lapsing into silence.

"I want the two of you to be friends."

Her pronouncement hung in the air. It was so quiet in the library that from somewhere deep in the bowels of the house, Virginia could hear the sounds of a vacuum cleaner. She waited patiently.

His eyes, so gentle and warm at times, hardened. "We'll never be friends."

Virginia stared at the man who had meant so much to her over the past three decades. She decided it was time to take off the kid gloves. "How often have I asked you for anything?"

Paul said nothing for long moments. Finally he spoke. "You win, Aunt Virginia. I'll be nice to her, even if it kills me."

"That's not good enough."

Again silence reigned for a long moment. Then, abruptly, he smiled, and his eyes lost their steely look. "You're a tough old broad, aren't you?"

Virginia grinned. "Yes, I am. How do you think I've survived everything that's happened to me all these years?"

He shook his head, his expression changing from amusement to affection. "All right. I'll also try my best to keep an open mind, and, because it seems to mean so much to you, I'll even try to become friends with Grace."

Virginia let out her breath, which she hadn't even been aware of holding. "Thank you, Paul."

"But in return, you've got to promise *me* something."

"What?" she said reluctantly.

"Don't do anything rash until we have the full report of the investigator Ned hired."

"Fine."

"You promise?" He didn't look as if he believed her.

"Of course." Virginia wasn't worried about her promise. She knew the investigator wouldn't turn up anything bad about Grace. How could he? Grace was Elizabeth. There was no doubt at all in Virginia's mind.

The lie detector test had taken place on Monday, three days after Grace's arrival in Rolling Hills.

Now it was Friday, and Grace had been at Hollister House for a week. The last couple of days had been much more comfortable for her, mostly because Paul's attitude toward her seemed to have undergone a change. Not that he was overly friendly, or anything like that, but he didn't seem so darkly suspicious of her any longer. He still watched her all the time, though.

She could feel his eyes, no matter what she was doing. Even when he wasn't in the same room, she felt his presence in the house. She had the feeling that he had suspended his disbelief, but only temporarily. One false move, and she would be the enemy again.

This morning, at breakfast, was a good example. When Grace walked into the sun room, Paul was already there, seated at the table. Dressed in dark gray pants and an impeccably laundered white shirt and striped silk tie, his suit jacket casually folded over the arm of the wicker sofa, he seemed engrossed in the morning paper, which was spread out beside him. Grace glanced at his plate and saw he was almost finished with his breakfast.

"Good morning," she said. She sat in her usual spot to his right. The smell of his cologne drifted across the table, its scent something fresh and crisp.

He looked up and smiled. The smile seemed genuine enough, yet there was still an element of reserve that he couldn't disguise. "Good morning. Sleep well?" He folded his paper and put it aside, politely giving her his attention.

"Quite well, thank you." That was true enough. Since she'd given him the locket to send off to be examined, her sleep was dreamless.

Paul handed her the bowl of fresh fruit, which was just out of her reach.

"Thanks." She helped herself to strawberries and orange wedges. Although she wasn't looking at him, she knew his gaze remained on her.

"Any special plans for today?" he said.

Grace wondered if his question was an attempt at pleasant conversation or if he had an ulterior motive for asking. "I don't know. Your aunt is the one who usually decides what we'll do."

He nodded, his eyes revealing nothing. "I understand you're staying with us longer than you first anticipated."

"Yes." Then, feeling the need to defend herself, even though he hadn't accused her of anything, she added, "Your aunt asked me to stay until we're able to prove something about my identity—one way or the other."

He nodded. "Won't a longer stay present a problem with your employer?"

For the first time that morning, there was a betraying flicker of emotion in the depths of his eyes, and Grace knew, no matter how hard he tried to pretend otherwise, that he was not happy about her continued presence in the house.

"I don't think so," she answered sweetly. "I have more vacation coming to me, and my boss said I could take another couple of weeks without pay if I wanted to." *Put that in your pipe and smoke it.*

Just then, Virginia, followed by Anna, entered the room. "Good morning," Virginia said, smiling at them. As she wheeled her chair into place at the table, Anna poured fresh coffee into Grace's cup, then Paul's. Once Virginia was settled, Anna moved to the older woman's side and filled her cup.

Virginia peered over at Paul's plate. "My goodness. You're almost finished. What time did you get downstairs?"

"About thirty minutes ago. I told Nora last night that I wanted to get an early start today." He picked up his coffee cup. "Have you forgotten? I'm driving into the city to meet with Ned."

"No, I hadn't forgotten."

Something in Virginia's tone alerted Grace to an undercurrent. She slowly looked at Paul. He returned her look. "Ned Shapiro and I have an appointment to meet with the jewelry expert this morning. We'll be getting a full report on the locket."

All day Grace felt anxious. Even though she told herself all she cared about was the truth, something had happened to her in the week she'd spent at Hollister House. She wanted more than the truth.

She wanted to belong to this family. She wanted to claim Virginia as her grandmother.

And she wanted to see the last of Paul Hollister's reservations about her disappear.

She knew that much of what she wished for hinged on the jewelry expert's report.

It was ridiculous to be nervous. The locket was genuine. She knew it was. If she'd ever harbored even the slightest doubt of its authenticity, the cessation of her dreams about Elizabeth the past five days would have been all she needed to convince her.

Grace was certain that the moment she had the locket in her possession again, the dreams would resume.

And that could only mean one thing.

The locket was the catalyst for the dreams. So there had to be a connection between the locket and Elizabeth.

Grace sighed and looked at her watch. Three o'clock. Paul had said he'd be home by teatime. She had an hour to wait. She wondered if Virginia was lying awake the way she was. Thinking, instead of napping, wondering about the outcome of the expert's examination of the locket.

When it was time to join the family for tea, Grace slowly descended the stairs. She'd changed her clothes because she'd felt the need to look her best when she faced Paul again, and this morning she'd been dressed in jeans and an oversize white sweater. This afternoon she wore a long navy wool skirt paired with a navy-and-white-striped blouse and a narrow gold belt.

She was the first one in the sun room, but Virginia entered only minutes later, looking chipper in a red wool dress. Grace thought Virginia looked stronger than she'd looked a week ago and wondered if her own presence in the house had something to do with it.

As they began to fill their plates, Virginia peered at her closely and said, "Don't worry, my dear. I'm not at all worried."

Grace met the older woman's comforting gaze. It wasn't the first time Virginia had instinctively known how Grace was feeling. Grace nodded and tried to smile. She took a deep breath and told herself to calm down. What would be, would be. There was nothing she could do to change it. There had never been anything she could do.

Grace cleared her throat. "I—is Paul back yet?"

Virginia nodded. "I think so. I thought I heard him talking to Wilbur as I came down the hall." At the sound of footsteps, she turned. "Here he is now."

Grace looked around. Paul, who had changed out of the dark gray suit he'd worn this morning, walked in. Although Grace never wanted to acknowledge the awareness he produced in her, she couldn't help noticing how attractive he was in his sharply pressed khaki slacks and dark green cashmere sweater.

She studied him, trying to fathom his expression. His face told her nothing.

He smiled at his aunt, walked over and kissed her cheek. As he straightened, his gaze met Grace's. The smile faded slightly.

Grace's heart beat faster.

Virginia looked up at him. "Come on, Paul, don't keep us in suspense. What happened today?"

Paul's gaze remained fixed on Grace. He reached into his pocket. When he withdrew his hand, the locket dangled from his fingers. He held it up. It caught a ray of late-afternoon sun, and momentarily blinded Grace.

She swallowed.

His tone was expressionless as he said, "As far as our expert could tell, this locket was made by the same designer who made Elizabeth's locket. The signatures were identical."

"I knew it! I knew it!" Virginia said, clapping her hands.

Almost reluctantly, Paul finally looked at his aunt. "There will never be any way to know for sure if this locket is Elizabeth's. The expert couldn't tell us what year it was made. Although it's unlikely, it could have been made years after hers."

"That designer was nearly seventy years old when I commissioned Elizabeth's locket." Virginia's smile was sunshine itself. "He was planning to retire that year. He told me so himself." She reached for the locket and held it tenderly. "It's Elizabeth's," she said softly.

Relief flooded Grace, even as she told herself not to attach too much importance to Paul's disclosure. After all, she'd always known the locket was Elizabeth's. That didn't mean *she* was Elizabeth. And from the reserved expression in Paul's eyes, she knew his thoughts matched hers.

"Oh, my dear, I'm so happy," Virginia said, a catch in her voice. She held the locket out to Grace.

"Mrs. Hollister, are you sure you want me to keep—"

"Oh, please," Virginia said, her voice trembling with emotion. "Don't call me Mrs. Hollister anymore. I want you to call me grandmother. I've waited thirty years to hear you call me grandmother." Bright tears shone in her eyes. "And yes, I'm *very* sure I want you to keep the locket. It belongs to you!"

Grace tried to swallow over the lump in her throat. Her hands trembled as she carefully laid her plate on the coffee table.

She couldn't look at Paul. She knew she should put up some kind of argument. She knew it was foolish to allow herself to fall deeper under Virginia's spell. For her own self-protection and emotional well-being, Grace knew she should gently but firmly refuse Virginia's request.

"Please?" Virginia said. She pushed her chair closer to Grace and reached for her hand, dropping the locket into it. "It means so much to me."

The moment Virginia's hand closed around Grace's, Grace knew she was lost. An image, diamond-bright, shimmered in Grace's mind: Virginia, younger, more vibrant, feeding Elizabeth cereal and saying, "Grandma. Say grandma, Elizabeth. Grandma..."

Grace blinked and the image faded. She took a deep, shaky breath. "I'll be honored to call you grandmother."

"Aunt Virginia, you promised!" Paul said, angrier and more frustrated than he'd been in a long time. "I've lived up to my end of the bargain, and you haven't!"

"Please don't raise your voice like that," his aunt said.

The two of them had gone from the sun room to the library after tea was over. It had taken all of Paul's self-control not to give way to his anger while Grace was still with them.

Paul dropped his voice. "You sat here not three days ago and promised me you wouldn't do anything rash until we had the investigator's report in hand. And what happens? You completely forget what we talked about, and you ask Grace to call you grandmother!"

"The investigator's report won't turn up anything."

"How can you say that? You don't have any idea what he'll find."

"He won't find anything." Her chin was set in a stubborn line.

Paul expelled a noisy breath. "I might as well save my breath. You're determined not to listen to logic. You want Grace to be Elizabeth, therefore, she *is* Elizabeth." He stood, walked to the window and looked out. He didn't know what to do.

"Paul..."

He turned.

Her eyes were clouded as they met his gaze. "I know you think I'm a foolish old woman. I also know you're disappointed in me, because you expect me to be logical about something that defies logic."

"I'm not disappointed in you. I'm worried about you. You're not being sensible."

"Haven't you always said I have good instincts about people?"

"Yes," he said reluctantly.

"Then trust me. Stop fighting me at every turn." She wheeled herself over to where he stood. "I don't want to hurt you," she said softly. "You've been the best part of my life for so many years, and I love you. But I also love Grace, and I won't lose her."

Their gazes locked, and he saw the steely determination in hers.

"Make up your mind to accept this," she said, "because Grace is here to stay."

For the next week, Grace and Virginia talked for hours, about everything. Grace told Virginia about her years at the convent. She told her about Sister Mary Clare and their special relationship. She told her about her roommate and best friend, Melanie. She even told her about Jason, her one serious relationship.

"Did you love him?" Virginia asked.

Grace shrugged. "Not enough to follow him all over the world." Jason was an engineer, and he'd wanted Grace to marry him and go with him to Venezuela, where he had accepted a three-year assignment.

"Then you didn't really love him. Not the way you should have," Virginia said. Her blue eyes became dreamy, and her voice softened. "I would have gone anywhere with Evan. Anywere. Into the jungle. Into the desert. To the ends of the earth."

Grace wondered if she would ever feel that way about anyone. She had cared for Jason, but she wanted security and a permanent home when she married. Someplace she belonged. Not traipsing from one country to another.

"And Evan felt the same way about me," Virginia said, breaking into Grace's thoughts.

"How did you meet him?"

"At my coming-out party. It was love at first sight. He was a friend of a friend and a last-minute addition to the guest list. I know it sounds corny, but the minute I laid eyes on him I knew he was the one."

"He sounds wonderful."

"Oh, he was. He was handsome and dashing and brilliantly clever." Virginia sighed. "He was also a fabulous lover."

Instead of being embarrassed, the way she normally would have been if someone said something like that in her presence, Grace felt wistful. A fabulous lover. Would she ever be able to say something like that, to feel something like that, about a man? For some reason, Paul popped into her mind. What kind of lover would he be? she wondered.

Now Grace *did* feel embarrassed. She also felt grateful that Virginia couldn't know what she had been thinking.

"The newspapers called us the match of the century," Virginia said.

Grace forced her mind back to the conversation and away from the dangerous turn it had taken.

Another day, Grace and Virginia spent the entire afternoon sitting in the sun room and looking through family albums. Virginia proudly identified each person. "This is my Evan—your grandfather. Isn't he handsome?"

Grace smiled. He *was* handsome. "Is this you?"

Virginia nodded.

"Oh, you were so beautiful," Grace said, looking at the beautiful young woman in the photo.

"I was, wasn't I?" Virginia said. Then she laughed. "I've never been very modest."

Grace grinned. She liked Virginia more each day.

"Here's your parents' wedding picture," Virginia said.

Grace stared for a long time at the beautiful blond woman in the satin wedding dress and the extremely good-looking man with the bold smile who stood beside her. Her chest ached because she'd never known them.

Beside her, Virginia sighed. "It nearly broke my heart to lose them."

"How *did* they die?" Grace asked.

Virginia's eyes grew bleak. "Their car was hit by a train."

Grace swallowed.

Virginia reached over and squeezed Grace's hand. "But they left you, the greatest gift anyone could ever have had, so I couldn't afford to be sad for long."

There were also pictures of Paul, lots of them. Grace could see that he'd been a pretty serious boy. She thought back to the things Virginia had told her about him and realized anew that his abandonment by his mother must have really affected him.

And then there were pictures of Elizabeth. Grace still had a hard time thinking of herself as Elizabeth, even though her desire to belong to this family grew stronger as each day passed.

Grace studied each picture for a long time, turning the pages of the albums slowly. Finally, near the end of one of the albums, a little plastic bag containing a lock of blond hair was taped to the page.

Grace looked at Virginia quizzically.

"Yours," Virginia said softly.

Grace gently fingered the bag. Her emotions had gone through a roller coaster of feelings during the afternoon, and she didn't trust herself to speak.

"Tell me about the day she disappeared," Grace finally said. She'd been wanting to ask about that day for a long time.

"It was a Friday. Well, you knew that, of course. It was the same day President Kennedy was assassinated."

"Yes," Grace said.

Virginia gazed out the window. "If the weather was nice, Josie always took Elizabeth for a morning walk in the park. That morning was beautiful, sunny. Josie and I got Elizabeth ready. It wasn't very cold, so I didn't think she needed to wear a coat. I got out a sweater I'd made her—one that had a matching cap—and put it over her romper suit." Virginia's voice broke. "She...she looked so cute. So sweet. She was grinning up at me when they left.

"The last I saw of her, she was sitting in her stroller, and Josie was pushing her down the driveway." Slowly, Virginia turned to Grace and gazed into her eyes. "You waved goodbye," she whispered.

Grace's breath caught.

"Elizabeth..." Virginia reached for Grace's hand.

"No, please," Grace said. "Please don't call me that. I can't let you call me that."

"Why not, my dear?" Tears shimmered in Virginia's eyes. "We both know you're Elizabeth."

Grace felt like crying, herself. "No, we don't know that. Not yet. I—I know you're convinced of my identity, but

I'm not. And I, well, I just can't think of myself by any other name except Grace.'' She squeezed Virginia's hand. "Please understand.''

Virginia smiled sadly. "I do. You're afraid. That's all right. I can wait. I've already waited a long time. The most important thing is, you've found your way home.''

That night, Grace had a vivid, disturbing dream. A pretty blond woman was wheeling a baby stroller around stone pillars and into a small park. The stroller contained a chubby little girl.

Elizabeth.

Elizabeth and Josie.

Josie walked down a wide path. Past a small pond where several small children were feeding the ducks. Josie didn't look at the mothers seated nearby. She walked briskly, her tan coat flapping around her legs. Dry leaves crackled underfoot.

Elizabeth squealed as a squirrel raced across their path.

Josie walked across the park, down a hill, past the playground area—again ignoring the children at play—and out the gates at the other end, the end farthest from the Hollister estate.

Grace saw the scene clearly.

The street bordering the park on that end was a hill. The entrance was about halfway down the hill. It was sheltered from the view of anyone in the park by high, thick hedges. As Josie exited the park, she looked up and down the street. No one was around. The nearest house was at the crest of the hill.

A dark sedan was parked at the curb close to the gate. The license plate was smudged with dirt so that it couldn't be read. The door on the driver's side opened. A swarthy, good-looking man got out. He had a cigarette dangling from his mouth, and his dark hair gleamed in the sunlight. He looked at Josie.

"Dammit, what took you so long?" he said. "I thought somethin' went wrong."

"I'm sorry, Frank. I—I got here as fast as I could." Josie's voice trembled. "I—I'm scared. Do you think—"

"Shut up and get that brat in the car," he said.

Josie lifted Elizabeth out of the stroller, and the toddler started to cry.

"Shh," Josie said, holding Elizabeth close. She climbed into the car.

The man opened the trunk, folded up the stroller and stuffed it inside. He slammed the trunk closed. Then he got into the car, started it, and it disappeared down the hill.

The next morning, Grace awakened before dawn. She lay in bed and remembered the dream. She reached under her pillow. Ever since the locket's return, she had slept with it there. As she stroked its surface, images crystallized in her mind.

The car speeding away. Josie, frightened, already sorry for what she'd done. Elizabeth, equally frightened, but not knowing why. A long drive, through several towns. A country road. A curve in the road. Grace's heart started to pound, and she abruptly let go of the locket. The image faded. She lay there until she felt calmer, then she swung her legs out of bed.

By seven-thirty, the sun was up, and Grace was dressed and ready for the day. She decided that as soon as breakfast was over, she would tell Virginia she felt the need for fresh air and was going out for a walk.

Paul excused himself from the breakfast table shortly after Grace arrived. For the past few days, he had fallen into the habit of coming down earlier than she or his aunt. Grace wondered if that was because he was trying to avoid spending too much time in Grace's company.

When Grace expressed a desire for a walk, saying she needed exercise, Virginia said, "Of course. I shouldn't have kept you cooped up in the house all week. You go on and have your walk. I'll be in the morning room when you return."

Fifteen minutes later, Grace walked slowly down the front driveway to the entrance of the Hollister estate. The gate opened automatically when someone or something approached it from this side. Grace walked through and around the corner. The park lay across the road.

She stood there for a long moment. Her heartbeat accelerated. Part of her wanted to cross the road and enter the park. Another part of her wanted to turn around and go back to the house.

Don't be a coward.

Taking a deep breath, Grace crossed the street. Just as in her dream, leaves swirled around her feet. She realized it was almost the same time of year as it had been when Elizabeth disappeared.

She entered the park. It looked different than in her dream, and she realized it was because some of the trees were so much bigger, and others were no longer there.

Still, she headed unerringly down the main footpath, which was paved and bordered by flower beds. Tiny chrysanthemums bloomed in a profusion of yellows and reds. She crested a small hill, and the duck pond lay to her left. To her right, a cluster of wooden benches sat facing the pond. She looked at the one farthest away and knew it was the bench where Josie always sat.

Grace walked slowly toward the bench. No one else was around, probably because it was only nine-thirty. Or maybe not many people used the park anymore.

When she reached Josie's bench, she sat down. She fingered the locket and was almost immediately overwhelmed by a feeling of sadness and desolation. The emotions were so strong, Grace trembled and closed her eyes.

Just then, the rustle of leaves underfoot alerted her to someone's approach.

She opened her eyes and turned toward the sound.

Chapter Seven

Paul had been sitting in his office, working, when he happened to look up and see Grace walking down the driveway toward the main entrance of the estate.

Where was she going? he wondered.

A second later, he'd jumped up, grabbed a leather jacket from the closet, ignored Susan's openmouthed expression and raced downstairs.

By the time he reached the main entrance of the estate, Grace was nowhere in sight. He looked up and down the street. There was a car at the bottom of the hill, but no pedestrians. Certainly no Grace. She couldn't have gone in either direction. There hadn't been time for her to have disappeared like that.

That left the park.

He crossed the road. Leaves swirled around as the wind picked up. He looked at the sky. It had clouded over, and it smelled like snow in the air.

He walked swiftly, slowing down only as he approached the duck pond and saw her sitting on one of the wooden benches. Something about the way her shoulders were hunched caused a hard knot to form in his chest. She looked so forlorn. So sad and vulnerable.

With a flash of pain, he was reminded of the way he'd felt the day his mother had left him. Suddenly, he had the wildest impulse to go to Grace and gather her close. He yearned to comfort her and tell her everything was okay.

Damn, you're a fool, you know that? What you should do is turn around and go back home. Get as far away from this woman as you can possibly get.

Even as he told himself what he should do, he walked forward.

She looked up.

Soft blue eyes filled with desolation met his.

The ache in his chest expanded, filled him, and rational thought disappeared. The next thing he knew he was sitting beside her, putting his arms around her, holding her close.

She offered no resistance. He tucked her head under his chin and smoothed his hand across her cheek. Her skin felt cold and soft, but as he stroked it, it warmed. He breathed in the sweet fragrance of her hair and closed his eyes for a moment.

A fierce protectiveness and something else—an impossible yearning that grew stronger with each moment—suffused him. Although he held her gently, she trembled.

"Tell me what's wrong," he murmured, opening his eyes. With his fingers, he lifted her chin so he could see her face.

To his consternation, tears filled her eyes, and her lower lip—full and tempting—quivered. "I—I had a dream last night. About...about Elizabeth. She...this is where she and Josie always sat. On this bench..." Her throat worked. The tears shimmered. "Sh-she was so afraid that day...."

Paul's arms tightened.

A lone tear broke away.

Mesmerized, he watched it trail down the slope of her cheek. His breathing quickened. "Grace..." With his thumb, he brushed away the tear. And then, before he could think, before he could be sensible, before he could remember who he was and who she was and all the reasons that this was a disastrous idea, he bent his head and captured her mouth in a kiss that was meant to be tender and soothing.

Her mouth, soft, yielding, and oh, so sweet, trembled under his. He slipped one hand under her hair and held her fast as his mouth slanted first one way, then the other.

She put one arm around his back. The other slid up to his neck.

He deepened the kiss, his tongue delving into her mouth, and at the touch of her tongue meeting his, a rush of hunger and need tore through him.

His heart banged away at his rib cage, and all he knew was that he wanted her.

The kiss lasted a long time.

When they finally broke apart, her eyes were filled with confusion. She stared at him, her mouth slightly open, her breath fanning out in front of her.

He didn't know what to say. He felt as confused as she looked. All of his savoir faire deserted him, and he felt the way he'd felt when he was sixteen and first kissed a girl this way.

He almost started to say he was sorry, then abruptly changed his mind. When he finally did speak, he knew he sounded gruff. "It's cold out. Let's go back to the house."

She nodded, and eyes averted now, she stood. He wanted to take her hand and tuck it into his arm as they walked toward the estate, but he felt awkward about doing it, so he didn't.

They didn't talk on the way back. When they reached the house, he opened the door for her, and as she brushed past him to enter the foyer, she said in a low voice, "I'm sorry I acted like such a crybaby."

"Don't be silly," he said, and again his voice sounded more stern and abrupt than he wanted it to.

Her gaze met his for a brief moment. He searched for something to say, but then the moment was gone. She looked away and headed up the stairs.

Nothing would ever be the same again. If Grace had been bothered by Paul's presence before he'd kissed her, it was nothing like the way she felt now.

She thought about him all the time.

And when they were together, she was so acutely aware of him, she was sure Virginia and the servants must be able to feel the tension in her body.

And even though Paul could usually mask his feelings, there were several times when Grace had caught him looking at her with something she'd have sworn was the same confusion and longing she was feeling.

She was bewildered by her feelings. How, and when, had they changed so dramatically? Before—or after—that devastating kiss? Surely one kiss couldn't have made such a difference.

Or could it?

She kept remembering the kiss.

Tasting it.

Tasting him.

Feeling the warmth and strength of his arms as he held her. Feeling the furious pounding of his heart as it beat against hers. Feeling the fire and passion and desperate need that had ignited between them.

She shivered. She hadn't known it could be this way. When she had dated Jason, his kisses had been nice, but they hadn't touched her beneath the surface.

She felt as if she'd been sleeping for thirty-some years. Like the kiss that had awakened Sleeping Beauty, Paul's kiss had awakened her. Awakened something that had lain dormant for her entire lifetime, something she'd never known she possessed. And now she throbbed with life and awareness.

She yearned for more. She wanted him to hold her again, kiss her again.

She thought he wanted her, too. She wished he'd say something, but both of them were pretending the kiss had never happened.

And what would she do if he *did* say something? What if he were to acknowledge the desire that had flamed into life? What would she do then?

Wouldn't it be absolute folly to go any further with Paul? Wouldn't she just be asking for heartache?

She had to be sensible. She knew the only outcome of an involvement with Paul Hollister was disaster.

He might be attracted to her, he might want her sexually, but he would never accept her. He'd made that abundantly clear on too many occasions for her to be fooled into thinking anything was different now.

No, what was more likely was that he'd momentarily felt sorry for her, and because of that strong sexual attraction between them, he'd kissed her.

That was all.

She would be all kinds of a fool to read anything more into that kiss.

On Thursday, almost two weeks after Grace's arrival, and exactly one week before Thanksgiving, Ned Shapiro called Paul.

"I've got the full report from the investigator," he said.

Paul tapped his Montblanc pen against his desk blotter. "Oh? And?"

"In a nutshell, he found nothing."

Paul let out the breath he'd been holding. A curious relief welled up in his chest.

"He checked her background, talked to the nuns at the convent, interviewed the only policeman involved in the investigation when she was abandoned, even talked to her dream therapist—who wouldn't tell him anything because she said it was patient privilege. Everything she told us checked out."

"No discrepancies at all?"

"None."

Paul swiveled his chair and looked out the window. As he watched, a cardinal landed in the big maple tree nearest his window. The bird preened, his scarlet feathers brightening the barren branches. "I don't understand why the FBI wouldn't have made the connection with Elizabeth?"

"Well, that's because the first police report wasn't filed until about six months after Grace was left at the convent."

"What? Why not?" Paul said incredulously.

Ned's sigh came through the wire clearly. "Paul, St. Mary's Convent is one of those nearly obsolete places where the nuns live a secluded life. According to Matt, my investigator, there's no television set, no newspapers delivered, very little contact with the outside world. Right now there are only eight nuns living there, and the youngest one is fifty-two.

"The way Matt tells it, when Grace was left on their doorstep, the nuns simply believed she'd been temporarily left in their care. They explained that they kept expecting her mother or father to come back at any time to claim her. It was only after about six months had gone by that they realized no one was coming. That's when they contacted the local police department, which is very small, even today.

"From what I can tell, the police made a halfhearted attempt to try to track down someone who knew Grace or her parents, but hell, the trail was cold by then. And they never thought about contacting the FBI. I kind of got the idea from the nuns that they loved Grace and considered her their gift from God."

Paul shook his head. "That's criminal, you know that?"

"I know, but what can we do about it now?"

"Nothing." He thought for a moment. "Listen, Ned, what's your feeling about all of this? Do you think Grace Gregory really is Elizabeth?"

"It's sure beginning to look that way, isn't it?" the lawyer hedged. "But you can make your own judgment. I'll overnight the complete report to you. Uh, do you want me to report to your aunt, or will you do it?"

"I'll do it." Paul slowly turned his chair to face his desk again, but the image of the cardinal stayed in his mind. Grace was like that cardinal, he thought. She had brightened his barren soul. As soon as the fanciful thought formed, he tried to force it out of his mind. What was wrong with him? He'd given up that kind of romantic nonsense when he'd given up his childhood. Still, the idea refused to go away.

After saying goodbye to Ned, Paul sat at his desk and thought for a long time. Then he slowly got up and walked downstairs to find his Aunt Virginia.

That night, Grace had a hard time falling asleep. She kept remembering the way Paul had looked at her at dinner.

Speculatively.

That was the word that had come to mind every time she met his gaze.

He'd looked at her as if he was trying to figure something out. Figure *her* out. And yet she felt no threat in his observation. There was none of the bug-under-a-microscope feeling of the past couple weeks.

Somehow, last night, even though he'd said nothing, Grace felt a glimmer of encouragement that Paul had finally begun to accept her.

And perhaps, after acceptance, would come belief.

She tried to banish the tentative happiness that filled her heart. *Don't count on too much,* she told herself. *Don't start to think there's any chance of a relationship between you and Paul. You'll just be setting yourself up for a big disappointment.*

Long after midnight, she reached under her pillow for the locket. She held it until she fell asleep.

The room was small and dark. Yellowed, pull-down blinds covered the windows. Elizabeth lay huddled under a brown blanket in one corner of a small crib. A pacifier protruded from her mouth, and she sucked at it noisily. Every once in awhile she whimpered.

Josie appeared in the open doorway. Her face looked strained and worried. She frowned, looking at Elizabeth and biting her bottom lip. Her fear was a tangible thing. "Oh, God, Frank," she moaned, "where are you? Why did you run out on me? What am I going to do? The damn kid is sick, and I don't know what to do." Her voice rose at the end.

Elizabeth's eyes opened. Her face crumpled, and she started to cry. "Mama, Mama." The cry was muffled because of the pacifier. Her child's mind was filled with confusion and fear. She hurt. She wanted her mama. When she breathed, her chest hurt. Her head, her ears, her throat—they all hurt. They hurt bad. Elizabeth started to cry in earnest, her voice rising to a wail.

Josie's blue eyes filled with furious tears. "Will you please stop crying? Please, please stop crying! I'm doing the best I can!"

Josie was scared to death. Her money was frighteningly low. Elizabeth was running a fever, and Josie didn't know what to do. Even if she could afford to, how could she take Elizabeth to a doctor?

She kept chewing on her bottom lip, the tears trembling on the brink of her eyelids. Desperation nearly choked her. What else could go wrong? First Frank had insisted they wait at least two weeks before making a ransom call. He'd explained that he wanted the Hollisters to be desperate so they'd agree to anything when he finally did call. Then he went off to make the phone call about the ransom and never came back. Two days later, the kid had gotten sick.

Josie knuckled away a tear and took a shaky breath. God, she needed to think. She walked over to the crib. She put her hand on Elizabeth's forehead. It felt like a furnace. "Mother of God," she whispered, "help me out of this mess."

Oh, why had she listened to Frank? She must have been crazy! She squeezed her eyes shut, as if shutting out the sight of the sick child would shut out everything that had happened. She wished she were thousands of miles away from here, her and Helen.

Oh, God, Helen. On top of everything else, how long would Mrs. Winsen keep Helen? Josie had been trying not to think of Helen. Helen was the real reason Josie was in this mess. Because she'd wanted to keep her, she'd allowed her better judgment to be overruled and had gotten tangled up with Frank.

Josie missed her daughter desperately. She'd never dreamed she'd be away from her so long. When this had all started, Frank had said it would take two months—

tops. But now it was almost Christmas, and she'd been away from Helen for eleven weeks.

"I should just go," she said. "Just go." She swallowed hard, fighting tears, knowing if she started crying she might never stop. "I could leave, call the police, tell them where they can find Elizabeth, then go get Helen and disappear." Josie had a bus ticket in her pocket. A way to get to Dobbs Ferry. And once she was there and had gotten Helen, she could figure out what to do next. She refused to believe she had very few options.

Elizabeth stood up in the crib. She screamed.

"Stop it!" Josie said, her control slipping. She raised her hand. "Stop crying, or I'll give you something to cry about!"

Grace cried out and sat up in bed, her heart pounding. Just as she did, her bedroom door opened, and light from the hallway spilled into the room. A man stood in the doorway.

"Grace? Are you all right?"

It was Paul. Grace sank back against her pillows. Her heart was still beating wildly, and she put her hand to her chest.

Paul walked into the room, quietly shutting the door behind him. The moonlight illuminated him as he approached the bed. Grace took a shaky breath.

"Y-yes, I'm all right," she said and willed her heart to stop its mad thumping.

He came closer and sat on the edge of the bed. He wore a dark robe. Moonlight played across his face, casting shadows along the planes and crevices. "I was walking down the hall when I heard you cry out. Did you have another dream?" His voice was soft.

"Yes," she whispered, remembering. She hugged herself.

He reached for her hand, enfolding it in his warm one. "Was it a bad one?"

She nodded, incapable of saying more. She couldn't stop shaking. Wordlessly, he tugged her forward. He stroked her hair, her back, all the while murmuring comforting words. Grace slid her arms around his body and closed her eyes. It felt so good to have him hold her. She wanted to stay here, safe in his arms, forever. She wanted to stop dreaming. To stop going into the past. She just wanted to go forward . . . into the future.

"Would you like to tell me about it?"

"I—I don't want to talk about it."

"All right."

He continued to stroke her. After a while, he put his fingers under her chin and raised her face. They looked into each other's eyes. Grace's heart, which had finally slowed down, picked up its tempo once more, but this time the acceleration wasn't caused by fear.

Slowly, Paul lowered his head.

Their lips met eagerly in a kiss of hunger and urgency that reached deep inside Grace and touched something elemental. She wound her arms around him and poured all of her loneliness and confusion and fear into the kiss, all of the need that had built up over a long period of time, all of the feelings of abandonment that had never completely disappeared.

One kiss became two. Two became three.

His mouth dropped from her lips to her throat, then lower still. His hands caressed her face, her neck, her shoulders, then moved to cup her breasts.

Grace moaned as his thumbs moved back and forth over the peaks, at first gently, then more demandingly. And when his mouth replaced his thumbs, she whimpered, her body leaping in response, her breath coming in short little gasps of pleasure.

Grace tunneled her hands through his hair as he lifted her gown, sliding his hands inside to touch her bare skin. She shivered as he caressed her, finding and igniting the exact places that yearned for his touch. She reveled in the feelings he elicited, wanted more and yet more. Her body strained toward him, an agony of tension building inside.

Suddenly, from downstairs, there was a loud crash, and they jumped apart.

Grace, heart pounding, sat up. "Wh-what was that?" she whispered, pulling her gown down to cover her body.

"I don't know." His voice sounded rough and not like him at all. He stood, retied his robe and padded silently to her door and opened it. He stood there listening for a long moment.

"It's probably one of the servants. Wilbur tends to roam at night."

Grace tried to calm herself. As reality pushed through the sexual haze that had enveloped her, she was horrified by her behavior. She pulled the comforter up again. What must he think? She had practically thrown herself into his arms and allowed him to...to...she couldn't even finish the thought. She knew her face was flaming and thanked God the moonlight would disguise it.

Paul slowly walked back to her bed, but he left her door open. "Will you be all right?" His voice sounded strained.

Grace nodded mutely. She couldn't meet his eyes.

"What...happened tonight," he said hesitantly, "I want you to know I'm sor—"

"It's all right," she said in an agony of embarrassment. "You don't have to apologize."

He seemed about to say something else, then didn't. A minute later, he was gone, shutting the door behind him. Grace buried her face in her pillow and wished the floor would open up and swallow her.

* * *

Grace slept through her alarm. When she finally awakened out of a deep sleep, her bedside clock read eight a.m. She sat up and stretched. Her breasts tingled.

In a flood, the events of the night came rushing back. Her cheeks warmed as she remembered everything. The dream. Crying out. Paul coming into her room. Holding her. And then . . . the intimate way he'd touched her. The places he'd kissed her. And the positively wanton way she'd kissed him back.

She closed her eyes. Oh, dear God. Had last night really happened? Had she really allowed him to do all those things? Even as she asked herself those questions, she knew the answers. She also knew that they had been only seconds from consummating their lovemaking.

She still couldn't believe it. Paul. She and Paul. And she had loved it! She had wanted more. The abrupt termination of their lovemaking had left her aching and frustrated.

And now, after all that, she had to face him over the breakfast table. She moaned and covered her face. She wanted to pull the comforter over her head and never emerge again. *Well, you can't. So get up and start figuring out how you're going to act when you see him.*

While she took her shower and dressed for the day, she thought and thought and finally decided she would take her cue from him. If Paul acted as if nothing had happened, so would she. But what if he acted cold and distant? What if he acted disgusted by her? What would she do then? Could she handle it?

I'll have to handle it.

She finished applying her makeup, then stood back and looked at herself. She had dressed carefully in a jade wool skirt and matching sweater vest over a cream silk blouse. She wanted to look her very best, and she knew the deep blue-green flattered her hair and eyes. She'd brushed her hair back from her face and tied it with a narrow black velvet ribbon.

Satisfied that she looked as good as it was possible for her to look, she started for the door. She took a deep breath to still the nervous flutter in her stomach.

You'll be fine, she told herself. She was late for breakfast, so Paul might have already gone to his office. If he had, that would probably be for the best. It would give her some time to adjust to everything that had happened.

Taking another deep breath, she opened her door and walked down the hall to the stairs.

Paul dawdled over his breakfast. He pretended to be absorbed in the morning newspaper as he ate his omelet slowly. Every so often he surreptitiously glanced at his watch. He wondered if Grace had purposely skipped breakfast to avoid being with him this morning.

He still couldn't believe he'd so completely lost his self-control and given in to the emotions storming through him as he'd held Grace and tried to comfort her.

He hadn't gone into her room with the intention of making love to her, he was certain of that. No, he just hadn't been able to sleep, the same way he hadn't been able to sleep for any of the nights since he'd first kissed Grace in the park.

He'd kept thinking about her and trying to figure out how he felt about her. Whether or not he believed in her. He'd finally got up, put on his robe and walked slowly down the long hallway to the other wing. He wasn't sure why, but he'd felt the need to make sure she was all right. To make sure she was safe.

Then, just as he'd passed her closed door, he heard her cry out. The cry was filled with fear, and he'd simply reacted, opening her door and walking into her bedroom.

And when he'd felt her tremors, known they were real, he had acted instinctively, drawing her into his arms to give her what comfort and assurance he could.

Touching her had been his downfall.

If there hadn't been that noise from downstairs, he would have made love to her. He wouldn't have been able to stop himself.

The feelings she had produced in him had completely overwhelmed him. There was something about the way she had responded to him that had shattered the invisible barriers he normally kept around his emotions. She was so sweet, so trusting, so giving. Her kisses had told him she needed him and wanted him just as much as he needed and wanted her. She'd felt so exactly right in his arms. As if she belonged there. As if she'd always belonged there.

"Grace is sleeping late this morning," his aunt said, breaking into his thoughts.

"Hmm?" He pretended to have been absorbed in his paper. "I'm sorry, Aunt Virginia. What did you say?"

She gave him a curious look. "I said, Grace is awfully late coming down this morning." The curious look turned into a frown. "Are you feeling all right, Paul?"

"I'm feeling fine." He folded up the paper and put it aside, then picked up his coffee cup and drained it. "Well, I guess it's time for me to get to—"

"Oh, here's Grace now," Virginia said, smiling.

Paul, feeling an unsettling and unfamiliar loss of composure, as well as a disturbing ripple of excitement, turned.

Grace, looking fresh and indescribably beautiful, smiled shyly at his aunt. "Good morning," she said. Then, slowly, her clear-eyed gaze met his.

Paul took one look into her beautiful blue eyes and knew he was in deep trouble.

Chapter Eight

How did he *do* that? Grace wondered.

For a fleeting moment, the expression in Paul's eyes was unguarded, and she had the feeling he felt as uncertain as she did. Then that mask of his dropped back into place, effectively blocking all emotion, and he was the same secretive man he'd always been.

Grace had learned enough about Paul and his childhood to understand that concealment of his feelings was probably a self-protective mechanism that was ingrained in his psyche. But knowing this didn't help when she was feeling so vulnerable herself.

If only he had given her one warm look, one tiny gesture of reassurance...anything to soothe her frazzled nerves and shore up her courage.

She took her seat at the table and told herself to be calm, but her pulse didn't get the message. Avoiding both Virginia's and Paul's gaze as Anna filled her coffee cup, she used the brief respite to attempt to shutter her emotions, too.

Anna moved to Paul's side. "More coffee, Mr. Hollister?"

"Thank you," he said.

Out of the corner of her eye, Grace could see his right hand, which rested lightly on the table. It was a strong-looking, long-fingered hand with a fine dusting of dark hair across the back.

She swallowed, remembering with vivid clarity how that same hand had felt last night, the things that hand had done and the places it had touched. Her heartbeat sounded too loud. Why had she come down for breakfast? She should have known she couldn't pull this off. She should have known her emotions were too chaotic to risk exposing them so soon.

"I've never seen you drink so many cups of coffee, Paul," Virginia commented.

Grace began serving herself. Her movements felt stiff and awkward, and she wished she could think of something to say. If she kept acting like this, Virginia was bound to guess something was wrong.

She didn't dare imagine what Paul must be thinking. How she wished she were worldly-wise and experienced enough to handle what had happened last night as if it were a brief indulgence of physical desire and nothing more.

The way she was acting, she was sure Paul thought she was the most unsophisticated woman he'd ever met. Probably, to him, making love to a woman wasn't a big deal. If she didn't get herself under control, he'd grow alarmed and think she expected him to make declarations of undying love.

That is what you'd hoped. Don't deny it.

Misery welled up in her chest, threatening to overwhelm her. What a mess she was! One night of almost-sex, and she was falling apart.

Grace buttered a blueberry muffin and took a bite. She chewed automatically, tasting nothing. She wished she had nerve enough to look at Paul. To say something breezy and innocuous. To show him she didn't care if he didn't love her. To show him that last night's events weren't momentous at all. To show him her emotions were just as unaffected as his seemed to be.

"You're very quiet this morning, Grace," Virginia said. "Did you have as restless a night as I did? I hope I didn't wake you when I dropped that pot."

Paul choked on his coffee.

Grace could feel her face turning red. "No, I—I slept just fine last night. When did you drop a pot?"

"Are you all right, Paul?" Virginia said as Paul continued to cough.

"I'm okay. My coffee just went down the wrong pipe."

Grace kept her gaze trained on her plate. She didn't trust herself to look at either one of them. She cut a bite of cantaloupe and ate it.

Virginia turned back to Grace. "For some reason, I kept waking up last night. I thought I heard someone walking around. Anyway, I couldn't go back to sleep, so I got up, wheeled myself out to the kitchen with the intention of warming up some milk and I dropped the pot. It made an awful clatter, and I was afraid I'd awakened the entire household."

"You didn't wake me."

"Or me," Paul said.

"Well, I'm glad of that. I felt so stupid that I never even made the milk." Virginia gazed out the window for a moment before speaking. "It's supposed to snow today." She smiled. "I've always loved the first snow of the season. Do you like the snow, Grace?"

Grateful for the impersonal question, Grace nodded. "I love snow. Winter's my favorite time of year."

"When I was younger, I couldn't wait until the pond froze over so I could ice-skate," Virginia said.

Grace attempted a casual smile and felt she'd succeeded. "When I first saw the pond out back, I could just imagine people skating."

"Do you like to ice-skate?" Virginia wiped her mouth with her napkin.

"I love it, but I'm not very good."

"Paul's a terrific skater. At least, he used to be. Why don't you skate anymore, Paul?"

Grace finally looked at Paul.

He shrugged. "It's not much fun skating alone."

"Well, Grace has just said how much she loves to skate. So now you've got someone to skate with."

Paul turned to Grace. His gray eyes softened as they rested on her face. "If the pond freezes over while you're here, we'll get you fitted for some skates."

"I'd like that," she managed to say.

He smiled.

Grace's pulse accelerated. She wished so much they were alone. If they had been, she might have been brave enough to say something. An awkward silence settled over the table. Virginia cleared her throat, and both Grace and Paul turned in her direction. The older woman studied them thoughtfully, an unreadable expression in her eyes.

After a moment, Paul pushed his chair back. "I've got a lot to do this morning, so I'd better head on upstairs."

"Paul, wait," Virginia said.

He stopped in midair, half standing, half sitting.

"When Grace has finished with her breakfast, I'd like the two of you to come to the library with me," Virginia said. "There's something I want to discuss with you."

Paul stood, his eyebrows knitting. "Maybe you could call me down when you're ready? Those Singer leases need to be—"

"It won't be long. You can wait, can't you, Paul?" Virginia looked at Grace's plate. "Grace is nearly finished."

Grace placed the remainder of her uneaten muffin on her plate. "I'm really not very hungry this morning."

"My dear, I don't want to rush you," Virginia said, frowning at Paul.

"No, it's okay," Grace said. She just wanted to get whatever it was Virginia had to say over with so Paul would go to his office, and Grace could finally relax and try to get her frazzled emotions under control.

When they reached the library, Virginia wheeled herself behind the desk. Grace and Paul sat in the two leather chairs facing the desk. As Grace settled back and crossed her legs, she was acutely aware of Paul to her right.

"The reason I wanted you both to come in here was so none of the servants would overhear us," Virginia began. Her blue eyes seemed very bright as they rested first on Paul, then on Grace.

"My dear," she said to Grace, "I'm sure you guessed that when Ned Shapiro called us about you, before we even invited you to come and visit, we hired a private investigator to look into your background and find out as much about you as he could."

Grace had suspected as much. In their shoes, she would have done the same thing.

"Well, we had the report from the investigator yesterday afternoon," Virginia continued.

Grace glanced at Paul. He was watching his aunt intently.

"Would you like to tell Grace what the investigator said?" Virginia asked Paul.

Paul said, "All right," and turned to Grace. His tone was even, noncommittal. "He told us he had uncovered nothing that would indicate you were doing anything except telling the truth."

Grace swallowed. Yesterday afternoon. Did this mean Paul finally believed her story? That all his doubts had been put to rest? Like Virginia, did he now believe Grace was Elizabeth?

Somehow, instead of making Grace feel better, this thought made her feel worse. Had Paul's lovemaking last night been calculated?

Grace had wanted to believe what happened between them was spontaneous. Now a niggling doubt whispered that perhaps the only reason he'd come to her room was that he was convinced she must be Elizabeth.

Maybe he's just covering all his bases, making sure his position is strengthened.

The thought hurt.

She searched his eyes, looking for a hint—no matter how small—of what he was thinking.

There was none.

There was also no warmth, and certainly no indication that their relationship had changed in any way. She must have imagined that earlier ripple of tenderness in his eyes. It had probably been a case of wishful thinking on her part.

All of Grace's tentative happiness vanished, leaving a raw pain in its wake. And for the first time since she'd arrived at Hollister House, she felt a hot rush of shame.

Had she allowed herself to be used by Paul? Were her feelings for him, her undeniable need of him, so obvious that he had known she would fall into his arms like a ripe peach?

Had his lovemaking last night been a carefully staged seduction for the sole purpose of furthering his own interests?

"Well," Virginia said, her face carefully devoid of reaction to the uncomfortable silence that had elapsed since
Paul's disclosure. "I am satisfied, beyond any doubt, that
you are my granddaughter, Grace, and I wanted you both
to know that I'm planning to make a public announcement."

Grace tried to shake off her misery. "No, please ...
Grandmother, I don't need that. I don't want that."

"I do," Virginia said stubbornly.

"It really is too soon," Paul said quietly. "Why don't
we give it a little more time?"

Virginia shook her head. "I'm not getting any younger,
and I want the world to know that Elizabeth has finally
been found. I want it to be official." Virginia's gaze softened as her eyes turned to Grace. "Come here, child," she
said softly.

Feeling very close to tears, Grace rose and walked
around the desk. Virginia took her hands. "Please don't
deny me this pleasure."

Grace swallowed against the lump in her throat. How
could she refuse? Virginia had been so good to her, so
welcoming and trusting from the first day. "All right,"
she whispered.

"I also plan to resurrect the Christmas Ball," Virginia
said happily.

"But Christmas..." Grace's voice trailed off. She was
supposed to go back to New York the first of December.
Her mind whirled. What did this mean? Did Virginia want
her to stay here, at Hollister House, permanently? Yesterday, Grace would have been thrilled by the thought.
Today...after what had happened between her and
Paul...she wasn't so sure she could stand living here, especially if he continued to behave in such a frustrating and
contradictory way.

Virginia gave Grace an understanding look. "This changes everything. You do realize that, don't you?"

Grace nodded slowly. She wanted to look at Paul, to see how he had reacted to his aunt's statement. Grace felt as if things were happening too fast. And even though Virginia seemed positive that Grace's identity had been established, Grace still wasn't sure what she believed, herself.

She remembered last night's dream. Elizabeth's illness, the daughter Josie had mentioned, the woman named Mrs. Winsen. She knew she should tell Virginia and Paul about the dream. And this was the perfect time to do so. But something held her back. She so desperately wanted to belong to this family. Wouldn't she be a fool to voice her doubts? To raise all these unanswered questions? What difference did it make that Josie had had a daughter? That Elizabeth had been sick? Why should Grace give Virginia anything else to feel badly about?

"Good," Virginia said happily, as if everything were settled. "Of course, I realize you'll need to go back to New York sometime, if only to wind things up, but from now on, I want you to think of this as your home. I want you to live here permanently."

"Grandmother...I—I've got to have time to think about all of this," Grace said. "I think Paul is right. Everything is happening too quickly."

"Not for me," Virginia said. "I've waited too long, as it is." She sighed. "But I understand how you must feel. You take all the time you need. Just know that I'm not changing *my* mind. The world will soon know my granddaughter has been returned to me, and you will take your rightful place in our family...and in our home."

Paul remained in the library after Grace left. As his aunt had been making her pronouncements, he had tried to determine exactly how he felt about them. He still wasn't sure.

He wanted Virginia to be happy, and obviously, believing she'd found Elizabeth had made her very happy.

Everything seemed to point to Grace's being Elizabeth.

Still, a tiny seed of doubt refused to go away.

Thoughts of last night spun through his mind. Had last night meant anything to her? Or had she simply taken advantage of his attraction to her, his obvious desire for her, and pretended a similar desire to strengthen her position? His mind immediately rejected this thought. She *couldn't* have been pretending. He was willing to stake his life on the fact that her responses to him had been spontaneous and deeply felt.

She's never claimed to be Elizabeth. She's gone out of her way to make it clear she has doubts.

Was Grace for real? Or was she very, very clever? Were even her expressed doubts part of a brilliant plan to ensnare his aunt... and him?

Although these questions plagued him, he knew he still wanted Grace. His weakness disgusted him. This was the first time since his disastrous engagement to Valerie that he'd ever allowed desire for any woman to cloud his judgment and put him in a vulnerable position.

Valerie Wentworth. He hadn't thought about her in a long time. He hadn't seen her in over six years, but he'd heard she'd married some Swiss tycoon and was living in Geneva in between jetting all over the world.

He was no longer bitter. After their breakup, he'd been hurt and disillusioned, but it hadn't taken long for him to realize Valerie had never pretended to be anything other than what she was: a woman who loved bright lights and brighter jewels. He had allowed his physical attraction for her to overrule his common sense. He had thought, once they were married, she'd be perfectly content to settle down at Hollister House and live the quiet life he loved.

She had also deluded herself into thinking he would change.

Paul thought he had learned from that experience.

Yet here he was, on the brink of making another mistake—this one with even more potential for disaster.

"Well, Paul," his aunt said, rousing him from his thoughts, "are you angry with me?"

"No. I'm not angry."

She regarded him thoughtfully. "There's something else. I think it's only fair to tell you I plan to change my will."

Paul nodded. Deep in his heart, he had known this would happen. If Grace really was Elizabeth, she was the rightful heir to Hollister House and the Hollister estate. He tried to ignore the acute sense of loss at the thought that sometime soon he might be expected to find somewhere else to live. He loved this house. It was his home. He fought against the negative feelings. He didn't want his aunt to know what he was feeling. She had been too good to him, too generous all of his life. She deserved his wholehearted support now.

"After some bequests, including an allowance for your mother, everything will be split fifty-fifty," his aunt continued. "Right down the middle. Half to you. Half to Grace."

Stunned, Paul stared at her. "Aunt Virginia, that's not necessary. I don't expect—"

She held up her hand. "I know you don't. And before you say anything more, let me say something else."

Paul subsided into silence, watching curiously as she wheeled herself over to the wall safe, spun the dial several times and opened the door. She removed something and beckoned to him.

He stood and walked over to her.

She held out her hand. In it was a gray velvet jeweler's box. "Open it," she said softly, eyes shining with eagerness.

Paul reached for the box and slowly opened the lid. Inside lay a three-carat, double-rose cut pink diamond ringed by smaller diamonds and mounted in an antique gold setting.

He stared at it. The Hollister diamond.

A priceless legacy that had been in their family for six generations, ever since 1850 when Elias Hollister had resigned from his position on President Zachary Taylor's staff and made his first million.

The ring had been passed from eldest son to eldest son and was the official betrothal ring of the Hollisters.

Paul tore his gaze from the brilliant jewel and looked at his aunt. There was an odd smile on her face as she met his eyes. The ticking of the wall clock seemed extra loud as they stared at each other.

"It would make me very happy if you and Grace were to marry," his aunt said, each word dropping like a bomb in the quiet room.

Marry Grace! Paul's heart lurched with a strange excitement. He finally gathered his wits enough to say, "What makes you think I'd want to marry her?"

"I know you're attracted to her. I can see it in the way you act around her, the way you study her when she's not looking." She smiled. "Grace thinks you dislike her, I'm sure, but you can't fool me, Paul."

Paul knew better than to deny the truth of her statement. He had never lied to his aunt.

Obviously knowing she had an advantage, his aunt pressed on. "And I'm pretty sure she feels the same way about you, especially after the way she acted this morning." She studied his face for a moment. "I know I've taken you off guard. You don't have to commit yourself right now. Just think about it."

Paul nodded slowly. Now that she had planted the idea in his head, he knew he would think of little else. He snapped the lid of the jeweler's box shut.

"And keep the ring," his aunt said, and now her smile was that mischievous one he'd always loved. "Just in case."

Chapter Nine

Virginia announced her intention to invite Ned Shapiro and his wife Deena, and another old friend, Cornelia Blake, a widow like Virginia, to spend Thanksgiving with the family.

"I want to show you off," she confessed to Grace. "Ned already knows about you, of course, and Cornelia can keep her mouth shut." Virginia smiled. "Because even though I can't wait to tell *somebody* our wonderful news, I do want the rest of the world to be surprised when we make our formal announcement."

Grace was really looking forward to the holiday, because the past week had been an anxious one for her. She hadn't slept well, and her appetite had fallen off. Her edginess resulted from a combination of uncertainty about Paul and his feelings for her and guilt over not disclosing the new information concerning Elizabeth and Josie.

Every night Grace lay in bed wide-awake. She deliberately put the locket on top of the dressing table at night. She didn't want to dream about Elizabeth anymore. She didn't want to find out anything that might change her status with the Hollisters.

She rationalized her actions by telling herself that Virginia never asked her if she was continuing to dream. Grace knew Virginia didn't want anything to upset the status quo, either.

Still, the names Helen and Mrs. Winsen refused to go away. At odd moments during the day, and certainly at night, the names would pop into Grace's mind, and she would feel sneaky and riddled by doubts.

If only Paul would talk to her. *Really* talk to her. If only he would acknowledge what had transpired between them. Maybe, if he gave her some indication that he cared for her, she could confide in him. But he hadn't, and she was sure now that he wouldn't. In fact, ever since the night they'd almost made love, he'd been avoiding her, she was sure of it.

Two of the days in the past week, he'd gone to Philadelphia for the entire day. One of those days, he'd even stayed in town for dinner, arriving home long after Grace had gone to bed. And on the other days, he'd been with them for meals and little else. The rest of the time he was closeted in his office.

Every night, Grace prayed he'd come to her. And every night, her prayers went unanswered.

As each day crept by, she became more and more convinced that she had imagined the entire encounter. Because if it had *really* happened, how could he just ignore it?

So, Thanksgiving and the guests that would be at Hollister House the entire weekend were a welcome diversion.

Cornelia Blake arrived on Wednesday evening in a flurry of noise and excitement. Grace immediately liked the elderly lady, who was tall, skinny and had eyes as black and shiny as onyx and a voice rough from years of smoking.

"Come here and give me a kiss," she ordered Paul.

Grinning widely, he complied.

After they'd hugged, she pushed him away from her and looked him up and down. "Handsome devil, isn't he?" she remarked to no one in particular.

Paul laughed. "Old flatterer."

Envy spiraled through Grace. What she wouldn't give to have him tease her and treat her with the same relaxed affection.

"And who's this?" Cornelia bellowed when she saw Grace standing in the background.

Grace smiled tentatively.

"This young lady," Virginia said proudly, reaching for Grace's hand and drawing her forward, "is Elizabeth."

Cornelia's eyes widened, and her mouth dropped open.

"That's the first time I've ever seen you speechless, Cornelia," Paul said dryly.

"Elizabeth?" Cornelia said. "Elizabeth *Hollister?*" When Virginia nodded, Cornelia let out a whoop. She rushed forward, grabbed Grace in a bear hug and squeezed her so hard, Grace couldn't breathe.

"I want to hear everything!" she shouted. "Everything!"

For the rest of the evening, Cornelia kept things in an uproar. Her exuberance, the recounting of everything that had happened since Grace first saw the locket, and the continued stress of Grace's uncertain relationship with Paul, all took their toll, and by ten o'clock, Grace was so exhausted, she knew she had to escape.

"I'm sorry," she said when there was a break in the animated conversation between the two women, "but I'm very tired. Do you mind if I go up to bed?"

"No, of course not, my dear," Virginia said.

Grace said her good-nights, first kissing Virginia, then shaking Cornelia's hand, then turning her gaze to Paul.

"Good night," she said softly.

He gave her a crooked little smile, and his eyes were understanding as they met hers. "Good night, Grace."

Grace lay awake a long time, remembering his expression and wondering what it meant.

Paul left his aunt and Cornelia about thirty minutes after Grace. He kissed both old ladies, then headed upstairs. He climbed the stairs slowly. When he reached the second floor, his eyes automatically turned right, zeroing in on the closed door to Grace's room.

Every night he'd fought the urge to go to her. Every night he'd battled his need to be with her against the certainty that he must be very sure about his feelings for her before he took any other action. Every night he'd lain awake, his emotions in turmoil.

Tonight would be no different.

He stood on the landing and imagined her behind that closed door. Was she already in bed? Lying against the pillows, her sheer nightgown caressing each curve, each hollow, the way he wanted to?

He swallowed.

God in heaven, but he wanted her.

He wanted her more every day.

He had never felt this kind of desire before.

Tonight had been agony. All evening he'd watched her, every subtle gesture, every fleeting expression. He'd seen her struggle to act normal—to smile, to answer questions, to pretend that all was as wonderful as his aunt was portraying it.

He had known the exact moment when weariness had claimed her, when the struggle had been too much to endure and he'd been filled with an aching tenderness.

She'd been through a lot in the past weeks. Whether or not Grace was Elizabeth, if she had been telling them the complete truth, the emotional toll on her must have been enormous.

So when she'd said good-night to him, he had been filled with the desire to take her in his arms and hold her close. To stroke her hair and comfort her and tell her everything would be all right.

Of course, he hadn't.

How could he have?

Even if his aunt and Cornelia hadn't been in the room, he had no right to touch Grace again until he figured out what future, if any, they had.

Just then, Cornelia's braying laugh rang out, and he realized he was still standing at the top of the stairs, staring at Grace's door like an idiot.

He shook his head in disgust and headed for his room. What was wrong with him? What if one of the servants had seen him? They'd think he'd gone nuts.

He laughed mirthlessly. Maybe he had.

If only he could come to a decision.

He slowly prepared for bed. After brushing his teeth, he snapped off the bathroom light and walked into the bedroom. His eye was drawn to the walnut bachelor's chest that doubled as his bedside table.

The top drawer beckoned to him.

Its contents beckoned to him.

As he had every night for seven nights in a row, Paul opened the top drawer and removed the small gray velvet box his aunt had given him.

He lifted the lid and stared at the glittering jewel. Its dazzling beauty never failed to stir him, especially as his mind envisioned the ring on Grace's slender finger.

He swallowed, mesmerized by the vision.

Hours later, still awake and tossing restlessly, he admitted how much he wanted to accept Grace without reservation. How much he wanted to forget all his doubts and let himself trust her and his growing feelings for her.

Should he?

But what if, in the end, she turned out to be an imposter? What if, even if she was telling the truth as she knew it, she *still* turned out not to be Elizabeth?

How would he feel about her then?

These questions had to be settled. And soon. Because until they were, he could not go near Grace again.

As Grace dressed for the afternoon, she decided that even though she had canceled plans to go back to New York the following week, she would have to go back soon. For one thing, she was running out of clothes. She put on the violet wool dress she'd worn her first night at Hollister House. She wished she had something new, something Paul had not seen her in before, but the only thing left in the meager supply she'd brought with her that filled that category was the dressy black crepe, and that was not a daytime outfit.

After one last glance at herself in the mirror, she headed downstairs. Before she'd reached the main floor, the aromas of roasting turkey and other holiday foods caused her mouth to water.

No formal lunch had been served today because the family was having its Thanksgiving dinner at three o'clock this afternoon, so Grace was hungry. She hoped she would be able to eat today. Having the distraction of company might help her relax.

When she entered the living room, everyone but Paul was already there. Grace smiled at Virginia, who looked lovely in a lavender dress trimmed in lace, then at Cornelia, formidable in black wool and diamonds. Finally, she turned to Ned Shapiro, who had risen as she entered the room.

They greeted each other, then he motioned to a small, plump woman with kind hazel eyes and salt-and-pepper hair who was seated nearby.

"This is my wife, Deena," he said.

"It's nice to meet you, Mrs. Shapiro," Grace said, walking over and holding out her hand.

"I've really been looking forward to meeting you, too," Deena Shapiro said. She smiled warmly. "Ned has told me so much about you."

They exchanged a few more pleasantries while Anna circulated with a tray of hors d'oeuvres. Then Grace accepted a glass of sparkling burgundy from a young male servant she'd never seen before, and as she turned back to the Shapiros, Paul entered the room.

Her heart skipped a beat. He looked so handsome. His dark gray slacks, white cashmere sweater and tweed sport coat set off his dark hair and gray eyes perfectly.

He headed straight for their group. His gaze connected with hers, and he smiled at her before he turned to the Shapiros. He stood talking to them for at least five minutes, smiling at Grace again before moving on to talk to the other guests. Grace was acutely aware of him for the rest of the cocktail hour, and once, when she glanced his way, she caught him looking at her. He quickly turned away, but the expression on his face and his obvious discomfort over being caught studying her, caused a fragile happiness to steal through her.

When they all went into the dining room for dinner, Grace found herself seated to Paul's left. Virginia, as usual, sat at the head of the table, but today Paul was at the foot. Deena sat on his right. Ned was at Virginia's right, Cornelia to her left. The table was festive with fall flowers and greenery.

There was a bewildering array of courses: wild mushroom soup to begin, followed by a Waldorf salad, and then the enormous turkey with all the trimmings.

The conversation was lively, and Grace actually began to relax and enjoy herself. Paul played the part of the charming, sophisticated host to perfection, and Grace realized there were many facets to his personality that she hadn't yet discovered.

He was actually witty, she found, and several times, when she laughed in delight over something he said, their eyes met and something sparked between them.

Just as the servants were clearing the dinner plates, Cornelia looked across the table at Grace and said, "Have you got a boyfriend, Grace?"

Grace was so unprepared for the question that it was a moment before she answered. "Uh, no, I don't." She willed herself not to blush.

Cornelia grinned. She looked at Virginia. "She'd be perfect for Craig, don't you think?" Then she turned back to Grace. "Craig's my son. He's recently divorced, and I think you'd like each other." Her head swiveled back to Virginia, who still hadn't answered the original question. "Wouldn't that be great, Ginny? Link up our two families?"

Virginia smiled. Her eyes reminded Grace of sapphires as they gleamed in the lamplight. "What do you think, Paul?" she said slowly. "Should we play matchmaker and introduce Grace to Craig?"

Grace couldn't believe this. They were all acting as if she weren't even in the room. She was especially surprised at Virginia. Cornelia seemed to enjoy saying outrageous things, but Virginia was such a sensitive woman, such a considerate woman.

"What I think," Paul said, "is that Craig and Grace are both perfectly capable of controlling their own affairs."

Grace looked at him, flustered by the unexpected subject, and what she saw caused her to become even more flustered. Paul's eyes glittered, and his jaw had hardened.

He didn't meet her eyes. Instead, he glared at Cornelia.

Why, he was angry!

A dizzying happiness flooded her. If Paul was angry, that must mean he was jealous. At that moment, Grace could have kissed Cornelia for inadvertently making him show some strong emotion where Grace was concerned.

For the rest of the day, she hugged her knowledge to herself. Even Paul's return, during the rest of the day, to a polite and casual friendliness didn't spoil her good spirits. She knew now that he had strong feelings for her. And she was confident that soon, very soon, he would express them.

During the next couple of weeks, Grace wryly remembered her optimism on Thanksgiving Day.

As day after day went by, and preparation for the Christmas Ball and the Christmas season accelerated, and still he made no move to initiate any kind of dialogue, her hopes waned.

She threw herself into helping Virginia with preparations for the ball. Extra staff were hired to help with the cleaning and refurbishing of the house. Drapes were taken down, cleaned and put back up. The hundreds of windows were washed until they gleamed. The chandeliers were washed, each individual crystal given careful attention. Mirrors, furniture and floors were polished. Rugs were shampooed. Hundreds of invitations were hand-addressed and mailed.

Then the process of decorating began. Boxes of glittering objects were hauled down from the attic by the servants, and Virginia supervised the hanging of each ornament. Heavy garlands of evergreens spiked with golden pinecones and threaded with satin ribbons were ordered from a local greenhouse, and soon the house smelled fragrant and wonderful.

Everywhere Grace looked, she saw something beautiful and sparkling, something that heralded the joyful season.

One day Virginia said, "You must have a new dress for the ball."

"Yes," Grace agreed. "I was planning to buy one when I go to New York."

Grace had finally scheduled a four-day trip to New York for the following week. She planned to give notice, pack her things, and—not without a pang—tell Melanie she'd have to find a new roommate.

"Oh, my dear," Virginia said, "please allow me to give you a dress."

"I can't do that."

"Of course you can. Rose, my dressmaker, is coming tomorrow, and we'll have her measure you the same time she measures me."

Grace finally acquiesced and soon found herself in the throes of picking out fabric and a pattern. The dress was going to be wonderful, she thought, the prettiest dress she'd ever owned—a filmy creation of ice blue lace and chiffon that Rose planned to sprinkle with hundreds of tiny rhinestones.

Grace knew that if she'd tried to buy a dress like it in New York, she would have had to withdraw her entire savings to pay for it. This incident, more than any other, brought home to her how different her future would be from her past. The thought was sobering. And a little frightening.

"You know, my dear," Virginia said, "this is changing the subject, but I've been wondering about something."

Immediately, Grace felt apprehensive and wondered if Virginia suspected how emotionally tormented she'd been lately. "What is it, Grandmother?"

"I noticed that you haven't been wearing your locket, and I ... I wondered why."

Grace swallowed. She didn't want to lie to Virginia. She chose her words carefully. "I just thought ... perhaps it was time to put it away."

Virginia studied her face for a moment. Then she smiled and nodded. "You're right. The locket belongs to the past." She reached for Grace's hand, clasping it warmly. "We don't need it anymore, do we?"

On the morning of Grace's departure for New York, Paul turned to her at breakfast and said, "What time does your train leave?"

"At one o'clock."

"I have to go into the city today, so I'll drive you to the station."

Excitement skittered through her. Maybe when they were alone in the car, he would say something about their situation.

He didn't.

All the way into Philadelphia, his only comments concerned the weather, the approaching ball, his aunt's excitement and happiness and Grace's upcoming trip.

When they reached the Thirtieth Street station, he pulled into the parking lot.

"You don't have to park. You can just drop me off in front," Grace said.

"I'll go in with you."

She didn't protest.

Inside the teeming station, he carried her bag and walked with her to her departure track. He set her bag down, and Grace looked up. Her heart knocked against her ribs as their eyes met.

"Grace," he said over the noise of an outgoing train, "when you get back, I think we need to talk."

She nodded, and her stomach felt hollow.

He gave her that funny little half smile of his, and just before he handed her her bag, he leaned forward and dropped a light kiss against her lips. "I'll pick you up on Saturday," he said. "Have a good time."

"Oh, Grace, I'm so glad to see you!" Melanie Beranchek exclaimed when Grace walked into their third-floor apartment. She rose gracefully from the sofa and threw her arms wide.

They hugged and when they drew apart, Melanie said, "I've missed you a lot."

"I've missed you, too," Grace said, realizing for the first time just how much she'd missed her friend. Suddenly, she wanted to tell her everything. For someone who looked the way Melanie did, all long legs and coppery hair and warm brown eyes, given to wearing flowing scarves and leggings and huge glittery earrings, she was one of the most pragmatic and sensible women Grace had ever known. You could always trust Melanie to cut right to the heart of something. On more than one occasion, she'd kept Grace's more romantic nature firmly grounded in reality.

For the next two hours, Grace talked and Melanie listened, only interjecting a comment here or there. When Grace finished, she sat back, completely drained. "So what do you think?"

Melanie twirled a long, gleaming strand of hair around her finger in thoughtful reflection. "It sounds to me as if Paul is in just as much turmoil as you are."

"Do you really think so?"

Melanie nodded. "Yes. I think that what almost happened between you, the things that *did* happen between you, have got him wrestling with as many conflicting feelings as you've been struggling with. After all, an involvement with you carries pretty heavy baggage with it, especially if he's still not entirely convinced of your identity."

"I know. I've been thinking the same thing, myself."

"And from the way you've described Paul, he doesn't seem like the impulsive type. It sounds as if he is very careful...about everything."

"He is."

"And even though I'm no psychologist, I think his adoption and his abandonment by his mother...all of that would make him especially cautious when it comes to emotional involvement."

Grace bit her lip and nodded slowly.

"You should understand how he feels," Melanie said softly.

Grace sighed. "Yes, I believe I do."

"My advice is, if you really care about him, be patient, and don't be too hard on him when he does make his move."

"He *did* say we needed to talk when I get back."

Melanie smiled. "See? What did I tell you?" Then she jumped up. "Now, I'm starved. Wanna head for China Palace?"

Grace grinned. China Palace was their favorite Chinese restaurant, only two blocks away from their Soho apartment.

As they walked down the three flights of stairs to the street level, Grace said, "How's Keith doing?" Keith was their landlord. He owned the gallery on the first floor and lived in the apartment on the second floor.

Melanie shrugged. "You know Keith. He threw Bruce out last week."

"Again?"

Melanie rolled her eyes. "Yes. Again."

While they walked to the restaurant, Melanie brought Grace up to date on their landlord's on-again, off-again relationship with his live-in lover.

The small restaurant was crowded and smoky, but Grace loved it, anyway. She and Melanie had spent many a happy evening here, surrounded by people who lived in the neighborhood.

Henry Lee, the owner, greeted them effusively and ushered them to a small corner table. Smiling, he handed them menus, saying, "So happy to have you back again."

After they'd placed their orders, Grace said, "You're going to be getting an invitation to the Christmas Ball my—" she hesitated over the word "—my grandmother is giving to announce my return."

Melanie eyed Grace gravely. "How do you feel about all this?"

Grace toyed with her water glass. "I don't know. Happy on one hand." She looked up, meeting Melanie's thoughtful gaze. "I love her. She's wonderful. And I love feeling that I belong at Hollister House, but—" She broke off.

"But?"

Grace sighed heavily. "But I just wish I was as sure of my identity as she is."

"So you still have doubts?"

Grace shrugged. "It's the strangest thing. I'm not sure how to explain how I feel. I... As much as I want to be Elizabeth Hollister... down deep, I still can't believe I am."

Then Grace told Melanie about her latest dreams. How she had, for the first time, become aware that Josie had a daughter, and that there was a woman named Mrs. Winsen who was somehow involved with Josie, too.

Melanie frowned. "The newspapers never said anything about a daughter."

"I know."

"If Josie had a daughter, where do you suppose she might be now?"

"I don't know."

"Josie was pretty young, wasn't she?"

"Twenty-five when Elizabeth disappeared."

"So she couldn't have a child that was very old."

"Well, we can't say that for sure. I mean, girls have babies as young as thirteen and fourteen."

"That's true."

Just then, their food arrived, and for a little while, they didn't talk. After they'd each served themselves a portion of the Szechuan chicken and the shrimp and lobster with black bean sauce, Melanie said, "What do Mrs. Hollister and Paul say about this new information?"

Grace looked down at her plate guiltily. "I haven't told them." When she looked up, she was relieved not to see any censure in her friend's eyes.

Instead, Melanie just seemed curious as she took a bite of her spring roll. "Why not?"

Grace shrugged. "I don't know." Then she sighed. "That's not true. I do know. But I'm a little ashamed of myself because of it." When Melanie waited silently, Grace continued, "It's just that, what purpose would it serve to tell them? It would disturb Virginia and it might get Paul all stirred up again, and, well—" She broke off.

"You don't want to rock the boat," Melanie finished.

"That's awful of me, isn't it?"

"No. It's practical. In fact, I think you did the right thing." Melanie dipped the last portion of her spring roll in hot mustard sauce, then popped it into her mouth.

"You do?" Relief washed over Grace.

Melanie nodded emphatically. "Yes. Wait until you have more concrete information. Have their names turned up in subsequent dreams?"

"There haven't been any subsequent dreams," Grace admitted.

"Oh?"

"I . . . uh . . . I put the locket away."

"I wondered why you weren't wearing it." Melanie took a bite of her chicken. "What have Mrs. Hollister and Paul had to say about that?"

Now Grace *really* felt guilty, because she'd deliberately misled Virginia. "She's such a wonderful woman. I know I should tell her the truth."

"Well, you'll tell her when the time is right," Melanie said.

Some of Grace's pleasure in being with Melanie again was spoiled by the reminder that she'd not been entirely truthful with Virginia.

"Hey," Melanie said softly. "It's okay. From what you've told me about her, she'd understand if you explained how you feel." She reached across the table and squeezed Grace's hand. "Now," she added brightly, "tell me about this Christmas ball. What kind of dress do you think I should wear?"

Chapter Ten

Grace stepped off the train in Philadelphia and searched among the faces in the waiting crowd for Paul. People jostled her as they greeted arrivals. Frowning, she looked up and down the platform. He'd said he'd be here, but she didn't see him. Paul was so punctual, so detail-oriented. It wasn't like him to forget or to be late.

A moment later, Tim, the Hollister chauffeur, waved from farther down the platform.

Grace's heart fell. Paul hadn't come. She had hoped that on the way home, they would talk, just as he'd promised.

"Hi, Miss Gregory," Tim said as he drew near. His freckled face broke into a welcoming smile.

"Hello, Tim." Grace tried to keep from revealing her disappointment by smiling brightly. As he picked up her two suitcases and started toward the exit, she casually said, "I expected Mr. Hollister to come today."

Tim nodded. "Yeah, he planned to, but this morning he was called away on some kind of emergency."

"I hope it's nothing serious."

"I don't know. It had something to do with the new store they opened in San Francisco a couple of months ago."

Business. Grace sighed in relief. For one crazy minute she'd imagined the unexpected trip might have had something to do with her.

During the drive to Rolling Hills, Grace decided that even though she had hoped to have her talk with Paul before telling Virginia and him about her latest dream, she would talk to Virginia as soon as she got to the house. For her own peace of mind she wanted to get it over with. She would bring Paul up to date when he returned.

With that resolve firmly in mind, as soon as she'd unpacked and found the gift she'd bought for Virginia, she immediately sought out the older woman.

Anna told her that Virginia was in her private sitting room, so Grace walked down the long hallway into the right wing and tapped lightly on the closed door.

"Come in," Virginia called.

Grace opened the door.

Virginia turned from her writing desk. Her eyes lit up. "You're back! I didn't hear the car!" She held up her arms.

Grace kissed and hugged her, breathing in the soft scent of roses. As always, she was nearly overwhelmed by the love she felt for this woman.

"I missed you," Virginia whispered, holding Grace's face between her hands and looking at her as if she would memorize every detail.

Grace swallowed against the lump in her throat. "I missed you, too." She gently extricated herself.

Virginia sighed. "Well, sit down. Tell me all about your trip."

"I will, but first..." Grace smiled and held out a box. "I brought you something."

"For me?" Virginia said delightedly. "I love presents!" She quickly tore off the wrapping paper and opened the lid of the blue Tiffany's box. "Oh, it's beautiful..." She reached inside and lifted out a crystal starburst paperweight. When she held it up, prisms of fiery color danced in the sunlight.

"I noticed you didn't have a paperweight on your desk," Grace said. "I hope you like it."

"I love it. It's wonderful. Thank you." Virginia turned and placed the paperweight on the desk, then looked at Grace. Without warning, her lower lip trembled. "It—it's my very first present from you."

Grace's eyes welled up with tears, and she had to blink rapidly to keep them from spilling.

Virginia sniffed and swiped at her eyes with the backs of her hands. She laughed shakily. "I'm sorry to be so emotional. Now tell me about New York."

Forty-five minutes later, after Grace had recounted everything, she nervously pleated her black slacks. "Grandmother, I...there's something else I have to talk to you about."

Virginia wheeled herself closer. "What is it, my dear? Is something wrong?"

Grace met her trusting blue eyes. "I should have told you about this weeks ago. I'm ashamed that I didn't."

Virginia waited quietly.

Grace took a deep breath. "Remember when I stopped wearing the locket?"

"Yes."

"The reason was, I'd had a dream that disturbed me, and I didn't want to have another."

"I suspected as much."

"You did?"

Virginia smiled gently. "I knew there was something you were keeping from me."

"Why didn't you say something?"

"My dear, you're entitled to some privacy. I figured you'd tell me when you were ready."

Melanie had said almost the same thing, but hearing it from Virginia made Grace feel as if a great weight had been lifted from her shoulders.

Grace started to talk, and the words tumbled from her mouth. She described her dream in detail, and in the retelling, she felt lighter and freer than she'd felt in weeks.

Virginia was quiet for a long time after Grace finished. Finally, she stirred and said, "This is very odd, you know."

"I thought so, too."

"Josie worked for my friend's son and his wife—Richard and Cynthia Chaney—for five years. If she'd had a child, surely Cynthia would have mentioned it to me when I called for a reference."

Grace nodded.

"I made a point of asking if Josie was the kind of young woman who would be likely to want to run around every night, and Cynthia said she was a very quiet girl. That she had rarely dated." Virginia's gaze met Grace's. "Are you *sure* about this, Grace? Could you by any chance have misunderstood?"

Grace shrugged. "I guess it's possible, but Josie's words came through to me very clearly."

"And who do you suppose this Mrs. Winsen is?"

"I don't know. She must have lived in Dobbs Ferry, though, don't you think?"

"It seems that way." Virginia stared into space.

"Wh-what do you plan to do?" Grace said after a moment.

Virginia turned slowly back to Grace. "I'm not really sure." She paused, then said, "Have you told Paul about this?"

"No. Not yet."

"Don't."

Grace frowned. "I thought you'd want him to know."

"Yes, well, let me tell him after I've had a chance to check a few things out."

"All right," Grace said reluctantly. She didn't like the idea of withholding this information from him and wondered what he would think when Virginia did tell him. Would the dark suspicion he'd exhibited when Grace had first arrived at Hollister House come back? She forced the dismal thought away.

"And until then," Virginia said, eyes filled with concern as if she could divine Grace's thoughts, "I want you to forget all about this. I want you to enjoy yourself and quit worrying."

"But what if—" She broke off. She couldn't voice the thought.

"Grace, I am convinced, beyond a shadow of a doubt, that you are Elizabeth. What you've told me today hasn't altered that conviction in the least. I'll investigate, because I know you'll feel better if I can allay your fears. But I'm not worried. There's bound to be a perfectly logical explanation for everything."

Paul returned home three days later, on the Wednesday before the ball, which would take place that Saturday. Grace waited for him to suggest that they have the talk he'd mentioned when he saw her off at the train station, but he seemed to have forgotten about it.

She wished she had nerve enough to remind him. If only she hadn't promised Virginia not to tell him about her latest dream, that would have been the perfect way to lead into a more personal discussion. But of course, she *had* promised Virginia.

By Friday, when he still had made no attempt to initiate a private conversation, Grace resigned herself to the fact that he had obviously changed his mind. She tried to put all of her worries out of her mind, as Virginia had advised, and give her full attention and energy to the upcoming festivities.

Out-of-town guests began arriving on Friday. Cornelia Blake and her son, Craig, were among the first to arrive, just before noon. They were staying with the family. They would accommodate as many guests as possible at the house, Virginia had explained earlier. The remainder were being put up at the Rolling Hills Inn.

Craig Blake resembled his mother—tall, angular, big-boned, with shrewd dark eyes and thick black hair streaked with silver. He looked to be in his late forties, Grace thought as they were introduced.

"Well?" Cornelia boomed, elbowing her son. "Isn't she just as pretty as I told you?"

Grace couldn't help but laugh. She wished Paul were there so she could see his reaction to Cornelia's blatant matchmaking, but he was upstairs in his office.

"Prettier," Craig said, bending over Grace's hand and kissing it. "Much prettier." His eyes said he was interested.

Grace wondered if it would help or hurt her cause with Paul for her to flirt with Craig. Not sure, she decided to be discreet—at least for now. She smiled. "It's nice to meet you."

By teatime, which Virginia had ordered served in the formal living room, there were a dozen houseguests. The only others Grace knew were the Shapiros, and she naturally gravitated to them. She and Deena Shapiro stood off to one side of the large room and discussed a mutual love for Broadway musicals.

While Grace talked, she watched Paul out of the corner of her eye. He was talking to a stunning woman named Olivia something. Grace remembered from the introductions that the woman was the daughter of Virginia's cousin from Vermont. Even so, she couldn't prevent the pinprick of envy when she saw Paul casually drape his arm around Olivia's shoulders and laugh at something she said.

Someone called to Deena, who smilingly excused herself, and Grace strolled over to the tea cart to refill her cup, then sat on one of the love seats. She looked at Paul over the rim of her cup. He was still laughing and talking to the beautiful Olivia. When his gaze turned in her direction, Grace hurriedly looked away. There was a painful knot in her chest.

When Craig Blake came and sat next to her, saying, "I can't believe my good fortune finding you alone," she was feeling just miserable enough to encourage him.

She gave him her most dazzling smile. "I was hoping you'd come and sit by me."

"I can see I'm going to have to come to Rolling Hills more often," he said, his eyes sweeping over her admiringly.

"Do you live in Cherry Hill, too?" Cornelia lived in Cherry Hill, which was only a few hours' drive away.

"Yes," he said. "Have you ever been there?"

"No, I never have." She was dying to look at Paul again.

"Well, we'll have to remedy that. I'll ask Mother to invite you, and I'll show you the town."

"I'd like that very much." If anything, the smile she bestowed on him now was even more dazzling than the earlier one.

He responded by putting his arm around the back of the love seat and bending closer. "You're very beautiful," he murmured.

Grace swallowed, her heart thumping. Maybe she shouldn't have encouraged him. Things were moving a little too fast for comfort. "Thank you," she managed to say, taking a sip of her tea and darting a glance at Paul over the rim of the cup. What she saw caused her to choke. He was looking straight at her, and he had one of the darkest scowls on his face she'd ever seen. As she watched, he said something to the woman named Olivia, then strode out of the room.

He didn't look at Grace as he passed by.

Melanie arrived Saturday morning. She said she would have liked to come earlier, but getting two performances off from her show was hard enough, because she'd used up all of her vacation. "They wanted me to come back tomorrow morning so I could make the Sunday matinee," she said with a grimace, "but I knew I wouldn't be worth two cents after being up half the night tonight."

"So are you going to stay until Tuesday morning?" Grace knew Mondays were dark at Melanie's theater.

"If you want me to."

"I want you to."

Grace spent a couple of hours that afternoon with Melanie at the Rolling Hills Inn, then returned to the house about four o'clock. She'd offered to help with last-minute preparations for the ball, but Virginia wouldn't hear of it.

"There are plenty of servants to do the work. You're the guest of honor. You just enjoy the day," she said emphatically.

After taking a nap and having a light snack of soup and a sandwich brought to her room at about six o'clock, Grace took a long, luxurious bubble bath, washed and dried her hair and began to dress for the evening.

While in New York, she'd purchased an underwire strapless bra and matching tap pants in pale blue satin.

She donned lace-trimmed, thigh-high, sheer white stockings and the expensive underwear, which she loved because it was so different from anything she'd ever owned before. Next, she slipped her feet into blue satin pumps with rhinestone buckles, then slipped on a floor-length taffeta half-slip.

When she was ready to put on her evening dress, she rang for Anna.

"Oh, miss," Anna said, eyes round, when Grace stepped into the gown. "Oh, it's so beautiful."

Almost reverently, Anna zipped her up, and Grace walked to the full-length mirror.

The vision in the mirror made her breath catch.

She looked like a fairy princess.

The dress shimmered in the lamplight, the hundreds of rhinestones hand-sewn into the filmy pale blue lace and chiffon twinkling like stars in the heavens.

The strapless bodice hugged her body to just below her waist, then the dress swirled into a froth of skirt whose scalloped hem skimmed the tops of her shoes.

It was a heavenly dress.

Anna helped Grace with her hair, which she'd decided to wear loosely piled on top of her head in a cluster of curls. The dressmaker had fashioned a hair ornament of tiny blue satin rosettes studded with rhinestones, and Grace carefully pinned it in place.

Tiny diamond stud earrings, a birthday gift from Melanie when Grace had turned thirty, and the locket completed her outfit.

After Anna left, still oohing and aahing, Grace looked at herself in the mirror again. Shining eyes filled with expectation looked back at her. The locket glowed, secure in its niche in the hollow of her throat. The dress undulated and sparkled with each subtle movement. Her hair, her makeup, her gown—everything looked perfect.

Somehow, Grace knew tonight would be a night to remember all of her life.

Smiling, she opened her bedroom door, and slowly
walked toward the stairs.

Paul, dressed in his evening clothes, a red carnation in
his lapel, was positioned at the foot of the stairs by seven-
thirty. He knew the invitations said eight o'clock, but he
wanted to be sure he was ready to greet guests if anyone
should show up early.

His aunt, beautiful in rose velvet and diamonds, and
more vibrant than she'd looked in years, joined him ten
minutes later. Some of their houseguests were already
gathered in the dining room, where the doors at the far
end had been thrown open to the ballroom.

Sounds of the band warming up filtered through the
laughter and conversation, joined by the tinkling of crystal as servants began circulating with trays of champagne.

The family's Christmas tree, trimmed all in gold, just
visible from where Paul stood, glowed from its place in
the front window of the living room.

The air was fragrant with the scent of pine and bay-
berry and candles and perfume.

Every inch of wood, every fabric, every surface, shone
from all the washings and polishings and cleanings.

"It's going to be a wonderful evening," his aunt said,
smiling. "And you look very handsome."

He returned her smile. "And you look very beautiful." Just then, she raised her eyes, looking toward the
staircase. Her smile faded, and her right hand trembled as
she clasped it to her chest.

Paul turned, and for one heart-stopping moment, he
couldn't breathe as his gaze fastened on a radiant Grace
slowly descending the stairs. His hand tightened on the

railing, and even if he'd wanted to, he wouldn't have been able to tear his gaze away.

With each slow, graceful step, her dress swirled and shimmered around her. She looked so impossibly beautiful, so exquisitely feminine and bewitching, it was as if she weren't a flesh-and-blood woman at all, but a fantasy who had stepped out of a dream.

As she came closer, he saw the rosy tint of her cheeks, the sparkling blue of her eyes and the alluring sweep of her eyelashes. His gaze traveled over the fullness of her rose-tinted lips, the graceful curve of her neck, the creamy slope of her shoulders and the tantalizing hint of cleavage in the cut of her gown.

God, she was incredible.

He held his breath as her gaze met his. Her smile, sweetly shy and sexy all at the same time, caused his heart to beat in slow thuds.

Their gazes held for what seemed like hours, but was probably only seconds. Still, it was long enough for Paul to know something he'd been denying for weeks.

He wanted her.

He didn't care who she was or why she'd come to Hollister House. He didn't care if this was a sensible decision or not.

He wanted her.

And he meant to have her.

The look in Paul's eyes made Grace's heart beat faster. She had to hold tightly to the banister because she suddenly felt light-headed.

When she finally reached the bottom of the stairs, Virginia said, "Oh, you look so beautiful! Doesn't she look wonderful, Paul?"

"Yes, she does," he said softly. His gaze swept her. "Perfect, in fact."

To cover her sudden attack of shyness, Grace bent to give Virginia a hug. "You look beautiful, too," she said.

She straightened, and Paul's gaze met hers again. "Save me a dance," he said.

Grace's heart soared. She smiled. "I will."

Only minutes later guests began arriving, and in the flurry of greetings and introductions, Grace got separated from Paul. By the time the dancing began, Grace had already promised the first dozen dances to other men.

Her first glimpse of the ballroom took her breath away. Her imagination hadn't done justice to the reality of its beauty with the chandeliers blazing, the Christmas decorations, the more than two hundred guests resplendent in their finery and the glimpse of a fresh snowfall, which had turned the landscape beyond the windows and French doors into a wintry fairyland.

Grace danced and danced. She had a bewildering array of partners and she knew she'd never remember all their names. All were charming and flatteringly attentive. She also drank several glasses of champagne, which made her feel as if she were floating.

She danced with Craig Blake four times in the first hour and a half. During each dance, at some time, she felt Paul's eyes upon her.

Why didn't he come to claim his dance?

That he was watching her, she knew for certain. It wasn't just when she danced with Craig that she felt his scrutiny. Dozens of times she caught him looking at her, and the expression in his eyes made her heart beat even faster.

Finally, just before ten o'clock, he approached her as she stood talking to Melanie, who looked spectacular in a flame-colored sequined dress slit up the front to expose her gorgeous legs.

"Hi," he said, looking into her eyes.

"Hi."

"I haven't met your friend," he said, looking at Melanie.

Grace introduced them, suddenly wishing she was as tall as her friend and had legs even half as beautiful.

Just then, the band struck up a waltz.

"Will you excuse us?" he said to Melanie. He turned to Grace. "May I have the honor of this dance?"

Grace smiled happily and moved into his arms.

He held her close, and as they glided into the waltz, and Grace felt the strength of his body moving against hers, she couldn't help but remember that night in her room.

When he looked down into her eyes, she knew he was remembering it, too.

"I didn't tell the truth earlier," he said, his voice husky.

"Oh?"

His arms tightened and drew her closer. His gaze swept her face. "Beautiful isn't the right word to describe the way you look."

Grace stared at him. Suddenly, she wished she hadn't drunk quite so much champagne. Her head was spinning, and she wasn't sure if it was the dark desire she saw in the depths of his eyes or the effects of the alcohol that made her feel as if she wouldn't be able to stand if not for his support.

His gaze dropped to her mouth. "You look irresistible."

Something warm and silky spread through her body. She could feel her heart racing, and wondered if he felt it, too.

He pulled her even closer, placing his mouth near her ear, and murmured in a rough whisper, "When you look at me like that, I want to kiss you senseless."

Grace's heart banged against her ribs. Desire spiraled through her, making her weak. She closed her eyes, felt his warm breath against her ear, the firm muscles of his legs brushing hers as they twirled and circled in unison to the strains of Strauss.

All she could think about was the promise in his eyes, the rough urgency in his voice and how much she wanted him. When the dance was over, he held her close for a long moment. Just before he released her and walked her over to the place where he had claimed her, he murmured, "Will you wait for me afterward?"

"Yes," she whispered.

For the rest of the evening, she was in an agony of anticipation. She danced, she ate, she talked, she drank more champagne and she remembered her promise.

At midnight, Virginia wheeled herself to the bandstand and the mike was lowered to accommodate her. As she had been instructed earlier, Grace stood on one side of Virginia, and Paul moved into place on the other.

The band played a drumroll.

Conversation died and an expectant hush fell over the crowd.

"My friends," Virginia said, "I invited you here tonight because something wonderful has happened to our family, and I wanted all of you share in my happiness." She reached for Grace's hand, then Paul's.

Grace smiled shakily. She'd been so aware of Paul, so excited by developments between them, she'd almost forgotten this moment was coming. Now she felt nervous and unprepared for the onslaught of questions and the media attention Virginia's announcement was sure to generate.

"All of you have met our houseguest, Grace Gregory." Virginia's smile expanded, and her eyes shone with happy tears. "It gives me the greatest pleasure to tell you that Grace is more than a houseguest. She is..." Virginia paused, and her hand tightened on Grace's. "Our long-lost Elizabeth—my granddaughter."

As the crowd gasped, and broke into an excited babble, Grace raised her eyes to meet Paul's. She was almost afraid of what she would see. Would this announcement change things again? Would that invisible barrier drop into place?

He didn't smile, but his eyes were filled with a fierce possessiveness, and her heart soared.

Flashbulbs went off and people surged forward. As Grace prepared to meet them, she knew that her entire life had been leading to this moment.

She had finally found a home.

A place to belong.

And someone to love.

Chapter Eleven

For the next two hours, Grace was surrounded by well-wishers and the society reporters who had been invited to come to the house in time for Virginia's announcement.

She didn't get a chance to talk to Paul at all, but several times she saw him standing nearby, talking to guests and watching her.

Twice he smiled at her. Each time, a delicious anticipation skipped through her, and she hugged the knowledge to herself that later they would be together.

She answered dozens of questions until finally, just before the band stopped playing at two o'clock, Paul broke through the crowd milling around her and took her arm. "That's enough questions for tonight," he said firmly. "Miss...Hollister is tired. My aunt said to tell you—" his gaze swept the reporters "—that there will be a formal press conference Wednesday afternoon in our lawyer's office in Philadelphia." He went on to give them details.

One of the pushiest of the reporters called out, "Tell us, Mr. Hollister, just how do you feel about the discovery of a new Hollister heir? Isn't that going to have an impact on your position?"

Paul's hand on Grace's arm tightened imperceptibly, but he smiled and said smoothly, "To repeat, no more questions tonight. Save it for the press conference." And then he led Grace away. Just before depositing her at Virginia's side, he leaned closer and murmured, "Do you want me to come to your room later?" Grace's heart knocked crazily at the expression in his eyes.

She wet her lips and nodded.

He gave her a slow smile filled with promise.

By three-thirty, all the guests had either departed the house or gone upstairs to their rooms, and the servants had begun the cleanup.

Virginia, looking tired but happy, said, "I'm ready for bed, I think. Brunch will be served at eleven-thirty in the morning. I'll see you then." She raised her arms for a hug, and Grace gladly complied. "This is the happiest day of my life," she said as they embraced.

Misty-eyed, Grace said, "It's the happiest day of mine, too." After Virginia left, Grace also headed for her room.

Her bed was already turned down, and the hurricane lamp on top of the chest cast a soft glow over the room. Grace walked to the windows, parting the drapes and looking out over the white expanse of snow glistening in the moonlight.

It had been such a magical evening—fulfilling all of her fantasies—and it wasn't over yet.

Her heart beat faster. Paul was coming to her.

And soon.

She didn't have long to wait. A scant ten minutes later, her door opened with only the tiniest whisper of sound. Pulse fluttering, she let the drapes fall into place and slowly turned.

Paul moved into the room silently. He closed the door behind him, and even though the *click* as the lock connected was almost infinitesimal, to Grace's sensitive nerve endings it sounded like a pistol shot.

She found it hard to breathe as Paul slowly walked toward her. He had removed his evening clothes and wore gray silk pajama bottoms and a loosely belted black velour robe that revealed bare chest. A tremor slid down her spine.

Wordlessly, he took her hand and drew her out of the shadows and into the pool of golden lamplight. His eyes, dark and glowing, never left hers as he traced the curve of her jaw, then her mouth, with the pad of his thumb. Heat, like quicksilver, raced through her veins as his fingertips grazed her shoulders, her collarbone, her arms.

"You're so beautiful," he murmured.

Grace trembled.

"So very desirable…" He leaned forward. Holding her shoulders lightly, he kissed her eyes, her cheeks, the tip of her nose.

And then his mouth sought hers, capturing it in a breath-stealing kiss. Desire arched through her as the kiss became more urgent, more demanding, more heated, and his hands roamed her bare back. He pressed her firmly against him, and she could feel the hunger pulsating between them.

Breathing hard, he finally released her. "I've been thinking about this all night," he said, his voice rough with desire. Then slowly, he began to undress her. First her dress, then her slip, were tossed onto the chaise.

His eyes devoured her as she stood before him clad only in her satin underwear and the sheer white stockings. Never breaking eye contact, he took off his robe, and threw it in the direction of her clothing.

Grace reached up and unhooked her bra. She started to remove it, but he said, "Wait. Let me." He opened it, baring her breasts.

She shuddered as his hands cupped them, his thumbs stroking until the peaks were hard and throbbing. Heat zigzagged through her.

With a groan, his own hands trembling now, he slipped her bra off, and together they hurriedly shed the rest of her clothing and his pajama bottoms. When all the barriers between them were gone, he lifted her in his arms and carried her to the bed.

He made agonizingly slow love to her, kissing and caressing and whispering endearments, until he had her trembling and weak. Almost senseless with need, she tried to hurry him by closing her palm around him, but he moaned deep in his throat and pushed her hand away. "Not yet," he muttered. A delicious tension built as his fingers worked their magic, and just when she thought she couldn't stand it another minute, her body shuddered under an onslaught of pleasure so intense, it was almost painful. She felt as if she were dissolving, completely coming apart inside.

Only then did he enter her, pushing hard and deep. Grace closed her eyes and received him gladly. He felt so good inside her, his heat and strength filling all the places that had been empty for so long. She lifted her hips and wound her legs around him.

He began to move, slowly at first, and then faster and harder, grunting with the effort. That unbearable tension began again, building, building. "Paul," she cried, and with one last mighty thrust, they each reached a shattering climax. For Grace, the physical sensations were almost anticlimactic compared to the fierce pride, the happiness and wonder and absolute certainty that she'd been right.

This was where she belonged.

They held each other until their bodies cooled and their heartbeats slowed. Then Paul propped himself up on his elbow and looked down at her.

He smiled tenderly. He traced the curve of her jaw with his finger, then touched her swollen lips. "I didn't hurt you, did I?"

Grace smiled. "Only in the nicest way."

"Grace..." The smile faded.

Grace tensed, an unreasonable fear gripping her.

"I'm sorry I ever doubted you."

Relief, like a sudden spring shower, washed over her. She captured his hand, brought it to her mouth and kissed it. She looked up into his compelling, mysterious eyes and thought about how strange love could be.

He bent over her and gave her a soft, lingering kiss. Then he whispered against her mouth, "I've fallen in love with you."

Grace's heart nearly stopped. Did he mean it? Did he really love her?

His thumb stroked her mouth, her cheek. He kissed her again, softly, gently, seductively. "Do you love me?" he murmured. "Do you?"

"Oh, Paul...yes! Yes, I love you. I think I've loved you forever...." She trembled as he gathered her close again, still unable to believe he really loved her.

He was smiling as he smoothed her hair back from her face. "Will you marry me, then?"

A wild joy spiraled through her. She could hardly believe she'd heard him correctly.

"Well?" he said. "Aren't you going to say something."

"I—I'm speechless."

He kissed the corner of her mouth, letting his lips linger there as he whispered, "I knew tonight that we belong together."

A dark, sobering thought struck her. *I knew tonight that we belong together.* What had brought on this sudden admission of love, this completely unanticipated proposal of marriage? *I knew tonight that we belong together.* Did the public announcement that she was Elizabeth prompt this? She wanted, she *needed* to believe he was sincere. Yet... an insidious doubt refused to disappear.

"Would you still want to marry me if I wasn't Elizabeth?"

He laughed softly. "What kind of question is that?"

"Please, Paul, I must know."

"Grace, it's *you* I love. *You* I want to marry."

"What if..." She hesitated. "What if, tomorrow, some piece of evidence turned up that showed I wasn't Elizabeth. What then?"

"You're being silly. The question is moot, because you *are* Elizabeth, aren't you?" He nuzzled her neck. "And I love you. Isn't that all that matters?"

Was he right? *Was* she being silly? Was it just her basic insecurity that had caused her to question his motives?

"You know how happy it would make Aunt Virginia if we got married," he said, his voice smoothly persuasive.

"Yes," Grace whispered. Her grandmother would be thrilled. Ecstatic, probably.

His hand caressed her breast. "It'll be perfect," he murmured. "The perfect merger." He lowered his mouth to her breast, his tongue flicking over the peak, then he nipped gently with his teeth.

Grace whimpered. But even as desire blazed again, part of her remained detached. She thought about his choice of words. *Merger* sounded so cold. So calculated.

Now his mouth moved to her other breast.

"Paul," she said weakly. "I can't think when you do that."

"I don't want you to think," he said. His tongue swirled around the hardened tip. "I want you to say yes."

Grace closed her eyes. She wanted to. She wanted to more than she'd ever wanted anything. If only she could be sure he loved her. She knew he desired her—his eyes had been telling her that the entire evening and his actions tonight proved it—but desire wasn't the same as love.

What were his *real* motives in asking her to marry him?

Paul raised himself over her, looking down into her eyes. "Let's tell Aunt Virginia tomorrow," he urged her, his fingers probing between her legs, then delving until Grace gasped.

"Say yes," he demanded.

"Yes, yes, yes... I'll marry you."

This time when he brought her to that starburst of sensation, she told herself she didn't care what Paul's motives were in asking her to marry him.

She loved him.

And she wanted to be Mrs. Paul Hollister.

The wonderful thing was that in marrying Paul, she could have it all. A home and a family. Her past and her future. Her heart swelled with joy as she imagined their lives together. They would fill this house with children and be wondrously, gloriously happy.

Later, he gently tucked the bedcovers around her. Grace watched him lazily as he walked to the chaise. He had a great body—long and lean and firmly muscled. She smiled. And he was going to be hers. All hers.

He picked up his robe. At first, Grace thought he planned to put it on and leave her, and she sat up to protest. But instead, he removed something from a pocket and came back to the bed. He turned on the bedside lamp, flooding the room with light. Then he sat down on the edge of the bed and looked at her.

Grace saw that he held a small jeweler's box.

He snapped it open.

Grace's eyes widened. The ring tucked into the satin folds was breathtaking. When he lifted it out and reached for her left hand, slipping it on the ring finger, Grace was speechless. She had never seen anything quite like the exquisite pink stone circled by diamonds.

"This is the official Hollister betrothal ring," Paul said. "It's a pink diamond, very rare."

"Oh, it's... it's gorgeous," Grace said, awed by its magnificence.

"No more than you are," he murmured.

And then he kissed her again, and Grace never even wondered why or how he'd come to have it in his possession. She only knew she was happier than she'd ever been and that from now on, she would always have a place to belong.

Virginia hadn't stopped smiling all day. From the moment she'd spied the betrothal ring on Grace's finger when Grace entered the dining room for brunch, she had been grinning from ear to ear.

She was especially pleased—and a little embarrassed by her pleasure—to see the wind taken out of Cornelia's sails. Cornelia, in typical Cornelia-fashion, was blunt. When Paul put his arm around Grace and told the assembled houseguests that he and Grace had become engaged last night, she said, "Oh, drat! And I wanted her for Craig!" Then she let out one of her booming laughs, swooped down on Grace and enveloped her in a bear hug.

"Are you happy?" she said.

Grace smiled shyly, looking up at Paul with adoration in her eyes. "Very."

Then Cornelia turned to Paul and said, "You sly thing. You misled me!"

Paul's smile was amused, and when Cornelia turned away, he winked at Virginia.

"So when's the wedding?" Deena Shapiro asked after congratulating Paul and hugging Grace.

Grace looked at Paul again. "I...we haven't talked about it."

"The sooner, the better," Paul said.

Virginia clapped her hands. "Valentine Day," she said. "Evan and I were married on Valentine Day."

"But that's only about seven weeks away," Deena said. "Weddings take a lot of planning. Believe me, I know. It took me six months to arrange Rebecca's wedding. Can you get everything ready by then?"

"Watch us!" Virginia said. Her mind was already whirling. She wondered if Grace would want her own wedding dress or if she'd consider wearing Virginia's. Come to think of it, Anabel's wedding gown was stored in the attic, too. Maybe Grace would prefer to be married in her mother's dress. And then there was the church. Would Grace and Paul want a church wedding at St. Martin's, or would they prefer to be married at Hollister House?

"What do you think?" Paul said, turning to Grace. "Do you want to be married on Valentine Day?"

Grace's luminous smile made Virginia's eyes mist over. "I'd love to get married on the same day as my...my grandparents." And then she walked over to Virginia and hugged her, and Virginia did start crying, but they were tears of joy.

Only one thing marred the day for Virginia. She couldn't help feeling a little sneaky for not telling Paul about the new information Grace had confided upon her return from New York. Virginia knew she should have— it wasn't fair to withhold this from him—but she hadn't wanted to burden him, especially when she knew the information had no importance whatsoever. After all, it was just a dream. And now he had more important things to think about. Like his wedding.

Still...she hoped Paul wouldn't be angry with her when he did find out. Well, she'd cross that bridge when she came to it. She *had* asked Ned Shapiro to put his investigator back to work and gave him all of the details Grace had given her. And Ned had assured her that the investigator was already checking every possible source.

Time enough to tell Paul after the investigator had unearthed the truth.

Grace moved through the next three weeks in a daze. With whirlwind speed, Virginia initiated the wedding preparations. She called a Philadelphia wedding consultant—a woman named Carolyn McNally—who arrived the morning after Paul and Grace had made their engagement announcement. Paul was invited to sit in on the consultation along with Grace and Virginia, but he declined.

"I'll leave the details to you and Aunt Virginia," he told Grace. "Whatever you decide is fine with me."

Grace couldn't believe how many decisions had to be made. The first was where they would be married, and she and Virginia quickly decided on St. Martin's, the church the family had attended for many years. Paul concurred. "I've always liked St. Martin's," he said.

"Well, why didn't you say so?" Grace said.

He kissed her cheek. "I wanted you to choose. If you'd have preferred to be married here at the house, I would have been happy with that decision, too."

The next decision concerned where they would hold the wedding reception. After much debate, Grace and Virginia settled on the country club.

"Even though I'd love to have it at Hollister House, having it at the club will mean much less work for the servants and less stress all around," Virginia said, and Grace agreed with her.

Invitations, flowers, music, an official photographer, size of the wedding party, how many guests, what kind of food—the list went on and on.

"What about your wedding dress?" Carolyn asked. "Are you having one made for you or buying something ready-made?"

"I don't know," Grace said. "I haven't had time to think about it."

"I'd be happy to help you with some ideas," Carolyn said.

"Before you start looking at designs, Grace," Virginia said, "I'll have Anna bring your mother's and my wedding dresses down from the attic. They are both very beautiful, and with only slight alterations, you could probably wear either one. Of course, if you prefer your own dress, I'll understand."

Grace was enthralled by the idea of wearing a dress that had belonged to either her mother or grandmother. For a woman who had never had a family, never known any tradition, the idea of walking down the aisle in a gown worn by a family member was irresistible.

The following morning, Anna told Grace that the gowns would be brought to her room after breakfast.

"Do you mind if I come up and watch while you try them on?" Virginia asked.

"Of course not!" Grace said.

So after breakfast, the two women headed for Grace's room. Both dresses were even more beautiful than they had looked in the photographs Grace had seen. Virginia's was an elegant, romantic lace creation fashioned along deceptively simple lines with a high, jeweled neckline, long sleeves and a slim skirt with a gently flared, scalloped hemline.

Anabel's dress was a creamy satin with a low-cut, sweetheart neckline, short puffed sleeves, molded bodice and an enormous skirt ending in a full train.

Grace tried on her mother's dress first. It was a little tight in the waist, but otherwise fit her nicely. "It looks beautiful on you," Virginia said. "And if you want to wear it, don't worry about the waist. Rose can let it out so it's comfortable."

The dress *was* beautiful, and Grace had a lump in her throat as she looked at herself in it. She remembered her parents' wedding photographs: her mother's radiant smile, her father's brash grin.

But as much as Grace loved the dress, she knew that if Virginia's gown fit her, that would be the one she'd wear. It didn't look like the kind of dress that could be easily altered, especially because the lace had yellowed over the years.

It fit Grace as if it had been made for her. Virginia looked at her, her eyes shiny with unshed tears. "It's perfect, isn't it?" she said.

Grace nodded, too emotional to speak.

Once the decisions about the wedding had been made, the family prepared for Christmas. On Christmas Eve, the three of them went to the candlelight service at St. Martin's, and Grace got her first look at the church where they would be married. It was also perfect, she thought—an older, traditional church with lovely stained glass and dark wood—just the kind of setting she had always envisioned when she dreamed about her wedding day.

"It *is* lovely," she whispered to Paul.

In answer he just squeezed her waist.

Christmas Day was quiet—just the three of them—but warm and happy and completely satisfying. They opened their gifts in front of a cheery fire on Christmas morning. Grace gasped when she saw the diamond bracelet and matching earrings Paul gifted her with, nearly passed out when Virginia, with a sparkling smile, gave her the keys to a sporty little green roadster.

Stunned, Grace hardly knew what to say. "But I never expected anything like this," she protested. "I just bought *small* gifts for both of you." She shook her head disbelievingly. "I don't need diamonds or a car."

"Nonsense," Virginia said. "Paul doesn't let anyone drive *his* cars, and I can't imagine you wanting to drive the Lincoln." She took Grace's hand. "I've missed so many of your Christmases and birthdays, my dear. Please don't deny me the pleasure of making up for some of them."

And Paul said, "I know you don't need diamonds, but I want you to have them. I had planned to give them to you as a wedding present, but then I thought you might like to wear them New Year's Eve." He insisted on putting the necklace on for her, and after fastening the clasp, his hands lingered on her neck and he bent forward to kiss her cheek.

Virginia beamed.

What could Grace say? How could she continue to protest without sounding ungrateful? Besides, the gifts were exciting. Thrilling. She had never owned anything like the diamonds or the roadster. In fact, she had received very few gifts in her lifetime. It was wonderful to be spoiled like this.

Two days after Christmas, Virginia told Grace about the changes she had made in her will. "I'm setting up a separate account for you. Starting now, you will receive a quarterly allowance that is yours to do with as you wish. The first payment has already been transferred to the First National Bank here in Rolling Hills. All you have to do is sign the papers, and you'll be able to draw on the account." She named a sum that seemed staggering to Grace.

"But, Grandmother, I don't need any allowance, much less such a large amount. Living here, I hardly spend anything at all. Besides, my former boss has asked me to do freelance work for him. I'm expecting several manuscripts to be delivered tomorrow, so you see, I'll have money."

"You are my granddaughter," Virginia said. "You're entitled to this money."

Even Paul seemed to agree with his aunt, saying, "Aunt Virginia's right."

Although intellectually Grace had known that if she was found to be Elizabeth Hollister, she would automatically become a very wealthy woman, she was still stunned by the enormity of the changes in her life—changes that were taking place so rapidly, her emotions were having a hard time keeping pace.

During this period, Grace and Paul spent a lot of time together, and each day her love for him grew deeper. He worked shorter hours so that they could take long walks, and one afternoon, when the temperature had been below freezing for several days in a row, he said, "Guess what we're going to do this afternoon." His hands were behind his back, and he had a mischievous gleam in his eyes.

Grace, who had been addressing wedding invitations, said, "What?"

"Ah, you're no fun. I told you to guess."

She rolled her eyes. "Okay. Okay. But I'm no good at guessing games. Let's see. You're going to take me somewhere fabulous for lunch."

His face fell. "Do you want to go out for lunch?"

She laughed. "No! But I told you, I'm no good at guessing games."

He produced a pair of ice skates from behind his back. "We're going skating!"

Grace was delighted. They spent a wonderful couple of hours skating on the pond, laughing and carrying on like kids. They chased each other, and Paul did figure eights and fancy spins, and several times Grace fell down. Each time she did, Paul would skate over and pick her up, and then he'd kiss her.

"Mmm," Grace said, "I think I'll fall down more often!"

After the skating session, Nora had hot chocolate waiting for them instead of their usual afternoon tea, and Grace thought the day was one of the nicest she'd ever spent.

In the evenings, she and Paul played gin. He was a very competitive player, Grace discovered. He always wanted to win, and he usually did. "You cheated!" she said one night after she had been sure she'd beaten him, only to have him declare gin first.

In answer, he gave her a sly smile and said, "I always get what I want." He reached under the table and slid his hand under her dress.

Grace blushed. "Stop that," she whispered.

"Stop what?" he said innocently, his hand moving higher.

Grace darted a quick look at Virginia to see if she was listening to them, but Virginia's head was nodding over her book.

Paul grinned and removed his hand. "Later," he whispered, and Grace blushed again.

A couple of nights, Paul took Grace out to dinner, but for the most part, they both preferred quiet evenings at home.

Grace was happier than she'd ever been. The only flaw in the perfection of the days was her inability to forget about the locket and her last dream.

Grace had again put the locket away. Only this time, it wasn't quite so easy to ignore it. Every time she was alone in her bedroom, she felt compelled to open the small vanity drawer where she'd secreted it. She would stare at it for long moments—at its glowing face, at the intricate scrollwork, and she would have an almost overpowering urge to pick it up.

She told herself to forget about it. She told herself that there was nothing else she wanted or needed to know. She was done with dreams. She wanted to put all of that behind her and get on with her life. She wanted to stop looking backward and look forward.

But none of her reasoning and rationalizing could hide the truth, and one night, about a week after New Year's, when Paul was out of town until the following morning and Grace was alone, she finally had to face it.

She had just finished her nightly ablutions, and she walked out of the bathroom and into the bedroom. She sat on the side of her bed and her eyes were instantly drawn to the vanity. The drawer that contained the locket beckoned to her.

"No," she said. "I won't. I can't." She turned off her bedside lamp and burrowed under her covers.

What are you afraid of?

I'm not afraid.

Yes, you are. Why won't you admit it?

There's nothing to admit.

Are you afraid of the truth? Is that it?

She put her hands over her ears and counted sheep.

Admit it. You're afraid the locket might reveal something you'd rather not know.

"I'm not afraid." Tears welled up in her eyes.

You like being Elizabeth Hollister. You don't want to find out anything that might even remotely suggest you aren't.

"That's not...true," she whispered brokenly. "It's not."

But the voice in her head would not let up. She lay there for hours and fought her private demons. Finally, wearily, she snapped on the bedside light and got out of bed. She walked to the vanity, opened the drawer and took out the locket. Then, resigned, she got back into bed, the locket clasped in her fist.

Josie was crying. Great, gulping sobs interspersed with hiccups, as if she had been crying for a long time. Slumped over in a chair, her hands cupped her face and her shoulders heaved.

Gradually, her cries eased, and she groped for the box of tissues sitting on a nearby table. She pulled several out, wiped her tears away and blew her nose.

Slowly, like an old woman, she stood and walked across the room. She looked down into the crib.

A child lay in the crib, as still and quiet as a doll. Her face looked porcelain pale, her hair lifeless and matted against her head.

Josie lowered the railing, then reached into the crib. Her face contorted as she touched the toddler. "You can do it. You can do it." Grimacing, she pushed her to the side of the crib, then picked up the blanket crumpled at the bottom of the bed. She spread it out, rolled the child over onto it, then started wrapping her up. The form never moved, not even an eyelash. Suddenly, Josie stopped. Her hand hovered over the child, then hurriedly, almost as if she were afraid she'd change her mind, she unfastened the locket around her neck and dropped it into her own pocket.

"If I need to, I can pawn it," she said.

Then she finished wrapping her, mummy-style, in the blanket. When finished, she left the room, returning dressed in a long black winter coat and a red woolen hat. She picked the child up and carried her out of the bedroom, down a hallway, into a small kitchen, and then outside.

It was nighttime, but the snow on the ground and the moonlight gave off enough light for her to see. Josie glanced around furtively. Her heart was thumping madly.

Nothing stirred. The nearest house was hundreds of yards away. She couldn't even see it from here, because it was around a bend. Taking a deep breath, she stepped off the porch into the backyard.

The yard wasn't very big, and it was surrounded by woods. Snow crunching underfoot, she tramped across the yard and into the woods. It was much darker now. She picked her way carefully, trying not to think about what she carried in her arms.

Before long, she reached a small clearing where there was an old, abandoned and boarded-up cabin. Next to the cabin was a well.

Josie's step faltered. Fear, thick and cloying, clogged her throat and roiled in her stomach. She closed her eyes and tried to keep the nausea under control. Then quickly, trying not to think, she walked to the well.

She looked down. She couldn't see anything. Only blackness.

She bowed her head. "Holy Mary, Mother of God, pray for us sinners, now and at the hour of our death. Amen."

Then, with an anguished whimper, she dropped the bundle into the well.

Chapter Twelve

Elizabeth was dead.

No matter how many times Grace told herself it wasn't true, that it *couldn't* be true—after all, wasn't *she* Elizabeth?—the knowledge of Elizabeth's death sat there like a great dark monster, smothering Grace, siphoning off every last bit of air until she knew she'd never breathe easily again.

Outwardly, she did all the things she always did when she awakened. She showered and brushed her teeth and put on her makeup and dressed and prepared herself to go downstairs to face Virginia across the breakfast table.

But all the while her mind churned. Over and over, like a needle caught in the groove of a record, the same scene played. Josie approaching the well with Elizabeth's lifeless body in her arms. The sick fear in Josie's stomach. The tormented prayer. And then Josie dropping Elizabeth into the well. Into oblivion.

No, no, no, it can't be true.

"... pray for us sinners, now and at the hour of our death..."

Grace pressed her hands against her eyes as if she could force the powerful images to disappear. They refused to go away. *She dropped Elizabeth into the well. Elizabeth wasn't moving. Elizabeth was dead. She dropped her into the well. You're not Elizabeth. You never were Elizabeth.*

How was she going to sit at the breakfast table and pretend everything was normal? How was she going to smile and talk about the wedding? And yet, she must, or Virginia was sure to suspect something was wrong.

Grace felt sick to her stomach. She had to pull herself together. She had to. Thank God, Paul wasn't due home until later in the morning. If she had to face him, too, she wasn't sure she could stay calm.

You have to tell them. You have to tell them about this dream. You can't pretend you didn't have it.

No! How could she tell them? How could she destroy Virginia's happiness?

And Paul.

What would he do if he found out she wasn't Elizabeth?

You'll lose him. You know you'll lose him.

Pain, diamond-hard, stabbed her temples.

She would lose everything. The home she'd found. The family she'd found. The love she'd found. Everything. And in the process, she'd break Virginia's heart.

Maybe there's some logical explanation for this.

Maybe there was. After all, if she wasn't Elizabeth, how had she come to possess the locket?

Yes. Yes. Grace grasped at the comforting thought. Surely there had to be something she wasn't seeing. Something she had misunderstood. Maybe the child Josie had dropped into the well hadn't been Elizabeth at all.

As she stood there grappling with her problem, her little bedside clock chimed the half hour. Eight-thirty. She had to go downstairs. It was time for breakfast, and after breakfast she and Virginia were supposed to go over some last-minute additions to the guest list for the wedding.

Grace massaged her temples, then went into the bathroom and gulped down a couple of aspirin. She took several deep breaths.

She'd come to a decision.

She would say nothing about the dream. Unless and until she knew more, she would keep quiet. Anything else would be irresponsible.

Thirty minutes later, Virginia, a concerned expression in her blue eyes, said, "You look tired, my dear. I'm afraid you're trying to do too much."

"No, no," Grace protested. "I just have a headache." *Why did you say that? Now she'll think you didn't sleep well!* She prayed Virginia wouldn't ask her if she was still dreaming.

Thankfully, she didn't.

The thought crossed Grace's mind that maybe the reason Virginia hadn't questioned her further was her own fear of finding out things she had no desire to know. But that was silly, wasn't it? Virginia was firmly convinced of Grace's identity. She couldn't have faked her unshakable belief—it shone from her eyes every time she looked at Grace. And since she *was* so firmly convinced, what could she possibly have to fear?

All morning, they worked on the last of the invitations. And all morning, Grace worried. She tried not to. She and Virginia were so in tune with each other, Grace was afraid Virginia would sense what was on Grace's mind.

But Virginia was still riding a pink cloud of happiness over the impending wedding and she didn't seem to notice Grace's preoccupation, or if she did, she probably attributed it to prenuptial stress.

By lunchtime, Paul had come home, and he joined them to share the meal. Grace had herself under better control by then, and there were moments she actually forgot about the dream. Being around Paul now always gave her a warm glow. He seemed like a different person from the one she'd first met. Every day he showed her new facets to his character, and every day she felt closer to him.

"How was your trip?" she asked.

He smiled. "Good. But I missed you."

Something painful knotted into Grace's chest. She tried to smile, but knew her effort was sadly lacking. "I—I missed you, too."

He frowned slightly. "Is something wrong?"

Grace shook her head. She could feel tears threatening. "I'm just feeling kind of emotional right now, that's all."

He nodded understandingly.

By now, he had finished his lunch. He kissed Grace lightly on the mouth and said, "I've got a lot of work to do this afternoon, so I probably won't see you again until dinner. Why don't you take it easy this afternoon? Read a good book, or something?"

She gave him a rueful smile. "I can't. I've got an appointment with the photographer, then a fitting for my going-away outfit." Using all of her self-control, she forced the dream from her mind, forced herself to concentrate on assuaging his concern over her. "Don't worry about me. I'm fine, really."

By the end of the day, she told herself she really *was* fine. All she had to do was forget the dream entirely and never go near the locket again. In fact, the wisest thing she could do was pack it away against the day she and Paul had a daughter of their own.

For an entire week, she was able to keep to the first part of her resolve. It wasn't easy. The locket called to her. She forced herself to ignore its mystical pull, the almost irresistible need to take it out and touch it.

Then, on the eighth night after her dream, when Paul had gone to Boston on business, the lure of the locket was simply too strong. Grace, frightened yet unable to stop herself, opened the drawer and stared at the golden oval inside.

Mouth dry, she picked it up.

She stood there, holding it, absorbing its warmth. It felt alive in her hand. Alive and full of secrets. She swallowed, and she could feel her heart beating.

Thump. Thump. Thump.

Almost as if her actions belonged to someone else, she slowly rubbed her thumb over the locket's face.

Images swirled.

Suddenly dizzy, she backed to the bed and sat down. She closed her eyes.

The house sat back from the road. It was a small, very plain, very ordinary frame house painted a muddy-looking brown. It had a steeply pitched roof and a narrow front porch. The blinds were pulled down over the windows.

All around the house were woods—dark and dense. There was no garage, and the driveway was unpaved gravel.

In the front of the house, right at the foot of the driveway, was a mailbox. On the side of the mailbox, there were words, painted in black.

Box 20, Old Dairy Road.

Grace gasped, dropping the locket as if it were a live coal burning her hands. Her heart raced. She must be crazy. Why couldn't she leave well enough alone?

She spent an agonizing night. She was afraid to close her eyes. Afraid the dream would start again. The picture of the house refused to go away. She felt as if it were burned into her brain.

Box 20, Old Dairy Road.

Josie, dropping a bundle into the well. The well that was somewhere behind the house on Old Dairy Road.

The next day, Grace told Virginia she had to get out of the house. She needed fresh air. She'd been cooped up too long. She knew she sounded desperate, because Virginia gave her an odd look.

Grace drove up and down the country roads surrounding Rolling Hills. For hours she drove, looking for Old Dairy Road, looking for the house in her dreams. There was no Old Dairy Road.

Exhausted, she finally returned to Hollister House. She was quiet and withdrawn at dinner. When Paul, who had returned from his trip at about five o'clock, frowned and asked her if she was feeling all right, she said, "I think I might be coming down with a cold."

"You should go to bed early," he said.

Grateful for the excuse he'd given her to escape his and Virginia's scrutiny, Grace said, "I think I will." She kissed them both good-night and went upstairs a few minutes after nine.

The next morning, when Paul headed to his office after breakfast, she told Virginia she was feeling better and thought she'd go out for another drive this morning. "I drove around Rolling Hills yesterday, and thought I'd like to explore the countryside today. Do you mind?"

"No, of course not. Was there anything in particular you wanted to see?"

"No. Just kind of get the feel of the area."

Virginia nodded. "It's pretty countryside. And if you're interested in history, there's a revolutionary war battlefield about thirty miles from here—near Johnson's Mill."

"That sounds interesting. You don't happen to have a map, do you?"

Virginia produced a map, and Grace took it to her room. She felt slightly guilty at how she'd let Virginia play right into her hands, even supplying her with a destination. Spreading the map out on her bed, she found Rolling Hills.

Yesterday she'd driven around in a panic. She hadn't planned anything logically. Today she realized, if she was ever going to find Old Dairy Road, she had to use her head. She thought back to the dream she'd had when Josie and the man named Frank had taken Elizabeth away in the car. They'd headed south on Park Drive, not north.

You wasted a lot of time yesterday driving around north of Rolling Hills.

With a red felt-tipped pen, Grace circled the names of two towns that lay to the south.

Hillsborough and Maple Creek. And there was the battlefield, clearly marked, only a few miles east of Hillsborough. Perfect.

Furtively, almost as if she were afraid someone were watching her, she removed the locket from the drawer, holding it by the chain, and stuffed it and the map into her purse. Five minutes later, dressed in black boots, her black coat and warm black leather gloves—another Christmas gift from Virginia—she was headed down the stairs.

"Where are you off to?"

Grace stopped, turning around to see Paul peering down at her from the second-floor railing. He had some papers in his hand and a quizzical expression on his face.

"I'm just going out for a drive. Thought I'd explore the countryside."

"By yourself?"

Grace smiled. "I'm a big girl."

He walked down the steps. "Why don't you wait until after lunch? I'll play hooky, too, and we can both go exploring." He had reached her side. "In fact, let's skip lunch here and we'll eat out." He smiled, obviously pleased by his idea.

Avoiding his gaze, Grace thought fast. "Oh, Paul, I don't expect you to neglect your work just because I've got cabin fever." She knew her answer sounded lame. Ordinarily, she would have been thrilled by his suggestion.

He frowned.

"But that does sound like fun," she said hurriedly. "Tell you what. I'll make sure I'm back by noon, okay?" She mentally readjusted her plan. Since she felt she had to go to the battlefield in case Virginia asked her about it, she would probably only have time to investigate the area around Hillsborough. If she had no luck there, Maple Creek would have to wait until tomorrow.

"All right," he said. "Have fun this morning." He gave her a quick kiss and waved her off.

Thirty minutes later, Grace, driving her new little car, was headed south on Park Drive. She went to the battlefield first and spent forty-five minutes walking the area, looking at all the markers and memorizing details. Satisfied that she could discuss the history of the battlefield, she proceeded to her real destination.

When she arrived in Hillsborough, it was already ten-thirty, and she knew she would not be able to drive around as she had in Rolling Hills. She also knew she would be extremely fortunate to find a map of a town as small as Hillsborough. But she had to try.

She stopped at the first filling station she came to. The lone attendant, a scrawny kid with friendly brown eyes, confirmed her suspicion that there would be no map available. He scratched his head when she asked if there was an Old Dairy Road in Hillsborough or the surrounding area.

"Don't rightly know," he said. "I just moved here 'bout a month ago, but Annie Humble, who owns the diner up the street, she's lived here all her life. She knows ever'body and ever'thing. You just go on up there and tell her Marsh Kovach sent you.''

Grace thanked him and drove to the diner. Even in her agitated state of mind, she was amused by its name. The Finer Diner. Finer than what? she wondered.

Annie Humble turned out to be a plump, rosy-cheeked, Kewpie doll of a woman with corkscrew gray curls and bright green eyes that studied Grace curiously. "No, hon, there's no Old Dairy Road around here, but there used to be a Dairy Road.''

Grace's pulse jumped. "Used to be?''

"Uh-huh. Now they're callin' it Country Club Drive. That's 'cause the developers bought up all the dairy farms and the country club and golf course got built and lots of new folks moved out there.''

"Can you tell me how to get there?''

The helpful Annie gave her directions, and Grace was soon on her way.

As soon as she turned onto Country Club Drive, she knew this couldn't have been the place from her dream. First of all, the terrain was too flat. Second, there was nothing that even remotely resembled the heavily wooded area she'd seen. Surely, if there had been a woods here, the Hillsborough Country Club builders would have found a different site for their golf course.

For a moment she was filled with giddy relief. The dream was wrong. It had to be wrong. And she'd prove it, too. Tomorrow, she'd make a quick trip to Maple Creek and eliminate that possibility, as well. Then she could *really* forget about the dream.

For the first time in a week, she actually felt happy. She was humming "Get Me to the Church on Time" as she turned her car around and headed home.

After Grace left for her drive, Paul continued on his way to his aunt's sitting room, where he was pretty sure he'd find her. Sure enough, she was writing letters at her desk. She signed the papers he'd brought to her, then said, "Grace went out for a drive this morning."

"I know. I saw her on the stairs a few minutes ago." For some reason, he still couldn't get the idea out of his head that Grace had seemed evasive this morning. In fact, she'd been acting strange for days. The word that came to mind was *preoccupied*. Worried, even.

He'd dismissed his vague feeling of unease by telling himself she was feeling the stress of trying to plan a wedding in such a short period of time. Especially a wedding on as grand a scale as theirs was shaping up to be.

Then, last night, when she'd said she thought she was coming down with a cold, he'd told himself that explained her lack of sparkle. She hadn't been feeling well and hadn't wanted to say anything.

But this morning, all of his antennae had picked up discordant vibrations. There was something not quite right in the way she'd reacted to his invitation to accompany her on her exploration of the countryside. Something downright suspicious about the way she'd avoided his gaze.

She didn't want you along.

For the remainder of the morning, the thought refused to go away. Paul dictated letters to Susan, he read through several contracts and made notes for his attorney, he made several phone calls and talked to two Hollister board members—and all the while, he kept remembering how Grace had avoided eye contact with him.

What was she doing that she didn't want him to know about? For the first time since the night of the Christmas Ball, some of his old doubts crept into his mind.

He hated feeling this way.

Hated the suspicion that she'd been hiding something from him.

Hated that the foundation of trust that had been building between them had developed a crack.

He decided he would not beat around the bush. He would come right out and ask her what was going on.

But at lunchtime, she talked animatedly about the battlefield and her exploration of Hillsborough and the countryside between the two towns. "It's so pretty around here," she said. "I'd forgotten how nice it is to live among so much green." She'd turned to him and given him one of her soft, sweet smiles. "This is a wonderful place to raise children, isn't it? Oh, Paul, we're going to have such a good life!"

Her smile disarmed him.

So he pushed his doubts away, and he didn't say anything.

The following day, Grace didn't make the mistake of trying to go out without telling Paul. At breakfast, she looked at Virginia and said, "Is there anything I need to do this morning?"

"Not a thing."

"Good. It was so much fun to get out yesterday, I think I'll go out again this morning. Maybe do a little shopping and explore some more." She deliberately turned her gaze to Paul. "Do you want to go with me?" She figured if he said he did, she would wait and go to Maple Creek tomorrow.

"Better not," he said. "I've got a transatlantic call coming through, so I'll need to stick close to the house."

By ten o'clock, Grace was headed for Maple Creek.

This time, when she stopped at a filling station to ask her questions, a garrulous old man with the name Skip emblazoned on his shirt pocket, said, "Yes, ma'am, the historical society, they put out a map of Maple Creek, but you can only get it at the drugstore. But you don't need no map. Old Dairy Road's out west of town. Just drive down

Maple Avenue until you get to the railroad tracks, cross the tracks, then hang a left at the first street and go about three, four miles, and when you come to Gil's Body Shop, hang a right and Old Dairy Road'll be the first street you come to."

"Is there a woods nearby?"

"Yep. Old Dairy Road dead ends into 'em." He frowned. "Pardon me for sayin' so, but that's not exactly the nicest part of town for a lady like you." His frown deepened. "Who ya lookin' for? Mebbe I can help."

"Thanks, but I just want to see the street." Then, feeling she had to say something to explain herself, she added, with an apologetic smile, "I think I might have lived there as a child. I just want to look at the area."

"It used to be real isolated out there. Only a few houses."

That fit. Grace thanked the old man and climbed into her roadster. Her heart beat faster—half in excitement, half in fear.

She had no trouble following Skip's directions. When she got to Old Dairy, she drove slowly down the two-lane road. Deep ditches rimmed either side, filled with mounds of dirty snow and litter.

The few houses on the street were dilapidated and neglected. Rusted cars were parked in the driveways, and one house even had an old washing machine sitting on the front porch.

None of the houses resembled the house in her dreams. Also, none of them seemed to have box numbers.

The woods started about midway down the road on the right. Suddenly, the road curved to the left, then stopped abruptly about a hundred yards away.

Grace stared. To her right, backed up by the thick woods beyond, was the house.

It was much older and the front porch sagged, but it had the same shape, the same placement of windows, the same steeply pitched roof. Her heart accelerated as she stared at it. There were no numbers on the mailbox, but she knew this was the right house.

Grace stopped the car and parked across the street. Her heart was pounding now. She slowly opened her door and got out. Telling herself it was ridiculous to be frightened, she walked across the street.

Then she saw the dog.

He saw her, too, and he snarled, lunging toward her. Fortunately, he was chained to a pole, and he couldn't lunge far. He was a Doberman, and Grace knew, if he'd been loose, he could have torn her apart.

She bit her lip. She wanted to walk around the back of the house, but she knew she'd be trespassing. The dog was sure to make a racket.

Maybe she should just knock on the front door, say what she was looking for and see what happened.

She took a hesitant step forward.

The dog growled deep in his throat. Then, leaping furiously against his restraint, he barked fiercely.

The front door opened.

An unkempt man dressed in a red plaid flannel shirt and dirty jeans stepped onto the porch. "Whadda you want?" His tone was not friendly. "Shut up!" he shouted at the dog.

The dog's barks subsided.

Grace wet her lips.

Just then, she heard a car screech to a stop. The man looked beyond her and frowned. The dog began to bark again.

Grace turned.

Her heart stopped.

Climbing out of his red Ferrari was Paul.

Chapter Thirteen

Paul grabbed Grace's arm. "What the devil are you doing here?" he asked, keeping his voice low so the man on the porch wouldn't hear him. "Are you crazy? This is a bad neighborhood."

Grace's face drained of color. "I—I," she sputtered. She looked stricken.

Paul almost felt sorry for her. Almost. Then he remembered that she had lied to him. She hadn't gone *exploring*. This wasn't an innocent, sight-seeing ride she'd taken. No one in his right mind would come to this neighborhood by chance. Something was definitely going on. Something she didn't want him to know about.

The dog snarled, straining at his leash. The man glared at them. "Do you want somethin'?" he shouted. "If not, git off my property or I'll let my dog loose!"

Paul didn't wait to see if the man would make good on his threat. He crossed the road, pulling Grace along with him. She didn't protest.

When they reached her car, he opened it. "Get in. Follow me home. We'll talk when we get there."

She nodded, her eyes wide and frightened.

"And lock your door," he said. He waited until he was sure she had followed his orders.

Paul climbed into the Ferrari. He turned the ignition and the car purred into life. He checked the rearview mirror. She was right behind him as he pulled out and headed down the road.

It took them nearly forty minutes to reach the estate. If Paul had been by himself, he would have made it a lot sooner, but he'd kept his speed down so Grace would have no trouble following him. The whole time he fumed, thinking about her evasiveness. What in the hell had she been doing at that house? He couldn't imagine. She had a lot of explaining to do.

He had followed her on a hunch. Although he didn't consider himself intuitive, the way his great-aunt was, he could usually tell when someone wasn't being entirely truthful with him, and there was something about the way Grace had answered him yesterday, when she'd gone "exploring" and again this morning, when she'd announced her intention to go out again, that didn't sit right with him.

So, because his transatlantic call came in right after breakfast, and because he happened to be looking out the window when Grace rounded the corner of the house and headed down the driveway toward the front gate, he had jumped up, grabbed his coat and dashed downstairs to the garage. Tim had looked startled when Paul hurriedly climbed into the Ferrari, waved and barreled down the driveway in pursuit of Grace.

At first, Paul was afraid he'd lost her, because he didn't see the little green convertible. He went south, because that's the direction she had gone yesterday morning, when she hadn't wanted him to go with her. Sure enough, a few minutes later he saw her car stopped at a red light. He hung back. He didn't want her to see him.

And when she stopped at that filling station and he saw the attendant gesticulating and pointing, obviously giving her directions, he knew his hunch had been right.

Thank God he'd followed that hunch. If not, no telling what stupid, fool thing she might have done. It scared him to think what might have happened to her. Yes, she had *lots* of explaining to do.

The gates to the estate swung open. He drove around back and pulled into the garage, then waited as she drove into her slot. When she climbed out of the roadster, she seemed more composed than she had in Maple Creek.

To her credit, she didn't try to avoid his gaze. "Paul, I know you're wonder—"

"Wait until we get inside," he said. He had no intention of carrying on this conversation in front of Tim, who had just walked into the garage.

Paul nodded to Tim, then took Grace's arm. He felt a tremor snake through her at the contact. She wasn't as composed as she'd wanted him to think.

They went straight to his office. Susan was at a doctor's appointment, so he didn't have to worry about his secretary's curiosity or the possibility that she might overhear them, which was a relief.

Once they were inside the office, he shut the door, and after they'd divested themselves of their coats, he motioned Grace to the love seat. He sat down next to her. He reminded himself that she was innocent until proven guilty, so he should try not to sound as if he were accusing her of wrongdoing until he'd heard her explanation.

"All right," he began. "Now you can tell me what you were doing in that place today."

She looked up. Her blue eyes were filled with regret. "I'm sorry, Paul. I—" She looked down, and he saw her lip tremble.

He willed himself not to touch her, not to be swayed by her obvious distress. *Remember, she lied to you.*

She took a deep breath, then met his gaze again. "I went there today because I—I had a dream, and I thought maybe that house was...was the one where Eliz...where I was kept after Josie and her accomplice abducted me."

Paul stared at her, shocked by her revelation. It took a few moments for the shock to abate before he thought about how she'd started to say *Elizabeth,* then faltered and said *I* instead. He realized it was still hard for her to think of herself as Elizabeth.

"How did you know where to go?" he asked, as if her statement had been perfectly ordinary.

She looked down at her hands. "I saw the address."

She spoke so softly he wasn't sure he'd heard her correctly. "You *saw* the address?"

"Yes."

"In your *dream?*" He knew he sounded skeptical, but this dream business had always seemed suspect to him. He knew that was probably because he had an analytical mind. If he couldn't see it or touch it, it was hard for him to believe in it.

She nodded, still not looking at him.

"Well, how did you know to look in Maple Creek? Did your dream tell you that, too?"

"No." Her voice sounded small.

Suddenly, Paul was ashamed of himself. He sounded just like a prosecutor. Did he have any right to be grilling her like this? Obviously, she was frightened. Obviously, her dream had disturbed her. But why had she hidden it from him? If she'd told him about it, he would have gone with her. It hurt his feelings that she didn't trust him enough to confide in him.

He softened his voice. "*Was* that the house you were kept in?"

She shrugged, finally looking up. "I don't know."

"Do you *think* it was?"

"I—I don't know what I think."

He stared at her, trying to determine if she was telling him the truth and wishing he hadn't started doubting her again. "How did you find the house?"

"I knew from an earlier dream that when Josie and Frank...when they t-took me, the car was heading south. When I checked, I discovered that there were no streets named Old Dairy Road near Rolling Hills, so I did the only logical thing I could think of. I decided to check the towns south of here."

"Which are Hillsborough and Maple Creek."

"Yes."

"Did you go to Hillsborough yesterday morning?"

"Yes."

"And you didn't find anything?"

"No."

He took her hand. It felt cold as he wrapped his fingers around it. "Grace, why didn't you tell me about this?"

She hesitated, then said, "I was afraid of what you'd think."

He gave a mirthless laugh. "Well, I guess you were right. I think the whole thing is crazy." Suddenly, the fear he'd felt for her when he first saw her approaching that disreputable-looking man and his vicious dog, made him angry all over again. "What did you hope to prove by finding the house, anyway? Surely there would no longer be any clues left. Hell, it was more than thirty years ago." He knew she could hear his anger and exasperation, but he simply didn't understand her thought processes. He couldn't believe how foolish she'd been, what an awful risk she'd taken in going to that unsavory neighborhood alone.

A sudden horrifying thought struck Paul, and he picked up her left hand. Relief rushed through him. She wasn't wearing her engagement ring.

"Give me credit for some sense," she said. "I'd never wear that ring when I'm out alone."

"I'm certainly glad of that. People have been killed for a lot less." He put his arm around her and tipped her face up so he could look into her eyes. "Grace," he said softly, "I'm sorry to have given you the third degree like this, but you scared me. I followed you today because I felt you were hiding something from me, and I'm damn glad I did. God only knows what would have happened if I hadn't shown up."

"I wasn't going to do anything stupid," she said, but her voice lacked conviction. He restrained himself from pointing out that she had already done something stupid in going to that place alone.

"All right, let's forget about today for a minute. Let's talk about tomorrow and the next day and the day after that."

"Okay," she whispered.

"I want you to promise me you'll never go back to that house again."

"I—"

"Promise me."

"I—I promise."

His arms tightened around her. "I love you," he said softly. "I love you, and I don't want anything bad to happen to you. Do you understand that?"

She nodded.

And then he kissed her and told himself that he could trust her. She had promised. Surely she would keep her promise. Funny then, that he still felt uneasy.

* * *

For the next couple of days, Grace felt the same way she'd felt when she first arrived at Hollister House. As if she was under constant surveillance.

Paul was watching her.

She knew he wasn't purposely spying on her, or anything, but she also knew he wasn't entirely satisfied by the story she'd told him and the promise she'd made to him. He was right to be suspicious, she thought wryly. Because she couldn't stop thinking about the house.

The house and the dream.

The woods and the well.

She knew, if she were smart, she would forget about them. She would put the locket away, as she'd decided to do once before, and she would stop worrying about the past. *Think about the future. Think about how happy you're going to be.*

She couldn't. The dream haunted her. The house haunted her. The suspicion that she had no right to be here, had never had any right to be here, haunted her.

The days marched on. The wedding was less than three weeks away. And still she was haunted by the dream. Sometimes, when she least expected it, when she was in the middle of some prewedding task, or sipping a glass of wine before dinner, the image of Josie walking to the well would suddenly superimpose itself on her brain. Her hands would shake, and she would feel sick to her stomach.

She didn't sleep well, either.

Even on the nights when Paul came to her room and they made love, she would lay awake afterward and her mind would churn. She knew she couldn't go on like this.

One morning, after a particularly sleepless and agonizing night, she decided she would go crazy if she didn't talk to someone. And the only person she trusted who didn't have a stake in the outcome of all of this was Melanie. So, after breakfast, Grace went to her room and placed the call to New York.

"H'lo?" Melanie's voice sounded blurred.

Grace looked at the clock. It was nine-thirty. "Oh, I'm sorry, Mel. It's Grace. Did I wake you?" Melanie was usually up by nine, at the gym by ten.

"Umph, s'okay." Yawning and stretching sounds followed. "Had a late night, that's all. What's up?"

"I—I just needed to talk to someone. Do you want to get a cup of coffee or anything before I start?" Melanie usually couldn't even muster a good morning before her first cup of coffee.

"Good idea. I'll call you back."

"No. That's all right. I'll give you twenty minutes, then I'll call *you* back."

Twenty minutes later, Grace launched into her story. She told Melanie everything, ending with, "And I promised him I wouldn't go back to the house again. But I..." She hesitated.

"You what?" Melanie said.

"I never said I wouldn't go into the woods."

"Grace! Don't you *dare* go there by yourself! It's dangerous! It's stupid!"

"But Mel, don't you see? I've *got* to find out if... if Elizabeth is really dead." Her voice broke, and she could feel the tears welling up in her throat and in her eyes. "Oh, God, what am I going to do? What if—" She couldn't continue.

"Listen," Melanie said urgently. "Do you want me to take a couple of days off? Come there?"

Grace brushed away the moisture creeping down her cheeks. She tried to think. "Y-you said you didn't have any vacation left."

"That was last year. On January the first I got two more weeks. And sweetie, I'll be glad to come."

Grace took a shaky breath. "It...it's sweet of you to offer, and I love you for it, but it's not necessary. I'm...I'm okay."

"Really okay?"

Grace sighed. "Yes."

There was silence for a moment, then Melanie said, "Grace, what are you really afraid of? Not being Elizabeth or losing Paul?"

Grace swallowed. "It—it's more than losing Paul. It's losing V-Virginia and losing my home." Her voice dropped to a whisper as pain flooded her. "It's losing my past...and my future." It was losing everything that mattered. It was the fear of being alone again after having known what it felt like to belong, to be loved, to have a place in life.

How could she chance it?

"If Paul really loves you," Melanie said slowly, "it won't matter to him whether you're Elizabeth or not."

If Paul really loves you...

The words echoed in her mind. She remembered the night he'd asked her to marry him. She remembered how she'd questioned him on exactly that point. She also remembered his evasive answer.

If Paul really loves you...

How could Grace ever know for sure? And could she spend the rest of her life not knowing?

About three o'clock that afternoon, Ned Shapiro called Virginia.

"I've got some news, Ginny."

Virginia clutched the phone tighter.

"I looked through the tax rolls for 1963 and found two Winsens listed. The first family I tried, the old man was still alive, but he had no idea what I was talking about, and I believe him.

"But the second inquiry I made turned up something. There was no longer anyone named Winsen in the house in question, but the woman who lives next door—one Frances Repasky—remembered the family. Mrs. Repasky said when she was a child, she used to play with Mrs. Winsen's daughter. She said Mrs. Winsen used to take in boarders and do baby-sitting. Evidently she was a widow, and that's how she supported herself.''

''Is she still alive?''

''No. The neighbor said she died awhile back, but Mrs. Repasky and Mrs. Winsen's daughter—Claudia Gillespie is her married name—have kept in touch. She said Gillespie lives in Albany, that they exchanged Christmas cards just this past Christmas. She gave me the address. I haven't contacted Gillespie yet. I decided it's best to do this in person, so I'm going to Albany tomorrow.''

After they hung up, Virginia sat thinking for a long time. She thought about telling Grace what Ned had told her, then decided against it. Grace seemed nervous and worried. Maybe her preoccupation was due to prewedding jitters, as Virginia had been telling herself, but maybe it wasn't. So why give her anything more to worry about?

This discovery of Ned's might yield nothing. Probably *would* yield nothing. In fact, Virginia was surprised he'd even found this much to investigate. Thirty years was a long time. It would be a miracle indeed if he were to actually track down the Mrs. Winsen that Josie had referred to in Grace's dream.

So, she would say nothing to Grace. After all, what purpose would it serve? Wouldn't they all be better off if they quit thinking about the past?

Her granddaughter had been returned to her. The circumstances surrounding her disappearance were no longer important. In just a little over two weeks, Grace and Paul would be married. If Virginia were very lucky, she might live to see a great-grandchild.

That was important.

* * *

Two days later, on a cold, blustery Friday, Paul announced that he had to go to Philadelphia that morning. "Would you like to go with me?" he asked Grace. "You could do some shopping while I meet with Richardson and MacAllister." He smiled. "Afterward, I'll take you to lunch at my favorite Italian restaurant."

"Oh, Paul, that sounds so nice, but I can't think of another thing I need, and I really had planned to begin writing thank-you notes today." Gifts had been arriving for weeks. There were already well over a hundred of them.

He shrugged. "Okay. I should be back about one."

After breakfast, Virginia headed for her sitting room, and Paul kissed Grace goodbye. "Don't work too hard," he said.

She waited until she saw his car disappear through the gates, then she raced to her bedroom. She removed her engagement ring and put it in her jewelry box, shoved the locket into her purse, put on heavy jeans, flat-soled boots, a heavy parka and gloves, jammed a black knit cap on her head and went in search of Anna.

"Anna, if Mrs. Hollister should ask, tell her I forgot to get something in town so I decided to go out, after all."

"All right, miss." Anna smiled.

Ten minutes later, Grace was on her way. She drove fast. She couldn't stay away too long. She didn't want to make Virginia so suspicious that she'd mention Grace's absence to Paul.

When she got to Maple Creek, she stopped at a big pharmacy. She bought some pain medicine—her excuse for going out—and the map the gas station attendant had mentioned on her first trip out here.

When she got back into her car, she studied the map carefully. She found Old Dairy Road and traced with her finger until she pinpointed the spot where the house must stand. The map showed the woods around it. It also showed a street on the other side of the woods. Just what she'd hoped for! She didn't dare go back to the house. Even if it hadn't been for the dog, she was technically trying to keep her promise to Paul. No, she had to approach the woods from the other direction.

She found the other street easily. Following the map, she also located the area she believed must be directly in line with the house. She couldn't be completely sure, but it looked right. Yes, there was the curve in the road up ahead.

She stopped, parked the car, took a flashlight out of the glove compartment, thought a minute, then removed the locket from her purse and shoved it into her pocket. She put the purse in the glove compartment. After locking the car, she took a deep breath for courage and entered the woods.

She tried to keep going in a straight line. She also tried to tamp down the fear that had her heart beating too hard. *There's no reason to be afraid.* She repeated the words like a mantra. Her plan was to find the back of the house on Old Dairy Road, then take out the locket and rub it. Maybe that way she would know which direction to go to find the cabin.

She walked carefully but steadily for fifteen minutes. The woods were denser than they'd looked on the map. When she came to a deep ravine, she almost cried. If the ravine had been marked on the map, she hadn't noticed it. How was she going to get across it?

She bit her lip. As she stood there trying to figure out what to do next, she heard a twig snap. It sounded like a gunshot in the quiet woods. She jumped and whirled. Her gaze swept the area. Nothing.

Oh, God, she really was crazy. Why had she come here today? This was stupid. Stupid. But even as she was telling herself this, she took out the locket. Shivering, cold as well as frightened, she slipped the locket inside her glove. Then she started walking, following the edge of the ravine to the right.

Only minutes later, she came to a bridge. It was old, but it looked sturdy enough. Besides, the ravine was only about six feet wide. Quickly, before she could change her mind, she crossed it.

Less than five minutes later, she found the cabin. The well was on the left. It looked exactly the way it had looked in her dream.

Goose bumps prickled her arms, and the fear she'd tried so hard to control welled up in her throat, choking her. She stared at the well, not moving, hardly daring to think.

Gripping the flashlight, she walked closer. Her heart was pounding so hard, she felt as if it might burst out of her chest.

The well was only a foot away. If she put her hand out, she could touch it.

She squeezed her eyes shut. The locket felt like a live coal in her hand.

Go home. Don't look.

She opened her eyes. She reached out, touched the rim of the well. She shuddered violently and nausea clogged her throat.

"No!" She whirled, nearly tripping on a rock in her haste to leave. She ran blindly, crashing through the woods, heedless of the branches whipping her face and the rocks underfoot. She tripped twice, and by the time she burst out of the trees and onto the road a hundred yards or so from where she'd parked her car, her chest heaved and she was winded and crying.

She staggered toward her car.

Paul watched her drive away. He waited ten minutes, then walked around the curve to where his own silver

Jaguar had been hidden from view. He thought it was damned fortunate for both of them that neither car had been stolen.

He still couldn't believe that Grace had once again lied to him. And he probably would never have known anything about her little excursion today if he hadn't forgotten an important paper this morning. He'd only been about ten minutes from the house when he'd remembered and turned around. He'd just crested the incline and was headed toward the entrance to the estate when he'd seen Grace's car come out of the gates and speed off down the street.

After telling him she planned to write thank-you notes all morning, he immediately knew she was up to something if she'd left the house so soon after him.

So he'd followed her again.

He'd kept well behind her in the woods, ducking behind trees and rocks to stay out of sight.

He'd seen the way she reacted when she came to that old cabin and the well. He would have liked to take a look at that well himself, but instead he decided he would call the offices of Richardson and MacAllister from his car phone, cancel his appointment, then go straight home and see what Grace had to say for herself.

Chapter Fourteen

Grace didn't remember the drive home.

One minute she was turning around, careening down the isolated road and heading for the highway back to Rolling Hills. The next she was pulling into the open front gates of the estate.

Her emotions were chaotic. She had been crying ever since she left Maple Creek. She knew she had to stop. She had to get herself under control. Her face was probably a puffy, blotchy mess.

She looked at her clothing, covered in twigs. It wasn't only her face that was a mess. If Virginia saw her, she would be alarmed, knowing immediately that something was very wrong.

Thank God Paul wasn't home.

Grace dug in her pocket for a tissue, wiped her eyes and blew her nose. She prayed she wouldn't run into any of the servants as she parked her car, entered the house and fur-

tively climbed the back stairs. When she reached the second floor, she headed straight for her room.

Luck was with her. She saw no one.

She locked the door of her bedroom behind her.

A half hour later, calmer, cleaned up, with fresh makeup on, she sat down at her writing desk. She had to put the
horrible morning behind her. She couldn't think about it,
because if she did, she would go to pieces again. She
couldn't afford to go to pieces. She had to write some
thank-you notes before lunch.

She'd no sooner gotten out the list of gifts and the stack
of engraved notes, when there was a knock on her door.
"Come in," she called, thinking it must be Anna.

The doorknob rattled. "It's locked."

She nearly fainted. Her heart knocked against her rib
cage. It was Paul! It was only eleven forty-five. What was
he doing home so early?

There was no way he could have gone to Philadelphia,
met with his clients and returned home already. *Calm
down. Calm down.*

"Just a minute," she called. She took several deep
breaths. *Calm down, or he'll know something's wrong.*
She walked to the door and unlocked it, pasted a bright
smile on her face and said, "Sorry. I forgot I locked it."
Then she frowned, as if she'd just thought of something.
"What are you doing home so early?"

"My appointment got canceled."

Why was he looking at her so intently? Why didn't he
smile? Oh, God, she was getting paranoid. She had a
guilty conscience, so she was seeing things that didn't ex-
ist, questioning things that were perfectly normal.

Instead of imagining he was looking at her in a strange
way, she should be thinking about how lucky she was that
he hadn't come back while she was gone.

He strolled into the room. "Did you get a lot of your thank-you notes written this morning?" Now he smiled, but the smile seemed almost challenging.

Grace felt chilled. She resisted the urge to hug herself. "No, not really. I, uh, started writing the notes, but then Melanie called, and we talked such a long time, and then, I don't know, I had a nasty headache and I decided to drive into town and buy some of that medicine I like. I'd run out. And then, when I came back, I just didn't feel like writing the thank-yous, so I took a nap." She knew she was babbling, but she couldn't seem to help it.

She could tell by the expression on his face that he didn't believe a word she'd said. Oh, dear Lord. What if he suspected that she'd gone back to Maple Creek? Her heart raced in alarm as her mind whirled.

What would she say if he asked her? She rushed over to her vanity. She picked up the bag from the pharmacy, intending to show him the medicine. Too late, she realized the name of the pharmacy was printed on the bag. Maple Creek Pharmacy. She hurriedly thrust the bag back, facedown, and prayed he hadn't noticed.

"Grace," he said, frowning and walking toward her, "you look feverish." He placed his hands on her shoulders and peered at her face. "I think you should lie down again. Your face is all flushed." He placed his cool hand on her forehead. "Yes. You feel hot."

Feeling as if he'd thrown her a life preserver, Grace seized on the excuse he'd given her. "Yes, yes, maybe you're right. I—I don't feel well."

That was no lie. She felt sick. She was also terrified. She knew she should tell both him and Virginia about the well. She'd been deluding herself, thinking she could forget all about it. Today had proven she would never forget it. Any of it.

The knowledge of the well and its possible contents would haunt her for the rest of her life. She would never be able to be happy.

Because she would be living a lie.

Somehow she endured his kiss on her cheek. Somehow she said the appropriate words in the face of his concern. Somehow she managed to hold herself together until she'd shut the door behind him.

Then, barely able to make it to the bed, she collapsed. She didn't cry. She just lay there, huddled into a fetal position, and stared, dry-eyed, into space.

After leaving Grace, Paul went into his office. He barely glanced at his secretary as he passed by. "No calls, Susan," he said.

"Yes, sir." She gave him an odd look.

He ignored it and shut the door of his office behind him. He sat down and stared at the phone for long moments.

She'd lied to him. Again.

And she'd been scared witless. She'd hardly been able to look him in the eye. And her face *had* been flushed, her forehead *had* been hot. Probably because she was so upset.

The anger he'd nurtured on the way home had evaporated. Now he just felt a steely determination to get to the truth.

He picked up the phone and called Ned.

"Why, Mr. Hollister," Peggy, Ned's secretary, said, "did you forget? He's in Albany today."

Paul frowned. "Forget what? Am I supposed to know why he's in Albany?"

"Why, I, uh," she floundered. "I just assumed, since your aunt is the one who—" She stopped abruptly. "I'm, um, sorry, Mr. Hollister, I obviously made a wrong assumption. Would you like me to have Mr. Shapiro call you when he gets in?"

"Yes, Peggy. You do that."

Paul hung up the phone and eyed it thoughtfully. *Since your aunt is the one who...* What the devil had Peggy meant by that remark? What was Ned Shapiro doing for Aunt Virginia that she hadn't told Paul about? And in Albany, of all places?

He drummed his fingers on his desk. His anger returned, swift and hot. Damn it! Was *everyone* in this house keeping things from him?

He jumped up, knocking his portable phone to the floor. He ignored it and stalked out of the office. He could sense Susan's shocked expression as he charged past her, heading for the stairs. Seconds later, he rapped on his aunt's sitting room door.

"Yes? Come in."

He opened the door. She turned from her desk and smiled. "Oh, you're back early! How was your appointment?"

"Aunt Virginia, what the hell is going on around here?" He pulled the door shut behind him and glared at her.

Her face reflected her bewilderment as her smile faded. "What do you mean?"

"I mean, why did Peggy Carlock tell me Ned Shapiro was in Albany as if I should know the reason why?"

His aunt grimaced. "Oh, dear," she said, sighing.

He waited.

She sighed again. "I wasn't going to tell you about this until I had something concrete to offer, but since you know about Ned..."

He listened as she told him about Grace coming to her, about the dream where Grace became aware that Josie had a daughter and that a woman named Mrs. Winsen was somehow involved. He listened as she told him about calling Ned and about Ned's call back to her yesterday. He listened as she apologized and explained that she'd asked Grace not to say anything to him, that she had planned to tell him everything herself.

She finished by saying, "I'm sorry, Paul. I shouldn't have kept this from you."

"No," he said. "You shouldn't have." His fury slowly evaporated, leaving a vague resentment and a gnawing disappointment that neither of the women he loved seemed to trust him enough to be honest with him.

He walked to the window and looked out. The day was bleak, as bleak as he now felt. For a minute he considered telling her about Grace's visit to the house on Old Dairy Road and about today's events.

Then he decided that he, too, would wait until he had something concrete. With that decision, some of his disappointment dimmed and he realized that's his aunt's failure to confide in him didn't mean she didn't trust him. It meant she probably hadn't wanted to worry him, just as he didn't want to worry her now.

He refused to think what Grace's silence meant, because he was afraid he knew.

Grace stayed in bed the rest of the day, huddled under the covers and full of misery. Paul looked in on her just before dinner. He sat on the edge of her bed and said, "Aunt Virginia's worried about you. So am I."

"I'm sorry." *I am so sorry, Paul. You'll never know how sorry.* She was glad the light in the room was muted. She was glad he couldn't see into her eyes.

He touched her forehead. "You seem cooler."

She swallowed. "Yes."

"Aunt Virginia wanted to call Dr. Joseph. Have him come and take a look at you."

"No! That's not necessary. I—I just have bad cramps, that's all." *You're getting to be a regular little liar, aren't you?* Misery choked her. Before now, she couldn't remember ever having lied. Little white lies, maybe. Tiny little untruths to keep from hurting someone's feelings, but out-and-out lies to protect herself? Never.

Paul left after promising to look in again before he went to bed. A very long time later, Grace finally fell into an exhausted sleep.

About midway through dinner, Anna came into the dining room and said Mr. Shapiro was on the phone for Mrs. Hollister. "I told him you were at dinner."

"That's all right, Anna. I'll take his call," Virginia said.

Anna handed Virginia a portable phone. Paul and Virginia exchanged glances before she pressed the Talk button.

She listened intently, nodding and saying "I see" a couple of times. Finally, she said, "Well, Ned, I don't know if I'm disappointed or relieved."

She listened for a minute, then looked at Paul. "Did you want to talk to Ned, too, Paul?"

Paul shook his head. "Tell him I'll call him tomorrow."

"Paul says he'll call you tomorrow. All right. Thank you, Ned. Goodbye." She deactivated the phone and set it down on the table.

"Well," Paul said, "what did he say?"

She sighed. "He talked with Claudia Gillespie today. He thinks her mother might be the Mrs. Winsen that Josie referred to in Grace's dream, but there's no way to know for sure. Claudia said that she did remember a little girl staying with them in 1963 and when Ned asked, she said her name might have been Helen. The problem is, at the time, Claudia Gillespie was only seven years old, so her memory isn't very reliable, and she couldn't tell Ned anything about the little girl's mother."

"Did she know how old the girl was?"

"No."

"Is that all Ned said?"

"No. Claudia also told him that in thinking back, she feels as if Helen was with them for a long time, but even a week or two might seem like a long time to a kid."

"Did she say that, or is that your interpretation?"

"Actually, Ned said that."

"Does she remember when Helen left?"

"Claudia said that one day when she came home from playing at a neighbor's house, Helen was gone. She remembers asking her mother where she went and her mother saying that Helen's mother had come to get her."

"And that's all?"

His aunt nodded. "I'm afraid so. Ned gave her his card and said if she should happen to remember anything else, to call him."

Paul thought about what he'd just learned. His aunt was quiet, too, lost in her own thoughts. Finally, Paul said, "Aunt Virginia, do you think Josie dropped Elizabeth at that orphanage, then went to pick up her daughter?"

"That seems logical, doesn't it? The orphanage isn't that far from Dobbs Ferry."

Paul frowned. Why would Josie have taken the risk of transporting Elizabeth to New York? Why hadn't she simply left Elizabeth at the house, made an anonymous call to his aunt, then gone on to New York herself?

He suddenly felt cold with the realization that he believed Grace's story about that house on Old Dairy Road. He believed that's where Elizabeth had been taken after she'd been abducted. In that much, at least, he believed Grace had told him the truth. About the abandoned cabin and the well that had so frightened her, he refused to speculate. Tomorrow, he would investigate both thoroughly.

After dinner, Paul excused himself, telling his aunt that he had work to catch up on. He kissed her good-night, then headed upstairs. Before going to his own quarters, he knocked softly on Grace's door. When there was no answer, he quietly opened the door and walked soundlessly across the room. Grace lay curled under the comforter. Her breathing was deep and regular.

He stood there a long time. He tried not to let himself be swayed by how defenseless and innocent she looked in sleep. Remember that she lied to you, he told himself. And people who lie have something to hide.

He left the room as silently as he'd entered.

After a night of exploring every angle of what had happened, Paul was left with a terrible suspicion. His suspicion wasn't based on anything factual; it was based on a combination of events and Grace's behavior.

He didn't wait until eight o'clock the next morning to call Ned at his office. Instead, at six, he called the lawyer at home. After explaining what had happened the previous day and why he hadn't wanted to tell Ned about it last night in front of his Aunt Virginia, he said, "Something's in that well, Ned. Something that frightened Grace so badly, she ran away."

"You're probably right."

"I think you should come to Rolling Hills this morning and we should go out there together. In fact, I plan to call the sheriff's office and get him and a deputy or two to accompany us."

"Yes," Ned agreed, his voice troubled. "I think that's a good plan."

"How soon can you get here?"

"I can be there by nine."

"Don't come to the house. Meet me in Maple Creek." They decided they would meet at the fire station, which was easy to find, and Paul gave Ned directions.

After saying goodbye, Paul went into his office and put on a pot of coffee. He waited until seven to call the sheriff's office. He knew Sheriff Evans personally and had no problem convincing him to send a couple of deputies to meet him and Ned in Maple Creek.

At eight o'clock, he buzzed his aunt's room on the intercom. "I won't be at breakfast this morning," he said when she answered. "I've got something I need to take care of. I should be back by noon."

"All right."

He was glad she didn't question him. He didn't want to lie to her.

"Have you seen Grace this morning?" she added.

"No."

"I hope she's feeling better."

"Yes. I do, too."

"Will you check on her before you leave the house?"

"Better not. If she's still sleeping, I don't want to disturb her."

"Yes . . . of course."

They hung up and Paul wondered if he'd imagined the slight hesitancy in her voice. His aunt really was intuitive. She'd probably sensed that something wasn't quite right between him and Grace. Well, it couldn't be helped.

When Grace awakened at seven-thirty, her head was pounding and she felt worse than she could ever remember feeling. She dragged herself out of bed, knowing she could no longer hide out. She had to go down to breakfast and face Paul and Virginia. And after breakfast, she had to take Paul aside and tell him where she'd gone and what she'd done yesterday.

She refused to think further. There was no sense in worrying. She'd worried for hours yesterday and what good had it done?

Once she told Paul about the well, matters would be out of her control. She reminded herself, as she had many times in the past, that she was strong. She was a survivor. She could survive anything. Even this. Still, she couldn't help the frisson of fear that whispered through her, and she said a silent prayer as she walked down the hall to the sun room.

"Oh, I'm so glad to see you're feeling better!" Virginia exclaimed as Grace entered the room. "Paul and I were both worried about you."

Grace looked at Paul's vacant chair.

"It's going to be just the two of us this morning," Virginia said. "Paul had some business to take care of. He said he'd be home by noon."

Grace's heart sank. She'd been bolstered to tell him everything now. She wasn't sure she could wait. She was afraid she'd lose her courage if she had to think about it until noon. But she guessed she had no choice. She would have to wait, like it or not.

It had snowed in the night. Paul wasn't sure if the road crews had been out early to clear the roads or not, so he drove the four-wheel-drive Bronco. He needn't have worried. The main roads were already plowed and salted.

When he got to the Maple Creek Fire Station, he had to wait about fifteen minutes, but by 9:10, Ned's big Cadillac pulled into the parking lot and the two men greeted each other. "Where's the sheriff?" Ned asked, his breath billowing in the frosty air.

"We're supposed to meet the deputies out there," Paul said. "Why don't you leave your car here? We can ride out in the Bronco."

Ned agreed, and ten minutes later they were driving slowly down the curving back road Grace had taken yesterday. Howard Evans, the sheriff, and a young red-haired deputy Paul didn't know, were sitting in the sheriff's cruiser, waiting. Paul pulled in behind the cruiser.

Car doors clunked as the four men got out of their vehicles and walked toward one another.

The county sheriff, a big, quiet man who had Amish ancestors, said, "Hello, Paul." He nodded to Ned.

Paul introduced them.

"And this is Deputy Grimes," the sheriff said.

The deputy, young and eager-looking, grinned.

"You ready to go?" Paul said.

"Soon as we get our equipment out of the trunk."

Paul led the way. The fresh snowfall had changed the landscape. Even so, he had no trouble finding the cabin again. When they arrived at the clearing, the sheriff walked around the site slowly.

"You two wait here," he said to Paul, "while Deputy Grimes and I check out the cabin." They set their equipment down on the ground and entered the cabin.

Paul and Ned didn't talk. Each was lost in his own thoughts. Five minutes later, the sheriff and his deputy rejoined them. "Nothin' in there," Evans said. "Just an old cot. Some empty tin cans and the like. Looks like maybe somebody, some drifter, might have used it to sleep in, but not lately." He picked up one of the bags of equipment. "Now let's take a look at that well."

The four of them walked to the well. The deputy had a big flashlight with a high beam, and he aimed it into the well. They all looked down. The well was deep and looked fairly dry. They couldn't tell what, if anything, was at the bottom.

"Hmm," Evans said. "Can't see much down there. Looks like there might be some trash or somethin'. No water, though. That's good." He looked at Grimes. "You ready to go on down there?"

"Yes, sir." If Grimes was reluctant, his expression didn't show it.

Paul helped them secure the rope ladder and lower it. Equipped with the high-beam flashlight, rubber gloves, a small shovel and a heavy-duty plastic bag, Deputy Grimes climbed over the side and began his careful descent.

The three of them waited silently. To Paul, the wait seemed agonizingly long. He tried to keep his mind empty. When the deputy reached the bottom, he was quiet for at least five minutes, then he shouted, his voice sounding hollow from the depths of the well.

Sheriff Evans leaned over the well. "Find somethin'?" he yelled down.

Paul stiffened.

"Might be a skeleton," the deputy called.

Sheriff Evans glanced at Paul, who felt chilled. "Human?" the sheriff said.

"Looks like it. Awful small, though."

For the next ten minutes, the three men waited. Finally, Deputy Grimes began climbing out of the well. When he reached the top, he handed his equipment and the plastic bag to Sheriff Evans. Paul helped him haul up the ladder while the sheriff peered inside the bag.

Paul had never considered himself squeamish, but it gave him a strange feeling to look at that bag. To think of the contents of that bag.

"Whadda you think?" Deputy Grimes asked eagerly.

Sheriff Evans shrugged. "Hard to tell. The experts'll have to make a determination."

Paul took a deep breath and said, "It's very possible those are the remains of Elizabeth Hollister, my great-aunt's granddaughter." He felt numb, and his voice sounded odd, now that he had finally said aloud the thought that had plagued him since the middle of the night.

Sheriff Evans stared at him. "I thought her granddaughter had been found."

Paul nodded slowly. "So did we." He couldn't think further. The implications of today's discovery were staggering.

"You serious about this?" Evans asked.

"He's serious," Ned answered. He looked miserable. "Unfortunately."

"In that case," the sheriff said, "you're probably gonna want to have some testing done."

"What kind of testing is possible?" Paul asked, trying to think only of the immediate problem instead of the problems facing him at home.

"Well, if you've got something to match it up with, we can send bone fragment to the FBI forensics laboratory for DNA testing."

"Something to match it up with?" Ned asked.

As they talked, they were tramping through the woods back to where they'd left the cars.

"Uh-huh," the sheriff answered, stepping around a rock. "A sample of hair or blood, for instance. It's just like fingerprints. Say you have a fingerprint. Although the fingerprint pattern is unique and can be used to positively identify someone, unless you can match it to a person, it's no good to you. So DNA testing is no good to you unless you can provide the lab with something that you know came from the person whose identity you're trying to establish."

Paul thought back. He seemed to recall that his aunt had saved a lock of Elizabeth's hair. In fact, weren't she and Grace discussing it that day they looked at Elizabeth's baby book? "I think a sample of hair might be available."

"Then you're in business."

"How long do you think it will take to do the tests?"

"Ten to fourteen days," Evans said.

Paul nodded. His mind whirled as he wondered what he would say to Grace and Virginia when he returned to the house.

The men parted company with Paul promising to bring the hair sample to the sheriff's office later that afternoon.

"Thanks again, Sheriff," he said. "I appreciate everything you've done today."

"No problem," Evans said. "I'm just sorry this had to happen at all. Seems a shame that after your aunt was so happy, now there's a chance that happiness will be taken away from her."

Yes, Paul thought bitterly, and he knew exactly whose fault that was. "Listen, Sheriff, I don't want my aunt to know about what we found today. Not until we're sure it has something to do with her."

"No problem. Although we'll have to make a full report, we'll leave names out of it. That way, if the TV people get a hold of it, they'll just say 'an unidentified skeleton.' Besides, we don't know for sure *who* this is, do we?" He looked at Deputy Grimes. "Right, Jack?"

Deputy Grimes nodded earnestly. "Right. Don't worry, Mr. Hollister. I won't say a word about your suspicions."

After the sheriff and his deputy left, Paul and Ned stood talking for a minute. They decided Ned should go back to Philadelphia. If he came to the house, Virginia would naturally be curious about his presence there. Both men thought it would be best to avoid questions altogether.

Ned said, "I hate this, Paul. I wish—" He sighed. "No use wishing." He hesitated, then said, "How do *you* feel about all this?"

Paul avoided Ned's eyes. "I'm fine."

Ned looked as if he wanted to say something else, but he didn't. They drove back to the fire station, said good-bye and Ned left.

Paul drove home slowly. He needed time to think and vent his emotions. When the others were watching him, he'd felt the need to hide his feelings. *I'm fine.* What a joke! He'd never been less fine in his life.

Bitterness twisted inside him. He'd thought he was miserable when his engagement to Valerie had gone up in smoke. That unhappiness was nothing to what he felt now. As his earlier numbness wore off, hurt and disap-pointment and a deep sense of loss had taken over, and now he felt like one raw, open wound. He couldn't be-lieve he'd allowed himself to be vulnerable again.

He thought of Grace, of how he had slowly begun to trust her, slowly begun to shed the layers of protective coating that he wore in any relationship.

No matter what she said when he questioned her, he couldn't see how they could salvage their relationship. She had lied, which meant one thing and one thing only.

She had known what was down there at the bottom of that well. And she hadn't wanted him to know.

Chapter Fifteen

Grace's nerves were shot.

All morning she'd both dreaded Paul's homecoming and wished he'd hurry up and get there so she could get her confession over with.

At eleven-thirty she was in her room, just finishing up the thank-you notes she should have done yesterday. She'd left her door open so she could hear Paul when he returned. She wondered where he had gone as she stacked the envelopes in a neat pile. They needed stamps. She wondered if Virginia had any and was just about to go and see when she heard footsteps on the stairs.

Her heart skipped and silently she rose, walking toward the door. She waited there for a moment, then taking a deep breath, she moved out into the hall. If this was Paul, she'd ask him to come into her room.

It *was* Paul. He looked in her direction. Their gazes met. Grace's stomach felt as if someone were jumping around inside of it. He didn't smile.

Grace's mouth went dry. The look in his eyes scared her. Her heart went *boom, boom, boom.*

"Paul," she said. "I—I wanted to talk to you."

His mouth twisted into a strange caricature of a smile. It chilled her. "I wanted to talk to you, too," he said, his voice colder than she'd ever heard it.

For the first time, she noticed how casually he was dressed. Jeans, a heavy dark blue sweater and some kind of hiking boots. She didn't have time to wonder about his choice of clothes, though. With only a few quick strides he was at her side.

She turned and walked into her room. He followed her and shut the door behind him. For just a second, she was afraid to turn and face him. *Come on. Don't be a coward. It's Paul, the man you love.* She turned. She looked up. He looked down. His eyes were like ice when the sun doesn't hit it—gray and cold—looking the way they'd looked when she'd first come to Hollister House. When he hadn't liked her and hadn't trusted her.

She swallowed, opened her mouth to speak. Her heart made little fluttery movements, as if it, too, was scared.

"I know where you went yesterday," he said, the words clipped and angry.

Grace stared at him, totally incapable of speech.

"I followed you. I saw you go into the woods. I saw you at the well. I saw how you ran, how frightened you were."

"Wh-why didn't you say—"

"I didn't say anything because I wanted to see if you'd tell me on your own. And you didn't, did you? I asked you what you did while I was gone yesterday, and you lied to me." He grimaced. "That was your second lie of the day. You lied earlier when I invited you to go into the city with me. You said you were going to write thank-you notes." His fists clenched. "You knew all the time that you weren't, didn't you?"

What could Grace say? *The truth. Tell him the truth.* "Paul, I was going to tell you. I intended to tell you this morning, right after breakfast. But you were gone. So I've been waiting for you to return. In fact, that's why I said I wanted to talk to you." His expression said he didn't believe her. Grace's voice had an edge of panic to it as she continued desperately. "I—I agonized over this all yesterday, all last night. I couldn't sleep. I knew I had to tell you, even though I was scared."

"I went out there this morning. Out to that cabin. Me and Ned and the sheriff."

His words shocked her. If she had been frightened before, now she felt terrified.

"Don't you want to know what we found?"

Grace wet her lips. Her heart pounded mercilessly.

"Or do you already know?"

"I—I..."

"We found a skeleton at the bottom of the well." He paused. "The skeleton of a child."

Grace gasped, her hand coming involuntarily to her mouth. "Oh, God."

"I think the skeleton is Elizabeth. What do you think?"

Grace knew the blood had drained from her face. She reached back and grasped the bedpost for support. Grace's eyes filled with tears. "I—I s-suspected." She fought the tears, took a shaky breath. "I didn't know for sure that sh-she was in the well, but I—I'd had another dream..." She couldn't hold the tears back any longer. They rolled down her face. She groped in her pocket for a tissue, her hand shaking.

"Something else you neglected to tell me." His face looked as if it had been carved from stone.

She swiped at her tears and tried to rid herself of the terror choking her. "Please, Paul, you must believe me. I wanted to. But I—I was afraid. I was so afraid I'd lose you."

"You were afraid you'd lose the Hollister money," he said bitterly.

She felt as if he'd slapped her. "I don't care about the money! I've never cared about the money. I love you, Paul. And I love Virginia. That's *all* I care about, all I've *ever* cared about." *Damn!* She was going to cry again.

His jaw clenched. "Give me one good reason why I should believe anything you tell me."

Grace stared at him. She searched his eyes for one spark of understanding, one tiny bit of warmth and love, anything to give her hope that this terrible anger of his would pass, that down deep he really loved her and that he would eventually relent and be willing to forgive her. She saw nothing except a stony dislike.

Her shoulders sagged. An overwhelming sense of futility pressed down on her, making it hard for her to breathe. It was no use. Nothing she said or did was going to make any difference to him. He would never believe her. If he had ever felt anything for her, it was gone. "Do you want me to leave?" she whispered.

"And what will we tell my aunt?" he countered.

She looked up. "Then what *do* you want?" Her tears had dried up. Now she just felt a dull acceptance.

"I've arranged for DNA testing of the remains. I'm told the results won't be available for at least ten days, maybe longer. I think the least you can do is stay until we know for sure whether the skeleton we found is Elizabeth's."

"How are you going to keep your aunt from finding out about this?"

"The sheriff has promised to keep our suspicion regarding the identity of the remains under wraps until the testing is completed." Now he did show some emotion — a weariness that made Grace want to reach out to him, even as she knew he would rebuff her. He ran his hands through his hair. "Lord," he said, "this is a real mess, and it's going to hit her hard."

Grace bowed her head. She knew he blamed her. And why shouldn't he? If she had never come here, none of this would have happened. Or if she had at least been honest with him... If, if, if. All the ifs in the world weren't going to change things. She *had* come. She *had* lied. And now she was going to pay the price. She was going to lose everything she cared about. Her past. Her future. She would have nothing.

"Until we have proof, I'll expect you to act as if nothing has happened," he said.

Grace looked up. "Yes, of course." Otherwise, what would be the point in her staying on?

His mouth twisted. "That should be easy for you. You're a very skillful actress. You must be. You suckered me in."

Suddenly, Grace had had enough. Yes, she'd made a mistake, but she had never, ever, lied about her feelings. Not for Virginia. Not for him. She stood, raising her chin and meeting his gaze squarely. "Think what you want to think, Paul. You will, anyway. You've set yourself up as judge and jury, and obviously you've rendered your decision. Fine. Now, if you don't mind, I'd like you to leave. I've got to repair my makeup and prepare to face my audience over the lunch table."

Then she swung on her heel and, head high, walked into the bathroom, shutting the door behind her.

The next week was the hardest week of Grace's life. For all her earlier bravado, several times she wasn't sure she was going to be able to carry on.

Having to pretend everything was fine in front of Virginia. Having to pretend she and Paul were still going to be married. Having to make last-minute decisions and continue to receive wedding presents and attend a luncheon in her honor given by one of Virginia's friends—all were excruciating for her.

One night she cornered Paul in the library. He stood in front of the shelves, a book open in his hands when she walked in. He looked up, an odd expression crossing his face, which he quickly masked. "Yes?" he said.

"I think we should just tell your aunt we've broken our engagement," she said angrily. "This pretending is awful. I'm not sure I can keep it up. And the longer we wait to call off the wedding, the worse it's all going to be. I think we should just tell her now."

"No." He went back to reading his book, just as if she weren't there.

Furious tears gathered in her eyes. How could he be so cold? So unfeeling? So completely detached? "You know, Paul," she said in a shaking voice, "you've accused me of being a good actress. Well, I think you're an even better actor!"

He looked up, eyes glittering. "Really?"

She walked closer to him. A recklessness seized her. She was tired of his censure. Tired of his superior sneers and wounding disinterest. "You *never* loved me, did you? It was all pretense. All of it. The only reason you ever asked me to marry you was because you thought I was Elizabeth!"

He smiled, his gaze raking her insolently. "That wasn't the only reason."

The smile, his insinuation, his contemptuous once-over, all were purposely cruel and degrading and cut deep into her heart. Humiliated, with nothing left to lose, she slapped him. Hard. The sound of her hand meeting his cheek was like the crack of a whip. She stared at him, shocked by how low she'd fallen.

Before she could move, he grabbed her wrist and yanked her to him. His eyes gleamed savagely, and his mouth twisted before he ground it down onto hers. The kiss was harsh, punishing, demanding, and it knocked the breath out of her. His tongue drove deep and his hands gripped her tightly as he took her mouth with unleashed fury and domination.

Grace's head spun, her blood raced, and even though she didn't want to, she responded to him. She kissed him back, pouring all her unhappiness and fear and misery into her response. Now he crushed her to him, one hand tunneling through her hair, the other cupping her bottom and bringing it close. She felt the heat of his arousal, and an answering heat raged through her. She wound her arms around him and pressed herself even closer. She'd missed this. She'd missed him. She'd been so lonely and unhappy.

With a sound that was half grunt, half groan, he shoved her away, so abruptly her knees buckled. His chest heaved as he stared at her, but his voice was quiet when he spoke. "I think you'd better go before we do anything else we'll be sorry for later."

Paul tried to stay away from the house as much as possible. He couldn't believe how difficult it was to be around Grace. And pretending that everything was wonderful in front of his aunt was almost intolerable.

The worst part of everything was that he still wanted her. He refused to call his feelings love. How could he love someone who had never been truthful with him? No. He wanted her. And that desire, that need, disgusted him.

The night she'd accosted him in the library was the low point of his life. He had allowed Grace to goad him into less than admirable behavior, and his actions sickened him.

Unfortunately, he couldn't forget how she'd felt in his arms. Her slender body, warm and trembling, her mouth, sweet even in anger, haunted him. He couldn't look at her without remembering what it was like to make love to her. His weakness disgusted him. What was wrong with him?

God, he couldn't wait until the DNA tests came back. He wanted Grace out of this house and out of his life. And the sooner, the better.

On the afternoon of the fifth day after they'd found the skeleton, Sheriff Evans called to report on what had happened when he and his deputies paid a call at the house on Old Dairy Road.

"Turns out there might be a connection between the man who's living there now and this Frank that you told me about," the sheriff said.

Paul stiffened. "Oh?" He hadn't really believed anything would come of the sheriff's investigation in that area.

"Yeah. The guy livin' there now, his name is Gene Caruso, and after he settled down and realized we weren't accusin' him of anything, he told us two things. The first is that the house has been in his family since 1946 when his daddy came home from the war and built it with the help of the G.I. Bill. The second is that he had an older brother named Frank who was murdered sometime late in 1963, he doesn't know for sure when."

Paul listened silently.

"Lemme back up and tell this from the beginning," the sheriff said. "The Caruso parents were both dead by 1959. Father died in an accident at the foundry where he worked. Mother died of cancer. Anyway, the house went to the boys. Gene enlisted in the navy in 1960, got out in 1964. Frank, the older brother, was some kind of legman for a bookie operation. Gene said he never really knew exactly what Frank was doing, 'cause the brothers weren't close. Frank was five years older than Gene.

"Anyway, Gene says he got notified in January of '64 that his brother's body was found stuffed in the trunk of his car in some junkyard. He was shot through the head. Police figured it was mob-related. I looked up the files, and it checks out. It also doesn't look to me like they made much of an effort to find out who killed him.

"Gene got out of the service in mid '64, came home, has been livin' in the house ever since."

It fit, Paul thought. From what Grace had told them, Frank had left the house to make the ransom call and never returned. Maybe he owed gambling debts. Or maybe he'd been siphoning off money he was supposed to have paid to his bosses, and they were lying in wait for him and killed him. Maybe that's why he'd come up with the kidnapping scheme to begin with. Who would ever know now? "Did you check out Caruso's story about his having been in the service."

"Yes. Everything checks out."

"Did you tell him we suspected his brother of having been involved in a kidnapping?"

"No, I didn't think there was any point to it. It's obvious Gene couldn't have had anything to do with it. I did ask him if, when he returned to the house, there was any evidence that a kid might have been living there."

"What did he say?"

"He said the house was a mess. Said it had been left open and vandals had trashed it, but he did say there was a rickety crib in one of the bedrooms, and for a while, he wondered if Frank had been living with a woman."

Paul nodded to himself. For a moment, both men were silent. Then the sheriff said, "If I come up with anything else, I'll call you."

Two days later, just one week before Paul and Grace were supposed to be married, Sheriff Evans called again.

"Paul, this time I've got some bad news."

Paul gripped his pencil tighter.

"The lab says they can't get a clear enough pattern from the hair you supplied."

"Why not?"

"There were no live hair follicles. Dead hair just doesn't work very well."

The pencil snapped in two. "Does that mean we can't determine if those bones are Elizabeth's?"

"Well, the lab said if they could get blood or tissue samples from her parents, but I told 'em her parents were dead." He paused. "You could exhume the bodies. Take a bone fragment from one of them. That would do it."

Paul felt chilled. Exhume the bodies? "I don't know, Sheriff. That's pretty drastic. Surely there's got to be some other way?" If he couldn't prove those bones belonged to Elizabeth, Grace would never leave. The thought of her here, taunting him, tempting him, was impossible. He would never be able to stand it. *He* would have to leave.

The sheriff said, "Well, they did say they could test your aunt's blood. It wouldn't prove identity conclusively, but if those bones are Elizabeth's, at least a quarter of the patterns should match."

Paul thanked the sheriff and said he'd call him back. He didn't know what to do. Either way, exhuming a body or testing his aunt's blood, would require her permission. And that meant he would have to tell her what they'd found.

How could he do that?

How could he not?

Damning Grace, damning the fates, damning the entire universe, he picked up the phone to call Ned.

An hour later, Paul found Grace curled on the window seat in the upstairs sitting room. A book lay open in her lap, and she was asleep, her chest slowly rising and falling, her breath coming in soft little spurts. Her eyelashes curved over her cheeks, and she looked young and sweet and impossibly beautiful.

Something sharp and painful stabbed his gut, and a deep yearning filled him. He closed his eyes. He would go crazy if he had to live the rest of his life this way.

"Grace." His voice was louder than he'd intended, and she jumped. The book fell to the floor. Her startled, confused eyes met his.

Quickly, he told her about his phone call from the sheriff. "We no longer have a choice. We have to tell Aunt Virginia."

Mutely, she nodded. She stood, smoothed her hands over her hair, composed her face. Her eyes looked bleak.

Pity twisted through him, but he hardened his heart. She had brought all of this mess upon herself. If she'd been truthful to begin with...

He walked out of the room. He could hear her following him. They found Virginia in the library. She sat behind her desk, reading glasses perched on her nose, papers spread out in front of her. She looked up as they walked in. She smiled, but her smile faded at their sober looks. "Is something wrong?" She removed her glasses, and her eyes, reminding Paul of bright blue marbles, scanned their faces.

Paul took a deep breath. He pulled a chair close to her and sat down. Grace sat in the other chair. Paul took his aunt's hand. "Aunt Virginia, there's something we have to tell you. I ... we ..." He stopped. This was going to be harder than he'd imagined. "Oh, hell," he said.

"Paul, you're scaring me!" Virginia said. Her hand trembled in his. "What *is* it?"

He made his voice as gentle as possible. "About a week ago, I found out...through Grace...where Elizabeth was kept after she was abducted." He paused. "A house in the country west of Maple Creek."

Virginia's eyes widened. She looked at Grace as if for confirmation, then slowly returned her gaze to Paul.

"There were...other things Grace revealed that led us—me, Ned, Sheriff Evans and one of his deputies—to an abandoned well within a mile of the house." He squeezed her hand tighter. "We found the remains of a child at the bottom of that well." Her face was very still. "A child we believe is Elizabeth."

The words were bullets that ricocheted off the walls.

Virginia's eyes widened in shock. She snatched her hand away. "Th-that's impossible." She looked at Grace. "It's impossible," she repeated.

Paul looked at Grace, too. Her eyes were filled with agony. The emotion looked genuine. Another testament to her acting ability, Paul thought bitterly. Of course, there was a hell of a lot at stake here, so she had powerful motivation to do her best.

"I don't believe you," his aunt said. Her face was white, her eyes like blue fire as they burned into his.

"Aunt Virginia . . ." He stopped. She was in shock. He would give her a few minutes before he told her the rest.

"Grace . . ." His aunt's voice broke. "This isn't true, is it?"

"I'm sorry, Grandmoth—"

Paul whipped his head around. How dare she call Virginia her grandmother? She knew damn well they weren't related. Not even remotely.

Tears swam in Grace's eyes, and as Paul watched, they slowly trailed down her face. She stood. Her face was whiter than Virginia's. "I'm afraid what Paul has told you is true," she whispered brokenly. She walked around the desk and threw her arms around Virginia. She kissed her. "I'll always love you," she murmured, so quietly Paul almost didn't hear her. "Always. But I can't stay here any longer." Then, twisting her engagement ring off her finger, she thrust it at Paul, then ran from the room.

* * *

Please, God, please help me. Please, please, help me.
Grace threw clothes into her suitcases. When she finished
packing, she called Melanie.

Please, Mel, please be there. The phone at the other end
rang twice, three times, four times. On the fifth ring,
Melanie's voice said, "Hello?"

Grace started to cry. Strangled sobs that choked her.
"Mel, Mel," she cried. "Mel..."

"Grace? Grace, is that you?" Melanie said, alarm
roughening her voice.

Grace tried to calm down. She tried to stop crying. She
finally managed to say, "I'm coming home. Can I come
home? You didn't rent my room out, did you?"

"Sweetie, you know you can come home. And no, I
didn't rent your room out. But what happened? *Why* are
you coming home?"

Grace's tears blinded her. She squeezed her eyes shut.
She had to stop. She couldn't afford to go to pieces like
this. "I—I can't tell you r-right now. W-will you be there
tonight?" She took a long, trembling breath. "I don't
know what train I'll be on. I haven't got a ticket yet. I'll
call you from the station when I get to Philadelphia and
know the schedule."

"All right. And Grace?"

"What?" Grace whispered.

"Sweetie, nothing could be this bad. You'll see. Everything's going to be all right."

Grace didn't answer. Melanie was trying to make her
feel better, but nothing and no one could ever gloss over
what had happened.

Grace had lost everything. And nothing would ever be
all right again.

Chapter Sixteen

After Grace left the library, Virginia glared at Paul. "What's wrong with you? Aren't you going to go after her?"

He shook his head, his face in its secret mode—a mode she knew well because he'd looked like that too often in his life. Even though Virginia understood Jennifer and what drove her, she cursed Paul's mother right now. With her abandonment of Paul, she had really done a job on him.

"Fine. Then I will." And with that, Virginia wheeled her chair out from the desk.

"Aunt Virginia, please let me finish telling you everything. Then, if you still want to go talk to Grace, I won't try to stop you."

"I'm listening."

She couldn't believe it when he told her about the DNA testing, how he'd found Elizabeth's baby book and removed the lock of hair without telling her. But that revelation wasn't the most upsetting. What he told her next made her feel nauseated. She stared at him, sure he'd lost his mind. "If you think I'm going to allow you to exhume Evan's and Anabel's bodies, you don't know me at all."

Before he could answer, she added, "And I have no intention of allowing my blood to be tested, either. I told you once before, and I'll tell you again, I'm perfectly satisfied that Grace is my granddaughter. Nothing you've told me today has changed my mind. And I intend to tell Grace just that."

She tried to roll her chair around the desk, but he was blocking her way. "Please move your chair."

He looked as if he wanted to argue with her, but he got up and moved his chair. Virginia wheeled herself out of the library. Just as she was turning to go to the elevator, Anna rushed down the hall, her face alarmed.

"Mrs. Hollister," she called. "Come quick. Miss Grace, she's leaving!"

Anna got behind Virginia's chair and pushed her toward the front entry. Virginia swallowed as she saw Grace's luggage piled there, and Grace herself, face pale, eyes swollen, standing next to it.

A few seconds later, Virginia heard Paul walk up behind her. No one spoke. Grace looked at Virginia.

"Please, Grace, don't go," Virginia said frantically. "Nothing Paul told me matters at all. Nothing has changed. This is your home. I love you. You'll always be Elizabeth to me."

Grace, face torn with misery, walked slowly toward her. She knelt in front of the chair. She took Virginia's hands in hers. Her lower lip trembled, but her voice was steady when she spoke. "I love you, too," she said. "More than I can ever express. But this isn't my home, not the way we thought it was. I don't belong here. Please try to understand. And please forgive me for hurting you."

If there was anything Virginia could say, anything she could do, she would have done it. But she could see the determination and the resignation on Grace's face, in her unhappy eyes. And she *did* understand. It was Paul. He had changed his mind about Grace, and Grace couldn't bear to stay under those circumstances.

Virginia's heart was breaking, but she knew she had to be strong. She didn't want to add to Grace's burden of misery and guilt, for she was sure Grace felt guilty. "My dear," she whispered, "there's nothing to forgive. But I will miss you so much."

Grace nodded. "I'll miss you, too."

They kissed again, and Virginia could feel the tremors in Grace's body. Five minutes later she was gone.

Tears blurred Virginia's eyes as the yellow taxicab sped down the driveway. She looked at Paul. To her satisfaction, she saw that he looked just as stricken as she felt. For once, he had been unable to hide his feelings. Maybe there was hope for him yet.

"Aunt Virginia," he finally said, "I'm sorry things have turned out this way."

"You should be."

He flinched. "This isn't my fault," he said.

"Are you sure?" She knew she was being hard on him, but she didn't care. She might not be able to force him to love Grace, to force him to see that he had just driven away the best thing that had ever happened to this family, but she didn't have to pretend she agreed with him.

"I'm not the one who pretended to be something I'm not," he said bitterly. "She betrayed both of us, even if you refuse to see it."

Virginia looked at him, this man she loved as much or more than she'd ever loved her own son. She knew his strengths, and she also knew his weaknesses. They had no secrets from each other. She considered trying to talk to him. Trying to make him see reason. Trying to make him go after Grace and bring her back.

Then she sighed. No. He would have to make that decision on his own. She only prayed, when he did—for she had to believe he would—it wasn't too late.

Paul was tired of the looks he'd been receiving. The servants, Susan, his aunt—all looked at him as if he had committed a crime. Why was he getting the brunt of everyone's unhappiness? Didn't they understand that he hadn't caused this problem? He was as much a victim as anyone.

Three days had passed since Grace's departure. Three achingly miserable, lonely days. Paul couldn't believe how much he missed her. He couldn't believe how solidly she had become entrenched in their lives. The house seemed empty without her.

Memories of Grace haunted him. Her smile, her beautiful eyes, her gentleness. Her kisses. Her passion. Why was it, he wondered, that people always remembered the good things about a person they'd lost?

He kept reminding himself that he had done the only possible thing. He kept reminding himself that Grace had never loved him. That she had never wanted him. All she had wanted was the Hollister money. And even there, she had managed to have the last laugh, he thought bitterly.

Yesterday, his aunt had informed him that even if Grace never returned, she intended to leave the changes in her will intact. "Grace will continue to share in my estate," she'd said, the expression in her eyes daring him to protest.

Paul knew protesting would do no good. When Aunt Virginia made up her mind, especially about something like this, nothing would change it.

He wondered if she was doing this to punish him. He could feel the weight of her disapproval every time they were together. He'd never thought his aunt was a cruel person, but since Grace had left, she seemed to go out of her way to make his life more miserable.

She refused to do anything relating to the wedding. "You're the one who broke your engagement. It's your responsibility to call everyone and cancel everything," she said flatly. Each time another wedding present was delivered, she had one of the servants bring it to him to deal with. She referred all calls to him, too.

In self-defense, he made Susan talk to the callers. By the second day, Susan was giving him dirty looks and muttering under her breath about people taking advantage of other people and not getting paid to clean up other people's personal messes. Finally, exasperated, he snapped at her—something he never did and for which he was immediately sorry. Now, instead of dirty looks, he was being treated to wounded looks and martyred sighs from his secretary.

He was damned sick of all of it.

On one thing, though, he and his aunt were in accord. When Paul called Sheriff Evans back to tell him they were not going to go further with the DNA testing, the sheriff asked Paul what he wanted to do about the remains. "I can take care of them," the sheriff said, "just like we would any unidentified body."

Paul knew that even if his aunt refused to acknowledge a connection between the remains they'd found and their family, they couldn't just turn their backs and walk away, pretending this had never happened. After all, he was the one who had initiated the search. "No," he said. "I'll arrange for interment in the family crypt."

Ned offered to tell Virginia, but Paul knew this was his responsibility.

She looked at him, saying nothing as he explained the decision he'd made. Then she nodded. "Although I don't believe the...findings...have anything to do with Elizabeth, you did the right thing." She thought for a minute. "We'll have a private memorial service, just you and me. Please make the arrangements."

Today, the fourth day after Grace's departure, was the day the memorial service would take place. Paul slogged his way through the morning, listless and feeling lonelier and more misunderstood by the minute. The service was scheduled for one-thirty that afternoon. After a quick lunch at his desk, he went to his room to change into a dark suit. He was dreading the ordeal ahead of him, dreading today and all the days to come.

As he walked down the hall toward the stairs, his steps slowed and his gaze slowly turned in the direction of the closed door of Grace's room. Like a man pulled by forces out of his control, he bypassed the stairs and walked down the hall to her room.

Quietly, he opened the door.

For a moment, he stood in the doorway and surveyed the room.

She'd left everything clean and orderly. The bed was neatly made, the pillows plumped, the spread smooth. He swallowed, remembering the last time he'd shared that bed with Grace.

He walked farther into the room. Someone had opened the drapes, and a ray of winter sunlight danced in the air. He drew in a deep breath, and it seemed to him that a faint trace of perfume, of Grace, lingered.

A terrible sadness gripped him. The room looked so empty. As empty as his heart.

There was nothing for him here. He turned around, intending to leave, when something sparkled in his peripheral vision. He turned. A small golden object gleamed on top of the vanity.

Curious, he walked closer. He sucked in a breath as he realized what that golden object was.

The locket.

Just as he'd been compelled to come into this room, he now felt that same strong compulsion pulling him toward the locket. He stood over it, nearly blinded by its brightness as the sunlight played across its contours.

Then he frowned.

Next to the locket was a small, folded slip of paper. He picked it up, opened it, read the words written in Grace's small, neat script: *This locket belongs with Elizabeth.*

The sight of the handwriting caused an ache in his chest. Yet even through his misery, he knew she was right. The locket did belong with Elizabeth. Gingerly, he picked it up. He might not have believed in the dreams when he'd first heard about them, but the fact that Grace had been able to find Elizabeth through them had convinced him that the locket did have certain powers. He started to drop it into his pocket, then that weird sense of compulsion overtook him again.

Slowly, he rubbed the face of the locket.

Heat flowed into his fingertips. And then, shocking him, images swirled in his brain like frames of a movie.

He swayed, steadying himself by holding on to the vanity top. His thumb continued to stroke the locket.

A young blond woman stood on the porch of a small, white frame, Cape Cod house. She rang the doorbell.

A minute later, a middle-aged, dark-haired woman answered the door. The woman smiled. "Joan!" she said. "You're back! I was gettin' worried. I didn't think you'd make it for Christmas." She opened the door. "Come on in."

The blond woman called Joan stepped into the house. "I'm sorry. I had some trouble, but I got back as soon as I could." She looked around. "Where's Helen?" Her voice had taken on a twinge of alarm.

"Helen's nappin', but I'll wake her up."

"I'll come with you."

The two women entered a small, darkened bedroom. The older woman opened the blinds. Sunlight poured into the room. Joan walked over to the crib. A chubby blond toddler lay curled under a pink quilt. A teddy bear was clutched in her arms. She was sucking her thumb. She stirred as Joan leaned over the crib, cooing, "Helen, Helen, sweetheart, Mommy's here."

The toddler opened her eyes. She looked up. Confused blue eyes studied Joan. Helen started to cry.

Joan's face crumpled. "She doesn't remember me."

"Well, it's been awhile," the older woman said. "She'll get over it once she gets used to you again."

"Sweetheart, I brought you a Christmas present," Joan said. She dug into her pocket. "Look. It's a beautiful necklace, a golden locket just for you. It even has your initial on it. See? An H for Helen." Joan lifted the toddler out of the crib, and even though Helen still looked wary, she allowed her mother to fasten the tiny locket around her neck. She smiled and touched it.

Paul blinked. The images faded. He rubbed the locket again.

Joan stepped off a bus. She carried Helen in one arm and a satchel in the other hand. She walked for a long time, past shuttered houses and closed storefronts. It was very early in the morning, bitterly cold and still dark, and there wasn't much traffic on the street.

She walked and walked, shifting Helen from one arm to the other. The child slept, sucking her thumb.

The farther she walked, the sparser the homes. Finally, she came to a large property surrounded by a tall brick wall.

She looked around, scanning the road in both directions. Nothing moved. She hugged Helen close and whispered, "I'm sorry, baby." Tears ran down Joan's face. "I hope someday you can forgive me for leaving you like this. I hope someday you'll understand that I couldn't take care of you the right way, that I made some terrible mistakes and hurt a lot of people, and I didn't want to hurt you, too.'' Helen yawned and opened her eyes.

Still crying, Joan silently opened the gate. She walked the few feet to the front steps. Then she kissed Helen's forehead and placed the little girl on the top step. The sun was just creeping over the horizon. She looked at the child. *''If Richard had ever seen you, he would have loved you,''* she whispered.

Then Joan reached for the doorbell. Her hand hesitated. The brass nameplate over the doorbell said St. Mary's Convent. She pressed the doorbell, then, crying, turned and ran down the walk and out the gate.

Helen stuck her thumb in her mouth and hugged her teddy bear closer.

The golden locket around her neck glowed in the misty morning light.

Paul was relieved when the brief memorial service was over. His aunt had begun to show signs of strain, and he knew that somewhere deep inside her subconscious, she had acknowledged that this was her granddaughter they were saying goodbye to.

"Before we seal the urn and place it in the crypt, is there anything you'd like to say or do?" the minister asked kindly.

Virginia shook her head.

Paul stepped forward. "I'd like to place something in the urn."

His aunt gave him a startled look.

He removed the locket from his pocket. He looked at his aunt. A shadow passed over her face, and her eyes were bleak. His thumb stroked the locket one last time, and a clear image of a forlorn little girl sitting alone on a stoop flashed through his mind. Her bright blue eyes seemed to be looking straight into his soul.

At that moment, a great peace settled over him and he knew the locket was trying to tell him something. His gaze met his aunt's and a silent message passed between them.

Slowly, he handed her the locket. She accepted it, wrapping her fingers around it and closing her eyes. Then she raised the locket to her lips, kissed it and dropped it into the urn.

Grace sat at the window and looked down at the street. It was a cold, overcast day and it matched her mood perfectly. She was alone in the apartment. Melanie had gone to dance class and would be back later that afternoon.

Grace was glad Melanie was gone. Even though she dearly loved her friend, and Melanie had been supportive and sympathetic to her, Grace had had to put on an act a lot of the time. With Melanie gone, Grace didn't have to pretend anymore. If she wanted to wallow in misery, she could.

She knew she couldn't keep this up. She would have to pull herself together soon because she had to figure out how she was going to survive the rest of her life.

At least she didn't have to worry about a job. She had called Phil, the editorial director at her publishing company, and he'd been thrilled to hear from her.

"I don't suppose my job is still open?" she asked.

"Nope. But I've got an even better opening, and you're perfect for it. In fact, if you'd have stayed on, I would have offered it to you as a promotion."

"Really?" she said, trying to muster up some enthusiasm.

"How does managing editor sound to you?"

"You mean Bonnie's job?"

"None other."

"But what happened to Bonnie?"

"She screwed up one too many times. I canned her. So what do you say?"

"I accept."

They had decided that she would start the following Monday. When Grace looked at the calendar, she realized that it was February the twelfth. Saturday was the fourteenth.

Her wedding day.

She stared at the date, and the full impact of her loss hit her again.

She started to cry, and nothing Melanie said helped. She had cried and cried and cried until there were no more tears left.

She wondered if she would ever be happy again.

After the memorial service, Paul called Ned Shapiro. "Ned, do you remember the name of the family that employed Josie McClure before she came here?"

"Certainly. The Chaneys. Richard and Cynthia Chaney."

Josie's words ran through Paul's mind. *If Richard had ever seen you, he would have loved you.* "Do you, by any chance, know how I can reach them?"

Paul knew Ned was dying to know why Paul wanted to talk to the Chaneys, but to his credit, he didn't ask. "Well, I know Richard Chaney's dead. He was dead when your aunt called for a reference on Josie. And I don't know if Cynthia Chaney is still living in the same place, but you can try." He gave Paul a Manhattan address.

"Thanks, Ned. One other thing. I'm going to be gone for a few days. Would you keep tabs on Aunt Virginia? The servants are good, but I'd feel better knowing you'll call her a couple of times."

"Where will you be in case I need to get in touch with you?"

Paul hesitated. "I'm not sure. I'm going after Grace. If I'm successful, she and I will both be back here soon."

"So Virginia told you about Grace's letter, did she?"

Paul frowned. "What letter?"

"Uh, I . . . never mind. I must be confused."

"Come on, Ned. What letter?"

Ned sighed, the sound clearly audible over the telephone wire. "Grace signed a release relinquishing all rights to the estate. She sent it to me with a registered letter. I called your aunt yesterday to tell her."

Paul smiled. He thought about the locket and the message it had sent him. "Thanks, Ned. I won't let on that you told me."

The following afternoon, a smiling maid let Paul into Cynthia Chaney's Park Avenue apartment.

Cynthia, a thin, elegant-looking woman in her late sixties, said, "Mr. Hollister, it's nice to meet you." She didn't rise from her seat on a yellow-and-white-striped satin sofa.

Paul walked over to her and shook her hand.

"Please, sit down," she said, indicating a blue and yellow abstract print chair nearby. As Paul turned around, his gaze was caught by a large portrait hanging over the mantel. He stared. A beautiful, dark-haired girl whose gaze bore an amazing resemblance to Grace, was the subject of the portrait.

"That's Meredith, my daughter."

Paul nodded and tried to tamp down his excitement. He was on the right track and this proved it. "She's lovely."

"Yes, she is." Pride rang in Cynthia Chaney's voice. She smiled. "Would you like something to drink?"

"No, thank you, Mrs. Chaney. In fact, I won't stay long. I just have a few questions."

"Well, as I told you over the phone yesterday, I don't know what I can possibly tell you about Josie that I didn't tell your aunt years ago."

Paul had rehearsed in his mind how he would say this. "Well, information has come to light that Josie gave birth to a daughter about six months after leaving your employ. That means she became pregnant while she was working for you. I'm trying to find out who fathered her child. I was hoping you might be able to help me.''

"*Me?*" Cynthia's eyes rounded into an expression of disbelief. "How would *I* know anything about that? If she was pregnant when she left here, that would definitely explain her abrupt departure, but she certainly didn't confide in me!''

Paul noticed how Cynthia's hand had clenched in her lap. He knew she was hiding something. He waited, having learned a long time ago that silence often worked better than innuendo or outright accusation.

His strategy was rewarded when she added defensively, "I don't know why you'd think I could possibly know anything about Josie's affairs. Why, she could have gotten pregnant by anyone! At the time she worked for us, we had at least three or four male servants, and I'm sure she came into contact with all kinds of men on her days off.'' She stared at him as if defying him to refute what she'd said. "I'm sorry. I wish I could be more help.''

Paul thought about telling her exactly what he suspected. He thought about showing her the picture of Grace that he carried in his wallet, one taken the night of the ball. Then he realized how futile it would be to try to browbeat her into confirming his beliefs. Cynthia Chaney was the type of woman who would go to her grave trying to protect her position and her dead husband's reputation. She would never acknowledge that he had probably fathered a servant's child, nor would she chance a possible claim to his estate. He rose. "I'm sorry, too, Mrs. Chaney. But I thank you for taking the time to talk to me today.''

It didn't matter that she hadn't admitted anything, he thought. He could still give Grace the gift of her ancestry.

An hour later, he stood on the sidewalk in front of the building where Grace lived. Pedestrians jostled him as they hurried along the street. It was a blustery, cold day, and people were in a hurry to get out of the wind.

He looked at the door to the right of the gallery. There were two buzzers on the left. Hoping he'd guessed right, he pushed the second one.

Grace frowned. Who could that be at the door? She dragged herself off the couch, where she'd been listlessly trying to read, and walked over to the intercom. She pushed the button. "Yes?"

"Grace? Is that you?"

Her heart stopped. That had sounded like Paul's voice, but it...it couldn't be! "Yes," she said, and her voice came out sounding like a croak. "This is Grace," she said, louder this time. "Who is this?"

"It's Paul. Can I come up?"

Now her heart was beating like a tom-tom. Paul. What did he want? Then fear nearly choked her. Virginia! Had something happened to Virginia? "Y-yes, of course. I'll release the lock."

Two minutes later, he knocked at the door. Taking a deep breath, she opened it.

For a long moment, they simply looked at each other. A crazy jumble of emotions cascaded through her mind. She searched his face. "Did...has something happened to Virginia?"

"No, no, nothing like that. Can I come in?"

Relief made Grace feel weak. "I'm sorry. I...you scared me. I thought...I mean, I couldn't imagine—" She broke off, rattled by the look in his eyes.

He walked closer. "Grace..."

Grace wet her lips. "Wh-what do you want, Paul?"

He reached out, his hand brushing her arm.

She trembled at the contact.

"I hardly know where to begin," he said.

She had rarely seen him so unsure of himself. She gazed into his eyes and what she saw caused her heart to lurch.

"I'm sorry," he murmured. He drew her closer, and then his arms were around her and he was kissing her. She clung to him as he kissed her again and again, saying between kisses, "I'm so sorry. I was hurt. That's why I said all those things. But I was wrong. I love you, Grace. I love you, and if you'll forgive me, if you'll still have me, I want to marry you."

Finally, he put his hands on either side of her face and looked down into her eyes. "Will you?"

"Oh, Paul!" she cried. "Yes. Yes. I will."

A long time later, Grace sat encircled in the warm security of Paul's arms and listened as he brought her up to date on everything he'd learned since she had left Hollister House.

"So you see, I believe that you are Helen and that Josie is your mother."

His revelation didn't shock Grace, and she realized that she'd suspected as much. "And that doesn't bother you?"

"No, my darling, that doesn't bother me, and if you're worried about Aunt Virginia, you don't need to be." He chuckled ruefully and nuzzled Grace's forehead. "She will never acknowledge that you are anyone but Elizabeth, so there's no point in even telling her."

"Do... do you think Frank was my father?"

"Frank was not your father."

Grace sighed in relief. That had been an unspoken fear ever since she'd figured out that she must be Josie's daughter.

Paul tipped her chin up. He was smiling. "But I think I know who was."

As he told her about his visit to Cynthia Chaney earlier in the day, Grace's heart filled to the bursting point. She couldn't believe that he had done this for her. She was glad to know about her parentage, but it was Paul's understanding and the love behind his gesture that really made her happy. It was ironic, she thought, that this knowledge had come when she no longer needed it. "Thank you," she whispered when he was finished. Tears blurred her eyes.

"I knew how important it was to you to know where you came from." He gave her a long, lingering kiss. Then he smiled. "Now let's go home."

Home.

It was the most beautiful word Grace had ever heard. She knew now that it didn't matter that she wasn't Elizabeth Hollister because home was more than a place, more than a name. Home was where we love and where people love us.

"Yes," she said joyfully. "Let's go home."

Epilogue

Three years later...
From the Society Pages of the *Rolling Hills Record*

Newest Hollister Arrives on Schedule
by Cookie Shephard

Mrs. Paul Hollister—the former Grace Gregory—gave birth to a seven-pound three-ounce baby girl yesterday, March 7, at Rolling Hills General Hospital. Virginia Elizabeth made her appearance into the world at seven minutes before noon, with the proud father assisting.

The baby is the first great-grandchild of Virginia Fleming Hollister, who will celebrate her 90th birthday in August. When this reporter called to congratulate the new great-grandmother and ask her how she was feeling, she said she hadn't thought anything could top the day her granddaughter was returned to her, but today's events had proven her wrong.

Congratulations and best wishes to all the Hollisters!

* * * * *

MILLION DOLLAR SWEEPSTAKES (III)

No purchase necessary. To enter, follow the directions published. Method of entry may vary. For eligibility, entries must be received no later than March 31, 1996. No liability is assumed for printing errors, lost, late or misdirected entries. Odds of winning are determined by the number of eligible entries distributed and received. Prizewinners will be determined no later than June 30, 1996.

Sweepstakes open to residents of the U.S. (except Puerto Rico), Canada, Europe and Taiwan who are 18 years of age or older. All applicable laws and regulations apply. Sweepstakes offer void wherever prohibited by law. Values of all prizes are in U.S. currency. This sweepstakes is presented by Torstar Corp., its subsidiaries and affiliates, in conjunction with book, merchandise and/or product offerings. For a copy of the Official Rules send a self-addressed, stamped envelope (WA residents need not affix return postage) to: MILLION DOLLAR SWEEPSTAKES (III) Rules, P.O. Box 4573, Blair, NE 68009, USA.

EXTRA BONUS PRIZE DRAWING

No purchase necessary. The Extra Bonus Prize will be awarded in a random drawing to be conducted no later than 5/30/96 from among all entries received. To qualify, entries must be received by 3/31/96 and comply with published directions. Drawing open to residents of the U.S. (except Puerto Rico), Canada, Europe and Taiwan who are 18 years of age or older. All applicable laws and regulations apply; offer void wherever prohibited by law. Odds of winning are dependent upon number of eligibile entries received. Prize is valued in U.S. currency. The offer is presented by Torstar Corp., its subsidiaries and affiliates in conjunction with book, merchandise and/or product offering. For a copy of the Official Rules governing this sweepstakes, send a self-addressed, stamped envelope (WA residents need not affix return postage) to: Extra Bonus Prize Drawing Rules, P.O. Box 4590, Blair, NE 68009, USA.

SWP-S295

MONTANA Mavericks™

Stories that capture living and loving
beneath the Big Sky, where legends live
on...and mystery lingers.

This February, the plot thickens with

WAY OF THE WOLF
by Rebecca Daniels

Raeanne Martin had always been secretly drawn to
the mysterious Rafe "Wolf Boy" Rawlings. Now they
battled by day on opposite sides of a murder trial.
But by night, Raeanne fought an even tougher battle
for Rafe's love.

Don't miss a minute of the loving as the passion
continues with:

> **THE LAW IS NO LADY**
> by Helen R. Myers (March)
>
> **FATHER FOUND**
> by Laurie Paige (April)
>
> **BABY WANTED**
> by Cathie Linz (May)
> and many more!

Only from **V** Silhouette® where passion lives.

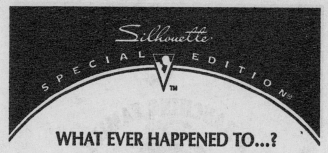

Silhouette

SPECIAL EDITION ™

WHAT EVER HAPPENED TO...?

Have you been wondering when much-loved characters will finally get their own stories? Well, have we got a lineup for you! Silhouette Special Edition is proud to present a *Spin-off Spectacular!* Be sure to catch these exciting titles from some of your favorite authors:

HUSBAND: SOME ASSEMBLY REQUIRED (SE #931 January) Shawna Saunders has finally found Mr. Right in the dashing Murphy Pendleton, last seen in *Marie Ferrarella*'s BABY IN THE MIDDLE (SE #892).

SAME TIME, NEXT YEAR (SE #937 February) In this tie-in to *Debbie Macomber*'s popular series THOSE MANNING MEN and THOSE MANNING SISTERS, a yearly reunion between friends suddenly has them in the marrying mood!

A FAMILY HOME (SE #938 February) Adam Cutler discovers the best reason for staying home is the love he's found with sweet-natured and sexy Lainey Bates in *Celeste Hamilton*'s follow-up to WHICH WAY IS HOME? (SE #897).

JAKE'S MOUNTAIN (SE #945 March) Jake Harris never met anyone as stubborn—or as alluring—as Dr. Maggie Matthews in *Christine Flynn*'s latest, a spin-off to WHEN MORNING COMES (SE #922).

Don't miss these wonderful titles, only for our readers—only from Silhouette Special Edition!

SPIN7

A RANCHING FAMILY

Though scattered by years and tears, the Heller clan
share mile-deep roots in one Wyoming ranch—and a
single talent for lassoing hearts!

Meet another member of the Heller clan in
Victoria Pade's
BABY MY BABY
(SE #946, March)

The ranching spirit coursed through
Beth Heller's veins—as did the passion she
felt for her proud Sioux husband, Ash Blackwolf. Yet
their marriage was in ashes. Only the
unexpected new life growing within Beth could bring
them together again....

Don't miss **BABY MY BABY,** the next installment of
Victoria Pade's series,
A RANCHING FAMILY, available in March!
And watch for Jackson Heller's story,
COWBOY'S·KISS, coming in July...only from
Silhouette Special Edition!

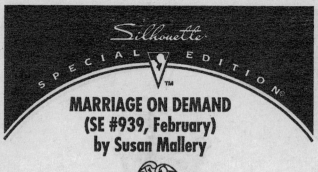

MARRIAGE ON DEMAND
(SE #939, February)
by Susan Mallery

Hometown Heartbreakers: Those heart-stoppin' hunks
are rugged, ready and able to steal your heart....

Austin Lucas was as delicious as forbidden sin—that's
what the Glenwood womenfolk were saying. And
Rebecca Chambers couldn't deny how sexy he looked
in worn, tight jeans. But when their impulsive
encounter obliged them to get married, could their
passion lead to everlasting love?

Find out in *MARRIAGE ON DEMAND*, the next story
in Susan Mallery's *Hometown Heartbreakers* series,
coming to you in February...only from
Silhouette Special Edition.

HH-2

A ROSE AND A WEDDING VOW (SE #944)
by Andrea Edwards

Matt Michaelson returned home to face Liz—his brother's widow...a woman he'd never forgotten. Could falling in love with *this* Michaelson man heal the wounds of Liz's lonely past?

A ROSE AND A WEDDING VOW, SE #944 (3/95), is the next story in this stirring trilogy by Andrea Edwards. THIS TIME, FOREVER—sometimes a love is so strong, nothing can stand in its way, not even time. Look for the last installment, A SECRET AND A BRIDAL PLEDGE, in May 1995.